MAFIA AND PROTECTOR

ISA OLIVER

MAFIA AND PROTECTOR

AN ITALIAN MAFIA ARRANGED MARRIAGE DARK ROMANCE

Copyright © 2023 by Isa Oliver

All rights reserved.

No portion of this book may be reproduced in any form without written permission from the publisher or author, except as permitted by U.K. copyright law.

This book features an Italian Mafia arranged marriage romance, an age gap, and a dark romance storyline.

CONTENTS

DEDICATION	V
AUTHOR'S NOTE	VII
SPOILERS - CONTENT NOTE	VIII
MAFIA FAMILES	IX
FACEBOOK GROUP AND ARCs	X
1. CHAPTER 1	1
2. CHAPTER 2	21
3. CHAPTER 3	30
4. CHAPTER 4	38
5. CHAPTER 5	48
6. CHAPTER 6	56
7. CHAPTER 7	63
8. CHAPTER 8	74
9. CHAPTER 9	82
10. CHAPTER 10	92

11.	CHAPTER 11	101
12.	CHAPTER 12	113
13.	CHAPTER 13	122
14.	CHAPTER 14	137
15.	CHAPTER 15	145
16.	CHAPTER 16	151
17.	CHAPTER 17	162
18.	CHAPTER 18	171
19.	CHAPTER 19	181
20.	CHAPTER 20	189
21.	CHAPTER 21	199
22.	CHAPTER 22	209
23.	CHAPTER 23	220
24.	CHAPTER 24	229
25.	CHAPTER 25	235
26.	CHAPTER 26	247
27.	CHAPTER 27	254
28.	CHAPTER 28	259
29.	CHAPTER 29	265
30.	EPILOGUE	278
31.	SNEAK PEEK	292

DEDICATION

I have been truly humbled by the genuine kindness and support that has been shown to me by readers during this scary publishing journey. Thank you from the bottom of my heart to each and every amazing reader who took a chance on a newbie author like me.

Thank you to all the Angels for so kindly supporting me. And a very special thanks to Kathy T (whose posts I love seeing as she is so enthusiastic and sunny and just a beautiful person), Zui S (for being so completely amazing and lovely and for the gorgeous picture edit you did for Mafia And Angel which even included a bow on Wilbur the cat), and Mihaela N (for your really awesome picture edits posted in my reader group and on Instagram).

And thank you to every ARC reader, blogger, and reviewer for giving up your time to read my books and share posts – you guys are truly awesome. Also, a huge thanks to the lovely Peachy Keen Author Services and also to Magan and Chrisandra.

Lastly, thank you to my beautiful family. I couldn't do any of this without your love.

Love Isa xxx

AUTHOR'S NOTE

Dear Reader, please note that while not wholly dark, this book is categorized as a dark romance due to some subject matter. Specific topics are listed on the next page. Please note that any beliefs, views, opinions, and statements in this novel are the views of specific characters as part of the storyline, and they are not the views of the author. Love Isa xxx

Marchiano Mafia Series (all can be read as standalones):
Mafia And Captive
(An Age Gap Dark Captive Romance)
Mafia And Protector
(A Dark Mafia Arranged Marriage Romance)
Mafia And Taken
(A Dark Mafia Romance)
Mafia And Angel
(An Age Gap Grumpy Sunshine Arranged Marriage)

SPOILERS – CONTENT NOTE

Topics referred to include:

...

...

...

Mafia violence and murder

Miscarriage

Pregnancy termination

Sexual assault (not committed by the hero)

MAFIA FAMILES

Santino Family: Società Mafia, Los Angeles
Emanuel Santino (Capo)
Ortensia Santino - wife
Gabriel Santino - son and heir
Rafael Santino - son
Natanael Santino - son
Nancia Santino - daughter

.

Bonardi Family: Società Mafia, Los Angeles
Cecilio Bonardi (Underboss)
Casmundina Bonardi - wife
Jacob Bonardi - son and heir
Juliana Bonardi - daughter
Jessica Bonardi - daughter

FACEBOOK GROUP AND ARCS

Facebook Group: 'Isa's Angels & Mafia Books'
https://www.facebook.com/groups/1409806332760996

Would you like to receive a free 'Advance Reader Copy' of Isa's next release before anyone else? Please see here:
https://isaoliverauthor.com/free-arcs/

CHAPTER 1

Santa Maria, Madre di Dio, prega per noi peccatori, adesso e nell'ora della nostra morte.
Holy Mary, Mother of God, pray for us sinners now and at the hour of our death.
— the words every Made Man recites upon a death.

JESSICA

"Jessica, your father wants to see you in his office." My mother, Casmundina Bonardi, had just dashed into my bedroom and was acting all dramatic as usual.

"You mean right now?" I asked her.

"Yes, straight away. What on earth are you wearing?" She grimaced as she saw me dressed in my lilac sundress, with my dark, wavy hair pulled back into a simple French braid that was already starting to unravel. "I thought I told you to get rid of that dress. It's shabby and does nothing to enhance your plain features."

It was a hot day here in L.A. and my outfit was perfect for the weather. "But, Mother, I like this dress and you know it's my favorite."

"You're eighteen years old now. That dress makes you look like you're fourteen and still a schoolgirl." She seemed to have forgotten that I *had* been a schoolgirl until just a couple of weeks ago when I'd finished high school.

"I thought it would be okay to wear it since I'm just spending the day at home—"

My mother cut me off. "There's no time to change now. You know your father hates to be kept waiting. You need to put some shoes on."

She threw open my closet door and grabbed a pair of five-inch spiky heels for me to slide my bare feet into. My mother had bought these shoes for me some time ago, though I had so far managed to avoid wearing them.

The sparkly gold shoes looked ridiculous with my dress, but there was no time to argue over her choice of footwear.

"*Pronti?*" My mother asked if I was ready. She always broke into Italian when she was nervous. Or when she was excited, or happy, or sad, or angry—so, basically, when any sort of emotion reared its head.

"I think so."

"Quickly now, you don't want to anger him."

She was right—I definitely didn't want to anger him. My father, Cecilio Bonardi, was a Made Man—a man initiated into the Mafia. He'd always been fairly short-tempered; however, after the recent kidnapping of my older sister, Juliana, he'd been as explosive as a piece of dry tinder. I really missed Juliana—I hoped she would be home soon and that things would go back to normal.

I rushed downstairs to the office.

As I hastened my step, I ran my palms over my wavy hair, trying to smooth any stray tendrils. Maybe if my hair looked half-decent, my father wouldn't notice my dress.

I knocked on his office door, waiting as always until I heard the deep 'enter'.

I opened the door to his office, hoping that he wasn't irritated with how long it had taken me to answer his summons. As I hurried into the room, I suddenly came to an abrupt halt as I realized that he was not alone.

"Oh, I'm so sorry, Father. Mother said that you wanted to see me? I didn't know that you had company. I'll come back later."

"No, Jessica, stay. We've been waiting for you."

My heart started pounding in my chest. In the room was the Capo, Emanuel Santino—he was the boss of the Società Mafia. From their base in Los Angeles, the Società ran their criminal empire and ruled over the West Coast.

The Capo sat in one of the wingback leather chairs in front of my father's desk. Standing by the fireplace was his oldest son and heir, Gabriel, and his second son, Rafael. My thoughts were racing through my mind. I hadn't done anything that could incur the wrath of the Capo...or had I?

I hated this room and had always tried to avoid this part of the house to minimize the chance of running into my father or any of the men who worked for him. And there were a lot of comings and goings, given that my father was one of Emanuel Santino's Underbosses, meaning that he held a powerful position within the organization.

"Sit down," my father commanded me.

In my haste to obey, I wobbled in my heels and lost my balance.

I managed to grab the edge of his desk in time, preventing me from falling flat on my face, although I couldn't stop the flush from rising up my cheeks.

I hoped that no one had seen, but one look at the expressions on the faces of the Santinos was enough to tell me that they had definitely noticed my clumsiness.

I silently cursed my mother for making me wear these ludicrous shoes.

I gratefully sank myself down into the second wingback chair, sitting on the edge of the seat with my hands tightly clasped in my lap. I swallowed the lump in my throat. "Is there something wrong, Father?"

"You must know that we have always hoped for a marriage bond between our family, the Bonardis, and the Santino family. We have now decided to go ahead with that union."

Oh my God. They'd found my older sister, Juliana!

My heart soared—they'd finally gotten my sibling back after her kidnapping a few weeks ago. Gabriel Santino was in love with Juliana. It had always been thought that they would marry, and now they finally could.

"You've found Juliana?" My voice was giddy with excitement.

"Do not mention that girl's name in this house! Everyone in the Società knows that she is a slut," thundered my father, the venom in his voice making me sink back into my chair. "Your sister means nothing to me now. She is no longer part of this family."

My father paused for a moment as if collecting himself, before continuing. "We have decided that you will marry into the Santino family."

"I'm to marry Gabriel?" I was dumbfounded.

"No, he's not interested in you." My father was as blunt as always. "Instead, Emanuel has suggested his second son, Rafael. You will marry him in two months' time."

I stole a glance across at Rafael, who stood leaning against the mantel of the fireplace.

Despite his casual stance, Rafael's whole demeanor was icy. He had handsome features and sandy-blond hair, but it was his dark blue eyes that I noticed as they radiated a stark coldness. A shiver ran through me.

The Società Mafia had started out by controlling the port and the drug trade in L.A. before extending its influence into other activities. Now it was one of the most formidable criminal organizations in the US, and the Santinos were some of the most powerful—and most feared—men in the country.

"What does Mother think about this?" I squeaked, forgetting my place. My father didn't like to be questioned about anything, even if it did concern my whole life.

"Your mother will do whatever is the best for this family and the Società, as will you," snapped my father. "We will sign the engagement contract today." The Mafia was still a traditional institution and families followed the custom of signing an engagement contract.

"Today?" I blurted out. My mind was scrambling, trying to calculate the age gap between Rafael and me. He was twenty-five years, if I remembered correctly, making him seven years older than me.

"Yes, today," interjected Emanuel Santino.

My gaze darted across to Rafael again and I wondered what he thought about this marriage. A black Brioni suit hugged his muscular body. Brioni and black: the typical Mafia uniform. And although his suit was obviously expensive, there was something untamed about him, and that sent a shiver through my body.

I knew that he couldn't be thrilled with me as his future wife. After all, I knew that everyone thought I was plain and unattractive. It was my older sister who was the beauty of the family, and she'd always been the one to draw admiring looks. I'm sure he had expected, as the second son of the Capo, that he would at least marry someone prettier than me.

Emanuel pushed the engagement contract across the desk until it was in front of me. He might be Capo, but he was also a slimeball who treated his wife with a complete lack of respect, sleeping around with a long line of lovers and prostitutes. I prayed Rafael did not take after his father.

"Um...please may I ask why we are signing this today? Usually, the contract is signed at the engagement party." I was unable to keep the bewilderment from my voice.

"The engagement party will be in a week's time; however, we want this finalized today," said the Capo. "Everyone is unsettled after the recent kidnapping of a Mafia daughter. We must focus on making the Società as strong as possible from within, and there is no better way than by a marriage between the families of the Capo and his Underboss. Once this contract is signed, we can announce the engagement to the rest of the organization. This union will be a demonstration of strength to the rest of the Società. And that should put a stop to the various jitters and rumors swirling around."

Great, I was being used as a means to quiet the gossipmongers and calm the over-wrought nerves within the Società, regardless of what I might actually want.

I worried my lower lip, trying to think of a way to delay the signing. I was told two minutes ago that I was to marry Rafael Santino, and now I was being asked to sign away my life to him via the engagement contract. I knew that once the contract was signed, there was no way out and that I would be bound to Rafael Santino forever.

But then, I thought to myself, I am a Mafia daughter—I had no choice in the matter of who I was to marry. Did it really matter if I signed the contract now or next week? There was no way out of this, no way to escape Rafael Santino, no matter what my wishes on the subject were.

I licked my dry lips and picked up my father's favorite fountain pen.

I looked up and in desperation said, "Wouldn't Gabriel prefer to wait for Juliana to return, and then he can marry her? And then our families will be united through that marriage?" I couldn't stop the words tumbling out—why couldn't I just keep my mouth shut?

"For God's sake, Jessica!" My father really lost it now. "She's obviously no longer pure. When we get her back, no decent man will look at her. She'll be worth no more than a used whore. Now sign the damn contract. We need to move on now that your sister is no longer of any use or value to us."

Gabriel's jaw tensed and his eyes darkened at my father's harsh words. It was obvious he was still interested in Juliana, and I was glad that someone else apart from me still believed in her and realized that what had happened wasn't her fault.

I signed my name slowly, all the while wondering if this was really happening. As I completed my signature, I laid the pen down carefully next to the papers.

Rafael prowled toward me, his jaw tightly clenched. He took the pen to sign his own name, and as he towered above me with his tall frame, I wished I had thought to push the contract toward him so that he wouldn't have to stand so near to me.

He was so close that I could smell him—a clean, masculine scent with a hint of cologne. As he wrote, I noticed his strong wrists. They were tanned and my eyes followed the trail of sandy hair which disappeared into the sleeve of his dress shirt.

After he had finished signing his name, I glanced down at my fingers, seeing that some black ink had leaked from the fountain pen and stained my fingers.

I felt like I wanted to wash my hands straightaway. In fact, I wanted to wash my whole body and try to wash away the stain of the Mafia, the stain of this life that I'd been born into. But I knew that even though I could wash away the ink, I could never get rid of my duty as a Mafia daughter. I could never get rid of my obligation to marry this man standing next to me.

After we had both signed the contract, I knew that there was no way out for me, and I was now bound to the Santino family for life.

I was marrying into a family where the father was a murderous psychopath, his eldest son was still in love with my older sister, and the man I was going to marry was...well, I don't know what he was because I'd never even spoken to him.

Emanuel stood. "We should leave the couple alone for a minute so that Rafael can present the engagement ring." With that, they filed out of the office while they carried on talking about business matters, leaving me sitting in the chair and Rafael standing over me.

This couldn't be any more awkward. Wasn't getting engaged supposed to be romantic?

But then, this wasn't the sort of engagement most people had. As was the norm in the Mafia world, our families had arranged this marriage. Rafael clearly wasn't interested in me—he'd never sought me out at formal Società functions to talk or ask me to dance. He was just marrying me to keep his father happy and the Società stable.

His whole energy filled the room, his proximity unnerving me and his scent consuming me. I didn't know where to look or what I was supposed to do.

"Stand up." His low voice penetrated the silence.

I would prefer to have remained sitting rather than risking standing on these heels again, but I guess he couldn't put the ring on like that. I slowly got to my feet, my left hand holding onto the edge of my father's desk for support.

He got out a small velvet box and opened it to reveal a large oval diamond flanked by two smaller sapphires, all set on a thin band of platinum. It was an exquisite design.

I watched as he removed the ring from the box and brought it toward me. "Give me your hand". Was anything he said not a command?

I hesitated, not wanting to let go of the desk in case I lost my balance again.

"Don't worry, I've got you," he said softly, as if realizing why I was reluctant to give him my hand.

I slowly gave him my hand, and as his fingers touched me for the first time, I felt a flush run up my cheeks and my heart thud too fast. It was the first time I had been touched by a man who was not a family member.

He slid the ring onto my left hand, but he didn't let go of it immediately. Instead, he admired the ring on me.

I discreetly looked at him. Up close, I could see that the stormy dark blue of his eyes was warmed by some lighter turquoise streaks. And as I ran my gaze over his hair, I thought somehow he was less scary than I imagined he would be. Yet I knew how deceptive appearances could be. And he was a Santino—there was nothing that wasn't scary about that family.

"I was taken by surprise when my father said our families want us to marry," I said in a rush.

"I could tell by your reaction."

"Oh, I don't want you to think it was personal against you."

"Don't worry, I've had worse said to me than someone indicating they'd prefer my brother marry into their family," he drawled.

I flushed. "I didn't mean any offense."

"I'll survive."

I fiddled with my hair, trying to tuck in the loose strands. "Sorry, I didn't get a chance to brush my hair before my father summoned me."

"No matter. It looks fine."

"Do you think? My parents like me dressed properly, especially in front of company." I realized then how that sounded and rushed on. "Not that I don't dress properly at other times." Jesus, why was I rambling in front of this man?

There was an awkward silence, and I willed myself not to fill it with any more of my gabbling.

"Do you always wear those shoes?"

I glanced down at my shoes and frowned, wondering if he was making fun of me.

Deep in thought, I startled when he brought his hand up to my face.

He ran his thumb over my brow and my eyes didn't leave his gaze. "You shouldn't frown so much."

I didn't know what to say, yet I felt the frown relaxing under his thumb. His touch was gentle, but I knew better than to be disarmed by small gestures. He was a Made Man, and his whole life was about violence and cruelty.

He slowly dropped his hand as our fathers returned to the room.

My father's voice broke the tension in the room. "That's all we need from you, Jessica." He was dismissing me. I should have been relieved that I could escape this room now. However, I was confused—was this all the discussion there was going to be about the biggest decision of my life? About whom I was going to marry?

I bit down on my lower lip, knowing there was nothing I could say now. So, I walked toward the door and let myself out quietly.

I ran up to my bedroom, keeping my head down and trying to keep my tears at bay until I was safely ensconced in my room. I didn't want any of the live-in staff to see my distress. My mother had always drummed into me the need to maintain appearances.

I didn't have long to myself before my mother appeared at my bedroom door, pouncing on me immediately. "I've been looking for you everywhere, Jessica! Why are you hiding yourself up here? Did you sign the engagement contract?"

"Yes, I did. Why didn't you tell me that Father wanted to see me to inform me of my engagement?" I had felt ambushed, and I couldn't help the hint of accusation in my voice.

"It wasn't my place to say. He wanted to tell you himself. What did Rafael think of you?"

"I don't know. We didn't speak much, and he barely looked at me. I've never spoken to him before, and I didn't even speak properly to him today."

"No, of course he wouldn't have noticed you before today. After all, you and Juliana were always joined at the hip, and standing next to her, it made you look even plainer." My mother really knew how to boost my self-esteem. "Really, Jessica, what were you thinking putting on that lilac dress this morning? It makes you look unsophisticated and insignificant."

My mother gave me no time to answer, however, and instead launched into wedding talk. "You will have to dazzle Rafael by wearing the most expensive wedding dress money can buy."

"I'd prefer something simple and elegant."

"Nonsense! People will be expecting something elaborate and opulent. After all, it will be the wedding of the year!"

I recalled her saying exactly the same thing about Juliana's wedding—and we'd all seen how that had turned out.

I knew there was no way out of this marriage now that the contract had been signed. Once we were married, I would do my duty as a Mafia wife and do what Rafael expected of me. I knew I was plain, shy, and uninteresting. However, if I was a good wife to him, he might treat me with respect and remain faithful to me. Some arranged marriages turned into love over time, and I was determined to work as hard as possible to achieve that within my own marriage. I wanted a loving husband with whom I could build a happy family life.

"Come along and change your dress right this minute," nagged my mother. "Then it is only fit for the trash can."

I would change out of my lilac dress to stop my mother from badgering me, but I definitely wouldn't throw it away—I wasn't going to give up my favorite dress so easily.

As I undressed, I couldn't help thinking to myself that soon I was going to lose even more control of my life, and that thought made my blood run cold.

***

"Ortensia Santino telephoned this morning," my mother informed me later that week. Ortensia was Rafael's mother. "She rang to arrange a doctor's appointment for you to start on birth control. The Santinos are sending a car tomorrow, which will take you to see their doctor."

"Couldn't I just get it from our own doctor?" Better still, I thought, we could just not consummate our marriage at all. But I didn't say that out loud because I knew that was out of the question.

Not only would I be expected to consummate the union on our wedding night, but also my husband would be expected to confirm to everyone the next morning that I had been a virgin for him.

Consummation on the wedding night was mandatory—it was my duty. If the marriage wasn't consummated, then it could be annulled. And an annulment would be a disaster, given that the marriage was a strategic business arrangement between the two families.

I shuddered at the humiliating thought of my first time having sex being discussed by the men in our families. To them, it was a business detail, but to me it felt like an invasion of my privacy.

"It's all arranged now, Jessica. Anyhow, the Santinos are only trying to help by making you an appointment with their doctor. Even if you don't seem to appreciate it, at least they recognize how much I have on my plate to arrange a wedding within such a short timescale," said my mother in a martyred tone.

She set a large box in front of me. "I've chosen what you will wear to the engagement party," she announced, sounding exceptionally pleased with herself as she proceeded to pull a dress out.

I looked at it with undisguised dismay.

It was completely over the top. It was obvious my mother had bought it at Signora Demonte's boutique, otherwise known as *The Desperate Brides Boutique*. It was where Società mothers went to get 'eye-catching', high fashion dresses for their unmarried daughters to wear at Società functions in the hope of snaring a good husband.

The more desperate the parents got, the more daring the outfits became. It was an embarrassment for a Mafia daughter to not be engaged by the time there was a '2' at the front of her age—in other words, by her 20th birthday. On the other hand, the men were permitted to get engaged at a later age and no one raised a single eyebrow at their sleeping around and sowing their wild oats.

This was clearly one of Signora Demonte's signature dresses: low neckline – check, high hemline – check, sequins – check, lace – check, bright screaming color – check, tight fabric – check, slutty – check.

My mother insisted I try on the dress.

"Mother, you know that this sort of dress really isn't my style."

"Jessica, first impressions count. And Rafael's first impression of you would have been awful in that dreadful lilac sundress you were wearing. We need to put you in a dress which will show him that you're not an unsophisticated young girl."

"But that's what I am," I wailed, although I knew I had no chance of changing her mind over the dress.

"Nonsense. This dress will transform his view of you."

"What does it even matter what I wear to the engagement party? Rafael has already seen me and he's signed the contract, so it's not as if he needs to be persuaded into marrying me."

"It's important he changes his view of you."

My heart sank to my stomach. "Did he say he wasn't happy with me...?"

"No, but of course he wouldn't have been happy—he wants a sophisticated wife. We can't do much about your disappointing looks, so we'll just have to try and impress him through your clothes. Even a plain Jane like you will look sensational in a dress like this."

Jesus, my mother was delusional.

***

The next morning, when it was time to leave for the doctor's appointment, I was surprised to see that my mother wasn't getting ready to leave. "Aren't you coming with me?"

"No, Ortensia said that Emanuel told her that he had arranged everything so that I wouldn't need to attend with you. He is even sending a car and two of his soldiers to escort you. The Santinos are determined to get all the preparations out of the way and keep the wedding date on track. They know that the only way the Società will get some stability after recent events is through a Santino-Bonardi marriage."

I worried my lower lip. "But I don't know the doctor and I really want you to come with me for this."

"You have to appear to be a grown-up, confident young woman. After all, you are marrying into the Santino family, the head family of the Società."

I looked at her doubtfully.

"For goodness sake, Jessica, you will do this and attend by yourself. You will not embarrass this family any further, especially after what happened with your sister, and not to mention your outburst at the contract signing when you suggested Gabriel might still want to marry Juliana."

"But I didn't mean to embarrass our family when I said that. I only meant—"

My mother cut me short. "Jessica, you are a smart girl, so try not to act like a tactless American tonight. Sometimes I think we should have brought you up more in the traditions of the old country."

The old country—Italy, of course.

My mother was always harking back to her land of birth, where she had lived until her parents brought her to America as a young child. She looked at life in Italy as the pinnacle of perfection, conveniently forgetting how much she enjoyed the trappings of her wealthy American lifestyle.

"Your father is still unhappy about what you said, so please think carefully before you speak today and make sure you do not cause any further shame to the Bonardi name."

I headed out to the car sent by Emanuel Santino, sitting in the back behind the two soldiers sent to guard me.

I was wearing a white tailored dress, although its formal style wasn't really to my taste, and I felt uncomfortable due to the neckline and cap sleeves being edged in scratchy lace trim.

I thought that white clothing always made me look washed out, my pale skin merging with the pale fabric, making me look sallow and tired. However, my mother had insisted that I wear white, cream, or ivory as much as possible in the run up to the wedding, so as to remind everyone that I was the bride-to-be. She definitely wanted to shout it from the rooftops and emphasize to everyone that I was marrying into the Capo's family. My siblings and I had always joked that our mother, Casmundina Bonardi, was a typical Mafia wife: obedient and demure, yet ruthlessly ambitious for her family.

When I arrived at the clinic for my appointment, I was shown into a sterile examination room and introduced to the doctor.

I wasn't sure why, but something about his demeanor set me on edge, putting my senses on high alert.

"I need to ask you some questions and then we can get on to the examination."

Examination? No one had said anything about any examination. I felt a chill spread through me.

The doctor took my medical history and asked me all sorts of questions about my periods and whether I was still a virgin.

After that, he handed me a paper sheet. "Take off all your garments, including your bra and panties."

"I don't understand...why?"

"Didn't your mother explain? You will need a vaginal examination before I can prescribe you birth control, and I'll also need to examine your breasts. The contraceptive pill can lead to a higher risk of breast cancer, so you will need to have regular check-ups. Once you have undressed, wrap the paper sheet around yourself and lie down on the examination table."

Once the doctor had left the room to give me privacy, I quickly undressed and wrapped the crackly sheet around my body.

I had never had an internal examination. The Mafia didn't allow a girl to have a pap smear before her marriage, so as to prevent any accidental damage to her hymen before her wedding night—they wanted to take no chances, given how important the blood on the wedding night was in proving the bride's pureness.

I looked down at the sheet. I assumed it was to provide some modesty, although it only came to mid-thigh and I wished it covered more of me.

A few minutes later, I heard the door slowly open and close, and then heavy footsteps came into the room.

The doctor was back.

The hairs on the back of my neck stood up as I sensed that something didn't feel quite right.

I looked up and felt the blood drain from my face as I saw Emanuel Santino standing in the room.

I quickly sat up and clutched the sheet more tightly to myself, being acutely aware that I was completely naked under it.

"I see you made it to your appointment," he rumbled.

I was too stunned to say anything.

"I came to check how everything is going."

My throat was dry and my heart felt like it had dropped to my stomach.

He took a step closer. "You must know, Jessica, that it is imperative my son marries a pure virgin."

His voice made my blood turn cold. "Y-Yes, sir, of course." My words came out in a hoarse whisper.

"Your family's reputation is somewhat sullied by the recent actions of your older sister, Juliana."

I flushed uncontrollably. "Sir, I can assure you I am untouched."

He paused, just staring at me. "It would be careless of me to just take your word for it, wouldn't it now?"

"I swear, I'm not lying." My voice was jittery and unnaturally high. "I would never lie to you, Capo." My chest felt constricted, like I could get enough air.

"I'm glad to hear it. I'll just need to find out for myself," he said.

I swallowed back the bile rising in my throat—I didn't know what was happening but I knew I had to get away from him.

I hurriedly swung my legs down from the examination table and as my feet touched the cold tile of the floor and I stood, he was instantly in front of me.

I dodged around him.

My heart pounded erratically. If I could get to the door I could call for the doctor or a nurse or just anyone to help me.

As I ran to the door, I cried out as I felt a searing pain tear through my scalp. He caught me by my hair and yanked me back toward his body.

"Scream all you like. There's nobody here that will help you. How do you think I got in here in the first place? Why do you think the doctor hasn't come back?"

I floundered as I tried to make sense of what he was telling me.

"They've all been paid off, so I can do whatever I want in here, no matter how much you scream out."

I felt my heart stutter. "Please, no..."

I attempted to fight out of his hold while at the same time my clammy hands tried to keep hold of the sheet around me.

He just laughed harshly at my attempts and while he restrained me with one hand, his other hand ripped the sheet away from me.

I screamed out again.

But he was right—nobody came to help me.

He pushed me back hard against the examination table, pain shooting through me as my body hit it at an unnatural angle. He pinned me to the table with his body on top of mine. I tried to fight him and gouged my fingernails down his cheek.

He seemed to hardly feel it. "You should know that it turns me on when a girl fights me during sex," he hissed.

I could feel the terror and panic taking over as he forced my thighs apart.

And when I felt the agony of him brutally penetrating me, I closed my eyes tightly and tried to force from my mind what was happening while the tears ran down my cheeks.

***

After Emanuel left, I hurried into the attached bathroom and shame washed over me as I looked at the blood on my upper thighs. I did the best I could to clean myself up, my hands shaking uncontrollably and sobs wracking my body. My mind was numb, and I couldn't even process what was happening.

I put my white dress back on, however, I was horrified to see in the mirror behind me a red bloodstain on the back of the skirt. I must have missed a bit when I cleaned myself, or perhaps, I was still bleeding.

I had a light overcoat with me and it came to just above my knees, so I put it on and let it hide my disgrace from the rest of the world.

After I had gotten my tears under control, I left the bathroom to find the doctor waiting in the examination room. He looked at me lewdly as he handed me a script. "Here are the birth control pills you will need to take."

I felt like refusing the piece of paper; instead, I clutched it in my fist as I rushed out of the room, degradation staining every inch of my being.

I rooted in my purse for my sunglasses, sliding them on in the hope that they would hide my red eyes. Thank goodness I wasn't being escorted by my own driver and bodyguard. They would surely have noticed that something was very wrong.

As I got back into the waiting car, I couldn't help looking with unease at the two soldiers Emanuel Santino had sent to escort me here.

After today, I knew that I could never trust any man associated with the Santinos, especially not Emanuel Santino, and most definitely not Rafael Santino.

CHAPTER 2

JESSICA

When I got home, I headed straight for my bedroom and locked myself in there for the rest of the day. I told a maid that I was feeling unwell and that I would skip dinner.

My mother was so preoccupied with her extravagant wedding preparations that she barely noticed my absence, and I was thankful for that because I couldn't face her or anyone else right now.

I could stop my body from shaking and my chest from aching. Shame washed over me in continual waves, drowning me completely with its weight.

The weather was hot in L.A. but I had never felt so cold in my life. Although I lay in bed huddled under my comforter, nothing could warm up the chill in my veins.

Every time I shut my eyes, images and sounds from earlier haunted me—the clink of his belt being unbuckled, the hiss of his zipper, the sounds he made while he did *that* to me.

I leapt off my bed and rushed into my bathroom, emptying the contents of my stomach into the bowl.

When I had finished, I sank down onto the cold floor and let my tears and humiliation overtake me.

***

The following day I stayed in my bedroom again, sending the maid with a message to say that I was still feeling unwell.

My mother briefly came in to ask how I was, and I pretended to be sleepy. I said little to her while she prattled on that she would have to choose the bridesmaids' dresses herself, given that I was too unwell to go shopping with her.

That suited me fine—right now I couldn't think about anything. The only thing I could focus on was trying to keep my mind blank and my memories of yesterday locked away.

***

The next day, I knew I had to get up, get dressed, and act like nothing had happened. I couldn't bear for anyone to suspect what had happened, and I knew I had to try and carry on as normally as possible if I was to keep what had happened a secret.

Today, the Santino family would be coming to our mansion for the engagement party. My mother was hosting a lavish dinner to celebrate.

All through the day, I wandered around in a daze, not able to focus on anything.

All I could think was that I couldn't face Rafael Santino or his father tonight.

Yet I had no other option, despite wringing my mind and trying to think of a way to get out of the party.

When it was time to dress for dinner, my mother brought to my bedroom the awful dress she'd chosen.

Over an hour later, I stood in the dress purchased by my mother, with my hair and make-up all done. I already felt horrific after the clinic incident, and this dress was making me feel even worse—if feeling worse was even possible. Inside, I felt broken. When I looked at my reflection in the mirror, all I could see was my shame.

At the appointed time, my mother went down to check on the dining room, while I made my way to the drawing room, where I knew the men would be having drinks while they waited for me. My back was damp with perspiration, yet I felt chilled to the bone.

At the door to the drawing room waited my older brother, Jacob. He was to escort me into the room. Thank God I wouldn't have to walk in by myself—although I knew that no one, not even Jacob, could protect me from Emanuel Santino.

"Wow, you look..." Jacob paused, unsure of what to say next.

"Ridiculous?" I supplied, not knowing what else to say.

"It's just that the dress is not really your style." I could tell Jacob was trying not to hurt my feelings.

I grimaced. "Jake, it's most definitely not my style."

"Mother chose it for you?"

"Who else?"

Jacob gave me a sympathetic smile. "We should go in. Rafael and Gabriel are waiting for us."

I stilled. "And...Emanuel?" My voice sounded strained even to me.

"Emanuel couldn't make it," Jacob responded, not picking up on my unease. "Although Rafael's mother is here."

I felt a sense of reprieve rush over me—*I wouldn't have to face my attacker today.* I would still have to see Rafael, but I knew it was too much to hope he wouldn't turn up to his own engagement party.

Tears of relief pricked at the back of my eyes as my emotions threatened to bubble to the surface. I had been trying so hard to contain my feelings, to keep my mind and sentiments numb, that this temporary respite caught me off-guard.

As I swept the escaping tears away with my hands, Jacob took me in his arms and gave me a hug. "Hey, Jess, it's okay. I'll be by your side tonight and we'll do this together." He gave me a reassuring smile, thankfully misunderstanding the cause of my anxiety.

If only he could always be by my side, I thought. But my nightmare at the hands of the Santino family had already begun, and I knew it would only get worse from here on in.

RAFAEL

We stood around in Cecilio Bonardi's drawing room, drinking whiskey and talking about business while we waited for Jessica to arrive.

Over the years, the families running the Società had become very wealthy. The Società had started out in L.A. by controlling the port and the drug trade, before extending its influence into various other enterprises. In recent years, the wave of indictments against Mob families in the north-east of the country had allowed Mafia organizations in other areas—such as Florida, L.A., and Vegas—to flourish.

I looked across at my future father-in-law. Cecilio Bonardi was a pretentious fool. I hoped his daughter didn't take after him, although she'd appeared pleasant enough from what I had seen of her at the contract signing.

The Bonardi's drawing room gave me a headache every time I had to come into it. It was straight out of the old country. The furniture was heavy and adorned with so many embellishments and flourishes that looking at it too long made one feel dizzy. Everything was either colored in garish gold or cringeworthy crimson, the décor screaming that the Italian inhabitants of this house had 'made it' out here in America.

The only exception to the color scheme was the green, red and white Italian flag in the corner of the room; however, even that shrieked tackiness, especially with a fan set up deliberately in front of it to make the flag flutter madly in its electric breeze. There was nothing Casmundina Bonardi didn't think of. She even had plastic covers on the chairs—her Italian relations would be so proud of her.

As I checked my watch, I heard the door open and turned to watch Jacob come in with Jessica on his arm.

Dear Lord, what *was* she wearing? Was this really the same demure girl who signed the engagement contract with me just a few days ago?

As she walked into the room, she was pulling hard at the bottom of her outfit, her actions drawing even more attention to the indecent hemline of her bright orange dress which violently clashed with the burgundy walls of the room.

I'd never spoken to Jessica before the day I gave her the engagement ring, but from what I had seen of her that day, she seemed to be a nice girl. However, if this was how she usually dressed, then maybe she wasn't the right girl for me.

She was also wearing the sparkly gold sky-high heels again—and she seemed just as unstable in them as last time.

They had seemed an odd combination with the simple lilac dress she had worn at the contract signing; to be honest, they looked no better with the current dress.

I sighed inwardly. My family ruled the Società Mafia; one day, I would become the Consigliere, and be second-in-command of the organization. My wife needed to be classy, not trashy.

The horrendous dress and shoes aside, she had a nice figure and a face with delicate features and huge gray eyes. She was wearing her dark hair loose over her shoulders, and as she walked toward us, the lighting caught the rich chestnut glints in it.

It was hard to know what to make of her. I tried to catch her eye, but she resolutely avoided my gaze.

Her mother placed Jessica and me next to each other at the dinner table. I would rather have sat where I could talk with the other men about business. That was the whole reason for this marriage, after all, not so that I could benefit from female company. There were plenty of attractive girls at our clubs who were more than willing to warm my bed.

I tried to engage Jessica in conversation, but she either ignored me or gave one-word answers as far as possible to any questions I put to her. The rare times I managed to catch her eye, her expression made it clear that she thought I was going to eat her alive.

After the meal, as we stood having coffee in the drawing room, Gabriel approached me. "So how was the dinner chat with your fiancée?"

"Far from a success," I said tersely.

Gabriel raised an eyebrow in question.

"She hardly said a word to me."

"Perhaps she's just nervous," suggested my brother.

"It's made more difficult by not having much to talk about. I don't even know the girl, so what are we supposed to talk about? I can hardly tell her that she looks nice in that dress."

Gabriel chuckled.

I looked across the room at Jessica. "This girl in front of me is completely different from the one I met a few days earlier. In her father's office, she was modestly dressed and demure in her demeanor. The girl in front of me now is dressed like a hooker, and she's either jumping out of her skin when I speak to her or being deliberately rude by ignoring me."

As the night wore on, I felt my blood pressure rising and eventually I pulled Jessica to one side.

As I laid my hand on her arm, she flinched and stepped back, and her reaction riled me even more. "We need to talk. Follow me."

She looked like a deer caught in headlights, her eyes huge and unblinking.

She followed me back to the dining room and I closed the door behind her; although knowing Mrs. Bonardi, she would probably within the next ten seconds have her whole body pressed up to the other side of the door, trying to listen in to what I had to say. Not that I cared.

I took a step toward her and her whole body tensed. I looked hard at my bride-to-be.

"You're fighting me," I told her. "Why?"

She looked at me with her wide gray stare, but her mouth remained resolutely shut. Getting her to talk to me was like drawing blood from a stone.

"This marriage won't work if you fight me."

"Said the predator to its prey." Despite the slight shake in her hands, there was an edge of sarcasm in her voice and that grated at me.

"I'm not the enemy."

"I know," she responded.

"It's good to hear you realize that—"

"You're the devil." She practically spat the words out at me.

I was stunned into silence for a moment—not something that happened often—then I felt my hackles rise. "Look, we're getting married, one way or another."

I saw a fire spark in her eyes. Perhaps she wasn't as docile as I had first thought her to be.

"I'm used to dealing with unwilling people, reluctant to do what they need to do. And you need to realize that you have no choice in this matter. It's been decided and the contract has been signed." These were the stark facts of the situation. "There's no way out for you now, and all the pouting in the world isn't going to change things."

"Pouting?" Her tone was incredulous.

"Yes, pouting. I won't stand for it now, and I won't stand for it once we're married."

"And what will you do if I *pout*?"

"You should know that I have no conscience," I advised her with a hint of warning.

"I've already gathered that. Is that all?" Her tone was angry, but I could see a faint glimmer of tears in her eyes.

I clenched my jaw. "For now."

She went to walk past me. I was standing right next to her, and she appeared to take great care not to touch me as she passed.

I sighed as I watched her go. Once she was gone, I went to the drinks cabinet and poured myself a glass of whisky, knocking it back in one go.

I knew I shouldn't be so affected by this girl, but it angered me that I was no longer in control of the situation. I prided myself on being in control of every aspect of my life and I thought I knew what I was getting when I'd signed the engagement contract. She had appeared pleasant and seemed the perfect bride to make a show of strength to the rest of the Società.

Now, however, I wasn't so sure. Having an out-of-control wife definitely did not fit in with my plans.

Jessica Bonardi certainly wasn't someone I would have chosen to marry. Although everyone referred to her as a plain Jane, she wasn't plain, but she sure as hell was awkward. I couldn't see our marriage being a pleasing relationship, nor the sex.

Maybe it was her age—she was only eighteen and seven years younger than me. Perhaps I should have insisted on a more mature bride?

What the hell had I got myself into?

CHAPTER 3

JESSICA

The day after the disastrous celebration dinner and Rafael's words to me, I finally plucked up the courage to tell my mother what had happened at the doctor's clinic.

As my words tumbled out, I saw her expression veer between incomprehension and anger.

She grabbed my arm and marched me into my father's office, repeating what I had just told her, while I stood next to her quivering and my face turning bright red through shame and embarrassment.

"For God's sake!" bellowed my father. "First Juliana, now you. Both my daughters are whores. Do you know what it would do to my standing in the Società if this got out?"

My mother couldn't help herself from interrupting my father. "Emanuel Santino is Capo, so he is justified in doing whatever he wants. But, Jessica, really you should have stopped him." She said this despite my telling her how I had tried to fight him off.

"What happens now?" I whispered through my tears. "I can't marry into that family."

"Of course you can!" thundered my father.

I was bewildered by my father's vehemence. "But I can't marry Rafael now...anyway, I'm no longer a virgin for him."

"When Emanuel took you, did you bleed?" Father grilled me.

I felt my cheeks flush a deeper shade of red. I couldn't believe we were having this conversation.

"Answer me, goddamnit!"

"Yes, I bled." My voice was a hoarse whisper.

My father nodded. "Then Emanuel knows you were a virgin and sufficiently pure for his son. At least he'll be satisfied that you weren't a slut before you spread your legs for him and will be satisfied that you are pure for his son. There is no reason to cancel the wedding. You will marry Rafael Santino if it's the last thing you do."

And I knew my father was speaking the truth—he would have no qualms in killing me if I disobeyed him. I would just be another murder to add to his long list of evil deeds. The only choices left open to me now were to marry Rafael or to die.

After that, my father dismissed me, and I crept back up to my bedroom. It was beyond comprehensible that after what Emanuel had done to me, my parents were still making me marry into the Santino family. I wished I could talk about it to my brother, Jacob, but I was too ashamed.

That only left my older sister, Juliana; but I didn't know how to get in contact with her.

***

As the days and wedding preparations went on, I felt as if I were in a trance.

I tried to keep my mind empty. If I didn't think, then maybe the pain would be less.

This morning was particularly difficult because it was Juliana's twentieth birthday. Juliana had always been there for me to lean on. This was the first birthday we wouldn't spend together, where we wouldn't even be able to talk to each other, and the thought depressed me immensely.

I was laying in bed when my cell phone rang. I didn't recognize the number and I didn't want to talk to anyone, so I ignored it, but it kept ringing insistently. With a sigh, I picked it up. "Hello?"

For a few seconds, there was only silence on the line.

"Jess? It's me. Please don't tell anyone I'm calling! Can you talk?"

Oh my God, it was Juliana. "I can talk." My heart leapt into my mouth. "Is that really you, Juliana? God, how are you?"

I heard her voice break with tears. "I'm fine, but I've been so worried about you. Are you okay?"

"I've missed you, Juliana."

"Oh Jess, it's so good to hear your voice. I've really missed you too."

"Are you okay, Juliana?"

Juliana went quiet, and I realized that she probably wasn't alone and couldn't talk freely. "I'm okay. I want to hear about you and what you've been up to. How are Jake and Mother?"

"Mother and Father have been keeping me busy. I'm getting married in a few weeks' time."

"What? What do you mean? To whom?"

"They're marrying me to Rafael Santino. We'll be married next month."

"But it's only been a few weeks since I've been gone." I could hear the shock in Juliana's voice.

"I'm eighteen now and therefore Father says I'm old enough to be married off. The Società has been in an uproar since your kidnapping. Emanuel Santino and Father thought a union between our families would send a signal of strength."

"What's Rafael like?"

I gave a hollow laugh. "Well, he's a Santino. They're all ruthless. I doubt he'll show me any mercy."

"He might be good to you, Jess. At least you will still be near Mother and Jake." After a pause, she carried on. "I wish I could be near you too. Jess, I miss you so much. I think about you and Jake every day."

I had tried so hard to keep the tears away over the last few days; however, speaking to Juliana today was too much. I couldn't say anything as my hot tears fell rapidly.

"Jess, don't cry. I'm okay, really. And you will be too, I know it. I wish I could be there on your wedding day."

"I wish that too." I couldn't say any more than that through my tears.

"Jess, is something else wrong?"

What could I tell her? She had enough of her own problems.

"Jess?"

"You can't help me. Nobody can. What's done is done."

"Jess, if you really don't want to marry Rafael, perhaps there is a way out of it."

I gave a humorless laugh. "As if Father or Emanuel Santino would let me off the hook. Anyway, the engagement contract has been signed, so it's all settled and there's no way out for me."

There was a pause from Juliana, and I heard someone murmur something to Juliana. "I'm so sorry, Jess, but I have to go now," she said quickly. "I'll try to call again soon. Take care of yourself, Jess."

"Happy Birthday, Juliana," I whispered.

"I love you, Jess."

"I love you too, Juliana."

As I hung up the call, I took some deep breaths and tried to stop the tears.

Today was a good day—I got to talk to my sister. Anything beyond that I wouldn't think about—if I didn't think about those other things, then I didn't cry.

***

A few days later, all hell broke loose.

I was asleep in bed when I heard something against my window. I got up to take a look and to my utter shock, found Juliana outside.

"Juliana, what are you doing here?" I said in a loud whisper. "Does Father know that you're here?"

"No. No one can know but you. Come down to the garden. I'll meet you by the big oak tree and I'll explain everything. Bring Jake with you."

I threw on my robe and sneakers and dashed downstairs. As soon as I reached the garden, I flew into her arms and started sobbing.

"I had to come and see you, Jess."

"Are you okay, Juliana? What did they do to you? I thought I would never see you again."

Juliana pulled back and searched my eyes. "It's you that I'm worried about. What's going on, Jess?"

I tried to avoid her gaze. "There's nothing wrong."

"Jess, I know you too well." Her voice was gentle. "Please let me help."

"It's just wedding nerves. You know how it is—you were nervous yourself before your wedding day."

"Is it really just nerves about the wedding? I know it's something more than that. Please tell me, please let me help you, Jess."

"There's nothing else, Juliana. It's been a lot lately. I lost you and there's been so much tension at home after your kidnapping, then the engagement suddenly happening and before I knew it, I was signing the engagement contract."

"You know you can still talk to me, don't you?"

When I didn't answer, Juliana asked me how Jake was, and I explained he was away for a few days on Società business. I was relieved to change the subject away from me. "Jake doesn't blame you, Juliana."

"Please tell him how sorry I am," she said quietly.

"It's not your fault."

"But it is my fault," she cried. "Everything is my fault, and now you're having to marry Rafael to strengthen the Società after my kidnapping. You and Jake are my siblings. I would do anything to protect you both."

We hugged each other again, both in tears by now.

She pulled back and after wiping her eyes, she continued to press me.

Before I could confide in her what had happened, a figure stepped out of the shadows. "What the hell is the meaning of this?"

Our heads whipped round at the sound of the voice.

"Father..." Juliana's voice shook as she addressed him.

"Jessica—go upstairs," he ordered.

"I love you, Jess," she said, quickly giving me one last hug. "Tell Jake I'm sorry. I never wanted him to get hurt."

"I'll tell him."

"Jessica, get upstairs now or I'll drag you up there myself!" bellowed my father.

I went inside with one last look over her shoulder at me. My father was furious, and dread filled me at the thought of what would happen next.

I couldn't see my father and Juliana from inside, so I went back to my bedroom. I wondered how Juliana had gotten here and if she was home for good now.

I couldn't sleep for the rest of the night, however, as my questions regarding Juliana went round and round my head.

***

Juliana stayed at our mansion for another day, although I barely had a chance to speak to her again.

The day after Juliana left, my father summoned me to his office. I knew Father was furious with me.

My father was openly seething. "You should also know that Juliana's reappearance resulted in Gabriel Santino being shot last night."

"Is Gabriel going to be alright?" My words came out in a rush. I was already on bad terms with Emanuel Santino; now Gabriel Santino was going to hate me too—after all, the only reason Juliana came was to speak to Jacob and me.

"Yes, of course he'll be fine." His tone was querulous. "What I want to know, Jessica, is why you keep attracting all these situations. As if what I've had to go through with Juliana wasn't enough, now you continually shame me—by acting like a whore with your father-in-law and then consorting with your sister when you know she is no longer welcome in our family."

I flinched violently at his use of the word 'whore'.

"I don't know why your sister wanted to come and see you, but you must have encouraged her in some way to come here."

"I didn't, Father." Technically, I hadn't asked Juliana to visit, although I couldn't deny that I had been so happy and relieved to see her. However, I wasn't about to tell my father about my earlier phone call with Juliana. I hoped that I would be able to talk to her again at some point, but Father would take away my phone immediately if he knew about this.

"I don't believe you, Jessica. You must have encouraged her to come here. For God's sake, the Capo-to-be was shot because of your stupidity! How do you think this reflects *on me*, although I presume you never thought to take your family into account before acting like this? Just as you didn't think about the family's reputation when you spread your legs in front of the Capo."

Father's reference to what had happened with Emanuel made my body clam up with shame.

But there was nothing I could say, so I just shrank into myself as my father continued his tirade against me.

CHAPTER 4

JESSICA

It was the morning of the wedding. The last few weeks had flown past in a fog of tears and terror.

Before I started to get ready, my mother came into my bedroom and shut the door behind her. "Jessica, I don't need to tell you about what will happen tonight in the bedroom. Given that you have already given your virtue away, you are well aware of what will happen."

My face reddened and I swallowed the lump in my throat. "What about Rafael needing to confirm tomorrow morning that I was a virgin for him?" I whispered.

"Emanuel will have spoken to Rafael to inform him that you were indeed a virgin, so you do not need to concern yourself with that. You need to concentrate today on looking like the happy bride."

So, I would have to put on an act.

She fixed me with her stare. "Do not let down your father or me. We have been very disappointed in you over the last few weeks, but today is your chance to redeem yourself in our eyes."

She walked out of my room then, and I let the tears slowly fall down my cheeks.

When it was time to leave for the church, Jacob came to escort me down to the waiting car. "Don't worry, Jess. We've got soldiers in other vehicles following the bridal car and more soldiers guarding the church and reception venue."

"Thanks, Jake," I replied as he squeezed my hand.

"I've overseen all the security arrangements myself. You will be completely safe—today will be nothing like Juliana's wedding day. I won't let you down in the same way."

I nodded as Jacob spoke. However, deep down, I knew that nothing and no one could protect me from the Santinos.

RAFAEL

It was the morning of the wedding, and I was getting dressed in my tuxedo for the ceremony. Gabriel came into my bedroom with our two other siblings, Natanael and Nancia.

Gabriel was the oldest at twenty-six years old, while I was just a year younger than him at twenty-five. Our youngest two siblings, Nate and Nancia, were twins and were only fourteen years old.

I noticed, as always, the similarities between my siblings. We all had dark blond hair, although the shade varied, with the twins having more bronze tones in their hair. We also shared the same dark blue eyes.

"For Christ's sake, are you still not dressed?" I asked Gabriel, seeing that he wasn't wearing his tuxedo and instead was still in his black business suit. He was a workaholic and I was surprised he'd actually taken time off today to attend my wedding.

"There's plenty of time. Relax, you're just getting pre-wedding jitters."

"As if," I chuckled.

"I don't see why I have to go to this wedding," complained Nate in his languid drawl as he tugged at the tight collar of his shirt.

"I've only got two brothers, you and Gabriel, so who else would I want to be by my side today?"

"It's not as though it's a special day," commented Nate. "You're just marrying that girl because you were ordered to."

"Wow, you're such a romantic," Nancia told her twin.

"I'm a boy—I'm not supposed to be romantic. Only girls are into all that mushy stuff."

"Even if you're not looking forward to it, I definitely am. This is the first time that I'm going to be a bridesmaid and I love my dress." Nancia smoothed down the skirt of her dress. "I can't wait until I get married one day," she said in a wistful voice.

"No one is going to want to marry you," shot back Nate.

I looked at Nancia's gold bridesmaid's dress with its garish color and plethora of frills and embellishments. It was a bit much, so I could see why a young girl like my sister might like it, but it seemed that Jessica had a thing with gold. First there were those gold shoes and now these gold bridesmaids' dresses.

I just hoped that the wedding dress wasn't going to be gold too. Mrs. Bonardi struck me as the traditional sort, so hopefully Jessica would go with the standard white dress to emphasize her virginity and pureness.

In response to Nate's insult, Nancia grabbed my bowtie from the bed and tried to swipe her twin with it as he dodged out of her way.

"Guys, seriously, I'm trying to get ready here," I said to my younger siblings.

"You're too slow to get me," challenged Nate to his sister, who responded by chasing him around the room.

"Okay, anyone under the age of twenty out of my room so I can finish getting ready!" I loved the twins, however you never knew if they were going to be getting on like best friends or fighting like arch-enemies.

When the door finally closed, shutting out the voices of the twins, it was just Gabriel and I left in my bedroom. I finished putting on my bowtie.

"You look good," commented Gabriel, looking over at me.

My black tuxedo was edged with a thin trim of red, which went with the red roses I had sent this morning to Jessica for her bouquet. It was customary in Italian families for their groom to choose the bouquet as a gift to his bride.

"Thanks, bro," I replied. "I think I'll do."

Gabriel raised an eyebrow at me. "Any nerves about today?"

I exhaled. "I just hope she doesn't try to ignore me like she did at the engagement dinner."

"She was probably just nervous."

"I get that she is young and only eighteen years old, but we spoke when I gave her the ring and she seemed pretty mature then. I don't want a silly, childish schoolgirl as my wife. We've got enough shit going on with the business and I don't want to be coming back to immature dramas at home."

"She's always seemed pretty quiet to me," remarked Gabriel.

"As if you've ever paid any attention to her. Your mind and eyes were always on Juliana."

"That ship has sailed," replied Gabriel curtly.

"Has it? How was it seeing her that night a couple of weeks ago when she came to see Jessica?"

"It was weird, I have to admit, but she's gone now, so there's no point discussing it further." That was typical of Gabriel. He compartmentalized his life and even his feelings—nothing got in the way of the Società or business.

"At least Jessica won't be able to totally ignore me today. She'll have to talk to me to make her vows at the altar."

"Unless she decides to refuse you."

"And why would she do that? She knows how much her family wants this union."

"She'd be mad to refuse you, but women are a strange breed."

"Gee, thanks for the pep talk. Isn't a groomsman supposed to bolster my spirits?"

"You'll be fine, Raf. You know I'm always here for you."

"Thanks, man." We embraced each other and then it was time to drive to the church.

The twins insisted on coming in the same car as Gabriel and me, and we had to put up with them bickering all the way to the church. "Do you two ever stop?" I asked my younger siblings.

"He started it," huffed Nancia. "He said that I look dumb in my dress."

"Hey, Nate, that's no way to speak to a lady," I admonished.

"She's not a lady. She's just a girl."

"I *will* be a lady one day, so you should speak to me with the respect I deserve," replied Nancia in a haughty tone.

"You don't deserve any respect wearing a dress like that," muttered her twin. "I deserve *your* respect as your elder."

"You're only older than me by seven minutes—that doesn't even count," disagreed Nancia.

I was glad when we arrived at the church. We all got out of the car, and Gabriel and I shook hands with various Underbosses and Captains before entering the historic church where we were met by the sight of a circus in full swing.

Gabriel looked at me. "Wow, your bride and mother-in-law have really outdone themselves."

"Christ, I know our families wanted to make a show of today to signify strength to the rest of the organization, but even I didn't expect them to go this far."

The cloying air overpowered my senses with the scent of hundreds of flowers. The church was rammed with people and it appeared that the whole Società had turned out in force for today's wedding—which I suppose wasn't surprising given that I'd heard Mrs. Bonardi had been telling everyone that this was going to be the 'wedding of the year'.

Mrs. Bonardi herself was dressed in what could only be described as a gold monstrosity. I hoped to God that Jessica would not be wearing gold today and her dress would be more tasteful than her mother's over-the-top outfit and the bridesmaids' flouncy dresses.

I made my way down the aisle to the front of the church. I had to push past the floral arrangements at the end of each pew, which were overflowing into and taking over the aisle. Some petals clung to my tuxedo and I brushed them off in annoyance. The wedding hadn't even begun, but I had already had enough.

While we waited for the ceremony to start, I greeted various guests and alternated business talk with polite chit-chat.

I checked my watch and clenched my jaw. Jessica was already twenty minutes late.

She knew the time that the wedding was due to start, and I expected her to show up on time.

When forty minutes had passed, the priest approached me and cleared his throat. "I have two more weddings to conduct this afternoon. I'm not sure how much longer we can wait. Do you think your fiancée will be turning up soon?"

"You'll wait however long I require you to," I growled at the priest, putting my hand on my revolver.

I saw the priest follow the movement of my hand. His face turned white, and he made the sign of the cross. Whatever—he knew the price of doing business with the Società. He might serve at the right hand of God, but that didn't protect him from the deadly hand of the Società.

As the priest scuttled away, Gabriel murmured, "Perhaps she's having second thoughts."

"She better not be. She's signed the engagement contract and she knows there's no way out from it—except through death." Those were the rules of our world and I wasn't going to apologize for it.

We continued waiting and Gabriel tried to distract me by talking about business matters. Business always managed to distract him, but I wasn't the same as my brother.

Fifty minutes after the scheduled start time, there was a flurry of activity at the wooden doors to the church and I focused my gaze on it, hoping for Jessica's sake that she had finally deigned to turn up.

My father came and joined me at the altar, and we all looked expectantly at the entrance.

The doors abruptly opened, and the organist began playing. A small figure dressed in white appeared, and as I watched her make her way down the aisle, I forced myself to unclench my fists and relax my muscles, but I didn't quite manage to remove the frown from my face.

I didn't like being kept waiting and as a Mafia daughter, she should have known better.

She walked toward me, and I watched her shoes crush the petals which had fallen from the arrangements onto the floor. Thank God she wasn't wearing those horrendous sparkly gold shoes again—that surely would have been the last straw for me today.

While she made the long descent to the altar, I could hear noisy sobs coming from the golden meringue—that is, her mother. But I shut my ears to it all and focused my attention on my bride.

Her dress was white with a high neckline and cap sleeves, showing off her slender arms. The dress flared around her delicate figure into an A-line skirt and there was a small train. My gaze rose to her face, and

I noticed that her hair was swept into an updo, its dark luster sharply contrasting with the veil covering it.

She came closer to me, and I could see that her father was tightly holding her hand and practically tugging her to the front of the church. She couldn't make it any more obvious to me and the whole of the Società that she didn't want to be here and that she didn't want to be marrying me.

Goddamnit, what was wrong with her? Didn't she understand what was required of her?

Jessica and her father reached my side. He pulled up her veil, revealing her soft gray eyes huge against her pale face, before forcefully putting her hand into mine as she tried to keep her distance from me. I closed my fingers around hers and I saw her flinch as I gripped too hard. I made myself loosen my hand, but only slightly.

Then her father shook the hand of my father who was also standing next to me. This was, after all, a business arrangement between our families.

I couldn't understand what Jessica hoped to achieve by making it obvious that she didn't want to walk down the aisle toward me. Surely, she must know that there was no way out of this for her?

The priest began his spiel about God, matrimony, and children. I felt like telling him to get a fucking move on. We all knew that this marriage wasn't about love or religion—it was about business and money.

The priest turned to me. "Rafael and Jessica, have you come here to enter into marriage without coercion, freely and wholeheartedly?" What a stupid question—everyone could see how my bride was.

"I have," I said firmly, and then I pointedly looked at Jessica who was hesitating.

The blood in my veins heated to boiling point and I tightened my grip around her fingers.

She replied in a tremulous voice, "I have."

"Are you prepared, as you follow the path of marriage, to love and honor each other for as long as you both shall live? And are you prepared to accept children lovingly from God and to bring them up according to the law of Christ and his church?"

I barely gave the priest a chance to finish his words before I impatiently barked out, "I am."

Jessica had gone deathly pale at this question. Perhaps she wasn't looking forward to the process of making children with me. Tough—she was going to become my wife today and I would be claiming her body tonight whether she wanted it or not. Jessica whispered, "I am."

For God's sake, she could at least have tried to sound a little more convincing. The girl before me today was a completely different person from the girl I had met at the contract signing. She blew hot and cold and could change from demure to prickly in a heartbeat.

But I wasn't going to play her game. She would be my wife and submit to my will, or she would reap the consequences.

We joined our right hands and made our vows to one another. When it was Jessica's turn, I listened in satisfaction as she quietly said the required words. "I, Jessica, take you, Rafael, to be my husband. I promise to be true to you in good times and in bad, in sickness and in health. I will love you and honor you all the days of my life."

It was time to exchange the rings and her hand shook uncontrollably as I slid the wedding band onto her slender finger. "Jessica, receive this ring as a sign of my love and fidelity. In the name of the Father and of the Son and of the Holy Spirit."

When the priest announced that I could kiss my wife, I didn't give my bride a chance to shrink away from me. Instead, I firmly grasped her in my arms and pressed my lips against her reluctant mouth.

As her sweet summery scent drifted into my senses, I felt her trembling in my hold—and I knew that I was definitely looking forward to later when I would have her in my bed.

CHAPTER 5

RAFAEL

At the hotel selected for the reception, we stood at the entrance to greet the endless line of guests, and again my bride avoided looking at me as much as humanly possible.

After we had finally done our duty to the arriving guests, we made our way to the head table. Every time I thought about my bride's behavior today, the blood heated in my veins.

As soon as we sat down at the table, Jessica reached for a glass of champagne.

I shot out my hand and I grabbed it away from her. "You're too young to drink," I growled, disregarding the fact that her parents had likely permitted her to drink wine with meals at home.

"So, I'm old enough to be married off to you but not to drink at my own wedding?" she snapped.

"Correct." At last, I had got a whole sentence out of her. To be honest, her drinking didn't bother me. Right now, however, I needed some outlet for my irritation with her.

Jessica glowered at me, but I couldn't have cared less at this moment.

Anyhow, I didn't want her drunk tonight—I wanted her to remember me taking her as mine, marking her with my cum, and making her submit to me.

All too soon, it was time for our first dance. As the music started, I stood up and held out my hand to my bride, but she deliberately looked away from me.

Christ, what the hell was she playing at? Her obvious unwillingness at the church had been bad enough, but she was my wife now whether she liked it or not. I couldn't understand the point of her games.

I reached down and took hold of her slender wrist, hauling her up to her feet and toward me.

"What are you doing?" she asked in a high voice.

"What does it look like? You're not going to get out of dancing with me that easily."

I tugged her behind me to the dancefloor, not slowing down my long-legged stride for her.

I could see she was struggling to keep up with me, but my grip around her wrist gave her no chance to slow down.

Once we were on the dancefloor, I pulled her small body into my hold. Despite not being a romantic, I would never have imagined my first dance with my bride being like this, with her caged in my vice-like grasp and being practically dragged around the floor by me.

"You're holding me too tight," she murmured.

"That's what comes of being difficult," I retorted.

"I wasn't being difficult. I just didn't want to dance."

"When will it get through to you that your wants are irrelevant now? You will do what is expected of you today as my bride, first at this reception and then in my bed tonight."

Her face blanched at my words. And I felt a surge of triumph that I was finally getting some reaction from her, rather than the distant, haughty bride she had been so far.

"You're hurting me." Her voice had taken on a pleading tone.

A hint of doubt crept into my conscience, and I relaxed my grip by the tiniest amount. I wasn't going to give her too much leeway, though—she'd shown me that she couldn't be trusted.

She avoided my eyes for the whole dance. She could do whatever she liked, but she wouldn't be able to avoid me tonight.

We finished the dance and I gladly handed her over to her father for the next dance while I had the dubious pleasure of dancing with her mother.

Mrs. Bonardi talked incessantly about the flowers, the dresses, the guests and the food. Christ, did the mouth on this woman ever stop?

"How wonderfully the wedding has turned out, just like I knew it would!" she exclaimed. She had obviously forgotten her daughter's childish display at the church, I thought.

I had never really spoken to Mrs. Bonardi in the past. Previously, I had been concerned that Jessica might take after her pompous father, but now I could see that I should really be worried about her taking after her tiresome mother.

JESSICA

Surviving today was a living nightmare.

I was terrified when I had to walk down the aisle—toward Emanuel who had been standing at his son's side, smirking an evil smile as his eyes burned into me. I'd been petrified that he would try to touch me in some way, but thankfully, he'd merely shook my father's hand.

Now, not only did I have to constantly monitor the position of my father-in-law in the ballroom, I was now also having to deal with my difficult husband.

Every look and touch from Rafael sent my pulse surging. Repeated waves of panic were threatening to overwhelm me.

I was the center of attention, and it was grueling trying to keep it together when all I felt like doing was huddling in a corner and bursting into tears.

Rafael and I carried on dancing with the required members of our families. After I had finished dancing with my father, it was the turn of the best man to lead me around the dancefloor. Gabriel Santino approached me and held out his arm. I didn't want to dance with any Santino men today, and that included him.

As we danced, I could feel his stare upon me, and the atmosphere was definitely awkward with my attempts to avoid his gaze.

"Are you okay?" His abrupt question made me jump.

I risked a glance up at him. He was looking intently at me. "I'm fine."

Neither of us said anything else for a while, although I was acutely aware that he was still staring at me, almost as though he were trying to look into my mind.

"Do you miss her? Juliana, I mean." I don't know what made me ask Gabriel this.

I watched as Gabriel gritted his teeth. "I worry for her, about what her captor has done to her already and what he is doing to her now. We won't stop trying to get her back. It shames us all that they took a Mafia daughter."

I noticed how he had cleverly avoided answering my question, no doubt a skill he'd acquired as Capo-in-waiting.

Next my husband came to collect me for photographs which were to be be taken outside. My feet were hurting in my new shoes and I longed to sit down.

Rafael led me outdoors without saying a word and that suited me fine, although I could feel his glare upon me all the while.

A number of guests were milling in the gardens which the banqueting suite opened into. As soon as we appeared, I felt everyone's eyes turn to us, and then they watched while we posed for the photos.

Once the photographer had finished, Rafael finally spoke to me. "Here comes my father now. He wants a photo with the bride. Make sure you behave—he won't put up with as much as I've put up with today. I'm going to get a drink."

Right then, Emanuel interrupted us. "I've come to claim your bride…" He openly leered at me.

My father-in-law's words and expression sent a shudder right through me. Suddenly I felt ice cold despite the hot sunshine blazing on my skin.

With the wedding taking up most of today, he probably wasn't going to get the chance to murder anyone today.

So, instead he was going to torment me to fulfill his daily quota of evil deeds…

"Claim her for a special photo, that is." His mouth twisted into a cruel expression as Rafael walked away.

Emanuel roughly grasped my wrist.

I tried to keep some space between us, but he held me too tightly and pulled me too close to him.

My skin crawled as he leered at me. I frantically hoped that no one would notice I was unraveling under the gaze of the Capo…

His proximity and the way he was gripping my wrist was unseemly, but no one would have the audacity to say anything to the Capo of the Società.

Even if people dared to mention it between themselves, no doubt his actions would be blamed on the effects of too much celebratory alcohol.

I felt a bead of cold sweat trickle between my breasts as I desperately avoided looking at him.

"You've been avoiding me, Jessica."

I felt my face flush. "I haven't…"

His fingers dug into my skin, reminding me of that awful day. My breath rushed out in a gasp.

"I like seeing the effect I have on you, Jessica."

I tried to steady my quick breaths.

"I've thought a lot about my time between your legs…"

Even though my breaths were coming rapidly, it felt as though the oxygen couldn't reach my lungs.

I started to feel lightheaded…

"…about how tight your virgin pussy was, about the sounds you made when I forced my dick into you…"

I was going to pass out…

He gave a cruel laugh. "I'm sure my son will enjoy your tight pussy—I know I certainly did. I'm so glad you are part of my family now."

I wasn't sure how much longer my legs could hold out. I turned my head frantically, attempting to find Rafael.

"I think you enjoyed it too, didn't you?"

Oh God, I couldn't see Rafael…

But then the photographer called that he was ready for us.

I felt my father-in-law wrap a sweaty arm around my waist and grip my hip too tightly.

Then I held my breath as he leaned in too close to me, my body rigid as I tried to stop him pulling me further into his hold.

I don't know how I carried on until the photographer was finished. When I heard him say he had all the pictures he needed, I felt like crying tears of relief.

Until Emanuel roughly maneuvered me behind some shrubs.

"Please, I need to sit down." I forced the words out.

Emanuel laughed at me again. "You should know from last time that your pleading doesn't move me, that your begging won't stop me."

"I'm n-not feeling well..."

"I am Capo, and you will do what I tell you to," he jeered.

He yanked at my dress...

I tried to scream.

But nothing came out.

My vision swam.

And then Rafael appeared.

Thank God!

"Jessica, what are you doing now?" he gritted out. "I've been waiting for you."

"N-nothing..."

"I was just letting your wife know what I expect from her now that's she's a member of my family," Emanuel smirks. "I was giving her some *fatherly* advice..."

"Jessica, you should probably sit down now," Rafael snaps. "You've been on your feet most of the day, and anyhow, they are serving the main course now."

I couldn't face food, but I eagerly clasped Rafael's outstretched hand in my desire to get away from his father's taunts.

During the meal, I could only push the food around my plate.

"You should eat," said Rafael tersely.

I shook my head at him. "I'm not hungry." If I ate, I was sure I would throw up.

All too soon, dinner was over and my husband turned toward me, looking intently at me. "Come, Jessica. It's time for me to take you upstairs."

And as Rafael spoke, I felt my skin heat and dread suffuse my entire body.

CHAPTER 6

JESSICA

Rafael stood up, his towering height and muscled physique emphasizing how much stronger he was than me—how easily he would be able to overpower me tonight if I refused him.

I felt my heart drumming too fast.

I slowly lifted my clammy hand and let him wrap his fingers around mine. I barely had the strength to get up, but he helped me to my feet with a strong hand under my arm. After I had stood, however, I couldn't move from my spot.

His warm hand at the small of my back urged me forward. He kept hold of my hand and with his other hand still on my back, I was compelled to walk toward the elevator.

I tried avoiding looking at anyone or listening to what they were saying.

I knew the men would be making lewd jokes about what would happen tonight, while the woman would be looking at me with a mixture of curiosity and pity—wondering if I would be strong enough not to show fear in front of the whole Società as I made my way out of the ballroom and up to our bedroom.

I was a Santino now—God, it was hard to believe even that—and, as such, there was a lot of interest in me. Some Mafia mothers were hostile because their own unwed daughters were not offered a marriage to Rafael Santino, while others were merely curious for the sake of gossip.

There was not a lot to occupy the life of a Mafia wife, meaning that gossip was rife amongst the females in our circle. As if a new Santino bride was not sufficiently gossip worthy, the fact that disgrace surrounded my older sister would be making all the gossips clap their hands in glee as they discussed and dissected my family later on.

They would analyze every look that had passed between Rafael and myself today, and the most bitter of the women would be wondering how awful my husband would be to me tonight, of course couched in words of feigned concern.

As we passed Emanuel, I tried to shut my ears, but it was impossible to avoid hearing him. "What I wouldn't do to have the delight of a fresh virgin tonight!" he declared loudly to his fellow men.

He was mocking me—he'd already taken me when I was a virgin. I felt a crimson tide rush up my cheeks and the prickle of tears at the back of my eyes.

But I couldn't cry, not in front of everyone, and definitely not in front of any Santino.

Rafael continued leading me out of the room. Just a few minutes longer, just a few more minutes, then I'd be away from the Emanuel, I told myself.

We were spending the night in the honeymoon suite of the hotel, and as the elevator whisked us upstairs, I was thankful that the jeers of the Capo and the other men were shut off from me now.

I didn't know how I was going to cope with Emanuel being my father-in-law, but right now I had to focus on getting through my wedding night.

When we reached our room, Rafael used the key card to open the door. The beep of the door unlocking seemed to echo in the hallway, making me shudder. The honeymoon suite was on its own private floor—there would be no one to help me tonight if I cried out for help.

Rafael held the door open for me, gesturing with his hand for me to enter first, and I felt myself shiver as I had to brush past him on my way in.

Once inside, I stood awkwardly in the middle of the large room, not knowing what to do next. The bedsheets taunted me with their dazzling white and pureness.

I knew that in line with the Sicilian tradition of *cunzata del letto*, the bed would have been prepared earlier by four unmarried girls because the wedding night bedlinen could only be touched by females who were virgins. They would have made up the bed with the pure white, hand-embroidered sheets. They would also have sprinkled rice between the sheets as good luck for the new bride's fertility.

I was supposed to consummate my marriage in this bed. But in the eyes of our traditions, I was not worthy of touching these sheets—because I was no longer a virgin. I was no longer pure.

Rafael took off his jacket and prowled toward me. I wished now that I wasn't frozen in the middle of the room. I should have stood next to the table or chair; that way, I would have had something to hold on to, something to steady myself against and something to put between myself and my husband.

Rafael walked behind me and I panicked that I couldn't see him or what he was about to do to me.

I tried to spin around to face him, but he stopped me by putting his hands firmly around the top of my arms—making me sharply inhale and forcing me to stay faced away from him.

"Easy," he growled into my ear, the soft caress of his breath on my neck making me jump. "I'm just taking off your necklace for you," he said as he undid the fastener.

I attempted to relax my muscles, but my sixth sense told my body not to relax—not to let my guard down around this man.

"As beautiful as this necklace is, I want to see you completely naked tonight."

Those words made me spring away from him just as he removed the necklace.

I backed away from him and felt myself lose balance as my heel caught in the hem of my long dress.

His hands clasped around my arms as I stumbled, catching me and tugging me into proximity with his body again. Before I could do anything else, he turned me around in his arms, further disorientating me.

I felt his fingers fiddle with the zipper at the back of my dress. I clenched my sweaty palms, telling myself that there was still the fabric between him and me, still some time and some protection before I would be forced to give myself up to him.

My dress's design meant that it dipped down to the middle of my back, and after he slowly undid the top part of the zipper, he let his finger stroke the sensitive skin there.

"No," I said in a strangled cry, managing to whirl around so that I could see him.

"No?" He narrowed his dark blue eyes at me in warning and his cold tone reminded me of my duty tonight. I willed my frantic heart to stop thumping and took a deep breath.

I forced myself to say as calmly as possible, "I need to freshen up first."

He regarded me for a few moments. He nodded toward the adjoining bathroom. "Why don't you get ready for bed," he said, his voice a command rather than a suggestion.

I fled to the bathroom, grateful that he hadn't undressed me—and hoping that the rest of the night would be as straightforward.

I took off my wedding dress, the simple task taking twice as long as it should have due to the trembling in my hands.

After getting the dress off and tossing it to one side, I put on a new silk nightdress which my mother had chosen. I looked at myself in the large mirror above the vanity. It was flimsy and had narrow spaghetti straps to hold it up.

Why on earth had I let my mother choose? I should have picked my nightwear out for myself, choosing the least sexy items I could find.

When I couldn't delay any longer, I returned to the bedroom. Rafael ran his gaze down my nightdress before heading into the bathroom. I heard the water in the shower run and ten minutes later he came back freshly washed and dressed only in a pair of black boxer briefs.

I looked at him for a couple of seconds and it was impossible not to notice his body. As he stalked toward me, muscles rippled across his tall body, defining his torso, arms, and legs and emphasizing his total power. His body was mostly tanned, like he was outdoors a lot, and hair and scars adorned his chest.

I could see the familiar Società tattoo on his arm—depicting a beating heart with the Società name emblazoned across it. I followed the sandy hair on his chest as it trailed downwards and disappeared into his boxer briefs, my face flushing as I darted my eyes away.

I was already laying in bed, with the covers pulled up to my chin. He walked toward me and turned off the lights, except for the two nightstand lamps. Why was he leaving the lamps on?

I laid on my back, looking at the ceiling and praying that he would turn off the lamps and go to sleep.

Instead, he reached for me.

Leaning over me, he caged me between his thick arms and his dark navy eyes stared at me. I felt myself hold my breath, trying to freeze time, trying to stop what was about to happen.

Then, very slowly, he stroked the back of his knuckles against my cheek. I averted my eyes and looked anywhere but at him.

He bent his face down to kiss me.

"What are you doing?" I blurted out, my voice unnaturally high.

"What do you think?" he smirked.

Maybe he just wanted a kiss and that was all. So this time, when he moved his face toward me, I let him press his firm lips against mine. I didn't respond, fighting the bile threatening to come up my throat.

My spine was ramrod straight. I could do this—it was just a kiss, I told myself.

His mouth played with mine, trying to get a response out of me, but I kept my lips clamped shut. His proximity was overwhelming my senses. My nostrils filled with his scent—soap and a trace of cologne overlaying something manly and dangerous. I held my breath, trying to close my mind and shut him out.

His tongue caressed my lips and I tried to push him away, but I had no strength in me. My hands were clammy and froze when I felt the fierce muscles of his bare chest under my fingertips—muscles that could hold me down and force me.

I hadn't been given a choice that day in the clinic. The choice had been ripped from my body and from my soul.

I wouldn't let that happen again.

I knew what my duty was tonight—to my husband, to my family, and to the Società. I knew what I had to do tonight, and I was making the choice to give myself over to that duty.

As long as it was my choice, Rafael couldn't hurt me.

I wouldn't allow anyone to hurt me ever again.

As I gasped for breath, his tongue slipped inside my mouth and stroked the sensitive nerve endings there. I gave myself up to the moment and let his mouth coax me into submission.

I heard him groan and I tried to ignore his hardness pressing against my thigh.

His hand moved and slipped inside my silk nightdress, cupping my bare breast, and the feel of his fingertips on my naked skin made me instinctively shove against him.

"Get away from me!" I cried out.

CHAPTER 7

RAFAEL

I looked down at Jessica, irritated at her return to childish games.

She was being coy and playing hard to get, but I wasn't in the mood for this again. I had already had enough of her games earlier in the day.

The sight of her in her silky nightdress, the thin fabric clinging to her breasts and highlighting her puckered nipples, had made me painfully hard—just as would have been her intention when she picked out the flimsy nightwear.

I let my stare linger on her curves. I was going to enjoy having her body under mine and making her submit to me.

"Surely your mother explained what is expected of you tonight?"

"She didn't need to." Jessica was equally terse with me, vexing me further.

I frowned, pausing for a few seconds, before I moved my hand toward her body again.

But she didn't give me a chance to touch her, instead pushing hard against me and scrambling off the bed. She ran and grabbed one of my knives that I had left on the dresser. "Touch me again and I swear I'll kill you." Her voice was full of hostility and vehemence.

My patience snapped. "What the hell, Jessica? Have you completely lost your mind?"

She held the knife in her violently shaking hand, its blade gleaming under the light of the lamps.

"Jessica, you know I will be asked to confirm tomorrow morning that you were a virgin and that we consummated our marriage. The Società expects it of all its newlyweds, and we are no exception. In fact, it's even more important that the Santinos, as the Società's ruling family, are seen to be following the organization's traditions."

Her eyes were huge in her face.

When she didn't answer, I slowly prowled toward her. "You know I must bed you and make you bleed tonight."

"Fuck you! You've already had my blood. You're all monsters."

"What are you talking about?" My voice was hard.

"Your family has already had my blood. What, do you want me to bleed again? Was once not enough for your family? Are you going to take me so roughly tonight that I bleed again?"

As unease prickled at me, I said in a low voice, "What do you mean, my family has already had your blood?"

When Jessica gave no answer, I carried on in a deadly quiet voice. "Jessica, tell me, are you still a virgin?"

She looked at me bewildered, her cheeks flushed red and her chest heaving with panicky breaths.

"Answer me." I took another step toward her. I was used to interrogating people, getting answers out of them even if they didn't want to talk. I wasn't going to let this girl keep secrets from me.

"You already know! Why are you tormenting me?"

"What do I know?"

She swallowed hard. After another long pause during which she looked carefully at me, she murmured, "You don't know?" The color drained from her face.

"I want you to tell me the truth—if I take you on this bed tonight, will you bleed for me?" I should have tempered my words with her, should have questioned her less harshly, but something was surging through me and making me lose control.

A tear rolled down her cheek. "How can I bleed for you if I'm not still a virgin?" Her voice was a whisper. "You obviously don't know...did your father think you wouldn't notice? Jesus, your family is beyond fucked up..." Her free hand flew to her mouth as if realizing she shouldn't have just spoken about my family like that and was afraid of my reaction.

Another thought crashed into my mind, and horror spread through me. I made my voice gentle. "What happened?"

She stayed silent.

I took a deep breath. "Did somebody force you?"

"Y-yes," she stammered, averting her eyes from me as her cheeks turned bright red.

I approached her in a wary manner. "Jessica, please give me the knife before you hurt yourself." I could easily get the knife from her, but I didn't want to scare her any further in her current state.

We were both silent for a long while. She looked like she wanted to tell me something but was too frightened to say anything more. My previous anger had scared her.

"Do your parents know about this?"

"Of course they know. Both our families know," she said bitterly, half laughing and half crying as she swiped her hand across her face.

"And they let this marriage go ahead?" I couldn't stop the steeliness creeping into my voice.

When she nodded, her voice broke down into rasping sobs and she sank into an armchair, her face in her hands. I wanted to ask her more, but she didn't look in any fit state to be questioned.

I needed to speak to her parents. I looked at my bride and faltered for a few seconds. Maybe I should call her mother to help her—but Casmundina Bonardi struck me as the sort who would probably get hysterical and make things worse.

"Stay here," I instructed Jessica. Throwing on some clothes, I added my knife holster and tucked a gun into the back of my belt before exiting our room.

I strode straight to the elevator and headed for the floor I knew her parents were on. We were all staying in the same hotel as it had been hired out exclusively over the weekend for the purpose of the wedding.

I pounded on the door of Cecilio Bonardi's room. I was raging and I had to force myself to breathe.

Cecilio answered the door in striped pajamas and with a gun in his hand. "What's the meaning of this? We were about to go to sleep."

"So I see," I gritted out, seeing Jessica's mother nervously hovering in the background, dressed in a nightgown and with cream spread all over her face.

"Is something wrong?" Cecilio barked at me, while his wife couldn't help looking as guilty as hell.

"We better talk inside." I pushed my way into their room. I didn't have time for polite formalities.

Once inside their room, Cecilio turned to me. "Well? Explain yourself," he demanded.

Fuck, he was a pompous jackass. "Bonardi, did you or did you not know that your daughter was not a virgin on the morning of her wedding?"

"Of course I knew." He didn't even hesitate before answering. "She told her mother and me. My daughter never lies to me."

My next words came out in a dangerously low voice. "And you didn't think to mention this? You didn't think that I, as her proposed husband, had a right to know?"

"I left it up to your father to tell you," Cecilio blustered.

"What the hell has my father got to do with this?"

Cecilio didn't answer, and he and his wife looked at each other uneasily.

I pulled my gun out and aimed it at Cecilio. "So help me God, tell me what the fuck my father has got to do with all this?"

Cecilio looked uncomfortable. "Well...he took Jessica...you know, bedded her. I thought you knew. It was at the doctor's clinic when she went to get her contraception."

Fury burned a trail through my whole body, ready to explode at the slightest ignition. "He bedded Jessica? Why?"

Cecilio threw his hands up. "Emanuel said it was his right as Capo, so that he could check she was still pure for his son."

"And you kept this a secret from me?" My voice was a harsh growl.

"I thought your father would have told you—you know, to not expect blood tonight and to lie when you are asked to confirm her virginity tomorrow morning. And I thought he would have informed you, of course, that Jessica was indeed pure." His voice quickened. "Let's be clear—she was definitely a virgin for your father, so your family can't claim she wasn't intact."

I could only stare at the arrogant bastard standing in front of me, while fighting down the urge to end his miserable life right now.

Cecilio, however, didn't know when to shut up. "I won't have our Bonardi family name called into question over Jessica's virginity, especially after what has happened with her older sister. Jessica was pure until your family got their hands on her. The Santinos got a virgin—whether it was you or your father who took her innocence, that's no concern of mine. I've done my duty and fulfilled my obligations under the marriage contract, make no mistake about that."

I should knife him in the gut right here and now, I thought. What monster wouldn't care that their daughter had been forced by a man twice her age?

I clenched my fists. As much as I wanted to murder the despicable man in front of me, I couldn't forget that he was an Underboss of the Società. And the person I really needed to take my burning rage out on was my fucking father.

Turning on my heel, I left their room. Swiftly making my way to Gabriel's hotel room, I banged on his door. I needed my brother.

He opened his door, and after one look at my face, he let me in and I informed him what Jessica had just told me.

"She's not a virgin, and her parents and our parents knew all along?" Gabriel said, clearly as surprised as me. The requirement for a girl to be a virgin on her wedding day was absolute in the Mafia world.

"I need to talk to our father."

We left his room and when we got in the elevator, I was about to hit the floor for my father's room.

But I stopped in my tracks. "What the fuck am I doing? I need to get someone to guard Jessica in our bedroom."

Gabriel frowned. "To stop her running away?"

I sighed. "I'll get Gianni to do it. Plus his wife, Lorissa, to sit with Jessica." Gianni and his wife could be be trusted to do what was needed and not gossip about it.

I rang Gianni and told him to meet me outside my room with his wife.

Once there, I instructed him to guard the door to my room and Lorissa to sit with Jessica.

He asked no questions, as I knew would be the case.

"Let me talk to my wife for a minute before you go in," I said to Lorissa.

Entering the suite, I saw Jessica shoot up from where she'd been sitting and take a couple of steps back.

"One of my men is guarding the door and his wife will sit with you."

"To stop me from running away?" she asked in a small voice.

"No." Fuck. First Gabriel thought this was my reason and now Jessica too. "It's to keep you safe."

After what Jessica had told me, I had stormed out of the room in my determination to get to the bottom of the situation. But I had left Jessica— a young girl who was in a vulnerable position— alone and unprotected. I berated myself for not thinking things through properly. I always took care to assess situations in my work rather than act rashly, but my emotions had got in the way of that this time.

"They will stay with you until I return."

She looked confused but gave the tiniest of nods. Then I went back to Gabriel and we proceeded to my father's room.

Gabriel looked me carefully in the eye. "Our father's gone too far this time, Rafael. He's always preyed on the weak. We should kill him now—tonight." He had given us a brutal upbringing, and there was no love lost between Emanuel Santino and his sons.

I exhaled as I shook my head. I'd like nothing more than to torture that fucker until he was screaming for mercy and then ending his measly existence. "If we do it tonight, people might try to find out why and then eventually find out about Jessica. I can't have that happen."

Gabriel frowned. "You mean you want to keep her?"

I gazed back at him, wondering what he'd do in the same situation. "She's mine now. She might not be a virgin, but that is through no fault of her own. I can't have people finding out about what happened to her. I won't do that to her, not after what she's been through. Anyhow, everyone will say the Santinos are out of control if we kill our father. Then there will be a power struggle, and other families will attempt to take over control of the Società. We'll get our vengeance. It just won't be tonight. Don't they say revenge is a dish best served cold?"

My mind started to think quickly.

"We need to be smart about this, Gabriel. I won't jeopardize the stability of the Santinos because that ensures the safety of our family: Mother, Nate, Nancia, and now Jessica." The last name I had uttered was the most important one to me now. "Through whatever means, I need to protect Jessica—she has to be my priority from now on. Even if that means vengeance has to wait for now."

Gabriel nodded. He knew what I was saying made sense. We would get our revenge, but it would have to be carefully planned and precisely executed.

Despite my words, I had to push down the extreme urge surging inside me to execute my father right here and right now.

We arrived at his room, and I banged on the door.

After a while, we heard him approach and open the door. "Ah, I thought I might get a visit from Rafael tonight, but not from the both of you," he smirked.

Gabriel and I stepped inside the suite. Our mother was nowhere to be seen. "Where's Mother?"

"Downstairs, checking on the arrangements for tomorrow's breakfast. So, did your bride please you between the sheets tonight?" he mocked.

I took a step toward him.

"You know, if you take her brutally enough, I'm sure you can get her sweet pussy to bleed again. She seemed to like it rough, given how much she fought me."

I clenched my fists as I thought about the violence Jessica must have endured. "Christ, you fucking disgust me," I hurled at my father. "What's happened stays between the Santinos and Bonardis. I won't have Jessica's reputation dragged through the mud. Is that understood?"

My father frowned at my tone. "Don't you forget I'm still your Capo."

Gabriel interrupted our father. "And I'm your heir. If you want the Santinos to stay as the ruling family of the Società, then you won't air our dirty laundry or your disgusting ways in public. Jessica is a Santino now, and we can't have our family look weak in the eyes of the rest of the organization."

"You're fucking lucky I don't cut your dick off tonight, Capo or not," I hissed at my father.

He laughed at me. "You're just a sore loser because I got the prize of the cherry between Jessica's creamy thighs. And let me tell you, her cherry was so deliciously sweet," he said, kissing his fingers.

I lunged for him, but Gabriel held me back. "Rafael, we should leave now."

Without a backward glance, I stormed out of the room. Once we were outside again, Gabriel put both his hands on my shoulders and looked me in the eye. "Like you said, we need to keep this quiet if you want to protect Jessica. We can't keep it quiet if we end up killing him tonight."

I nodded at him. Our father would get what he fucking deserved if it was the last thing I ever did. A battle was raging within me, but I had to focus on Jessica right now and put her first.

Returning to my room, I found Lorissa outside with Gianni. She told me that Jessica had asked to be alone.

Entering the room, I found Jessica was curled up on the small couch and crying.

When she saw me, she scrambled to sit up and pressed herself back against the seat, trying to get as far away from me as possible. "I'm so sorry," she sobbed. "We can start annulment proceedings tomorrow."

She thought I was angry with her. I was still furious at my father, but I attempted to calm my expression.

"You have nothing to be sorry for. We will stay married. There will be no annulment. Nobody knows about what has happened outside our two families." I raked my hands through my hair. "Look, you should get to bed. We still have to get through tomorrow morning and the whole virgin confirmation thing."

"What are we going to do about that?" she whispered, her voice quivering, obviously thinking I might still try to touch her tonight.

Nothing could have been further from my mind right at this moment.

She watched me warily, her breaths coming erratically.

"Don't worry about that. I'll make sure that everything goes fine tomorrow."

She gave a small nod, biting her bottom lip.

"You should sleep." When it became clear that she wasn't going to move, I slowly walked toward her, watching while she held her breath.

"Up," I instructed. "You need to get some rest."

She rose and scurried toward the bed.

As she reached it, I pulled down the comforter. "In you get." I watched while she climbed in and then pulled the comforter up around herself.

I reached across the bed and she recoiled from me, scrambling back against the headboard. "Hey, I'm just grabbing a pillow—I'll sleep on the couch. Now get some rest."

She looked at me hesitantly, but eventually laid down again, all the while keeping her eyes on me.

I sat on the edge of the bed, careful not to touch her.

I looked down at the terrified girl next to me. "Just know, Jessica, that I will kill that bastard for what he did to you. If I do it tonight, people will talk about nothing else and there's a real risk that they will eventually find out the reason why I did it."

It was very difficult keeping any secrets in our close-knit organization. And I didn't know yet who else knew about this—if my father had boasted about it to anyone else or if the soldiers guarding Jessica that day knew what had occurred.

"But, Jessica, if you want him dead tonight, just say. I will do it for you. Because I need to make things right for you."

She frantically shook her head. "Please—I can't have anyone knowing what happened to me..."

"You want me to hold off on killing him?"

She nodded. "Yes," she whispered. "No one can ever find out my secret..."

I understood. It was Jessica's secret and I would do whatever she needed.

"But I will kill him soon..."

She nodded again.

I stood up and walked over to the couch, Jessica watching me with huge eyes.

I leaned my head back on the armrest.

I had to wait a long time for Jessica's breathing to slow into the steady rhythm of sleep.

I could tell she was afraid of me. I was used to men being afraid of me—my own men and also men belonging to rival organizations. They feared my name, my reputation, and my Società tattoo. I could sense fear in the way someone breathed, talked, and looked at me. I didn't want my wife to ever be afraid of me, though. She was mine—mine to protect.

Once I was sure Jess was asleep, I texted Gabriel and told him to meet me downstairs.

We were going to pay a visit to the clinic doctor. He had been complicit in my father's plan to defile Jessica.

The doctor's torture, and his life, would have to satisfy my bloodlust tonight.

CHAPTER 8

JESSICA

I found it impossible to fall asleep.

I was shocked that Rafael had been unaware of what his father had done. Even though I felt some relief that Rafael hadn't been involved in his father's plan to rape me, that relief was short-lived.

Rafael now knew that I was not a pure virgin for him. The latter was an absolute requirement in the Mafia world, and I had failed to be an adequate bride for him.

I was unworthy in his eyes.

The events of the last few weeks kept haunting my mind, no matter how much I tried to block those thoughts.

I must have fallen asleep finally in the early hours.

***

The next time I woke, I could see that it was light outside. I felt the strange sheets around me as soon as I woke, and the memories of yesterday came tumbling back to me.

I cringed, thinking about not only last night, but also what I would have to go through this morning.

I slowly got up and sat on the stool in front of the dressing table, looking at my pale face and red eyes in the mirror opposite.

Rafael was already up, and I could hear him in the shower.

A couple of minutes later, he walked back into the bedroom with only a towel wrapped around his waist, his sandy hair wet and darkened from the water. "How did you sleep?" he asked.

My body tensed. "Um…it was fine."

I wasn't really sure where to look or what we were supposed to talk about. I still couldn't believe that we were married and that the last few weeks had really happened.

I took a deep breath. I was physically exhausted from yesterday and mentally drained from the last few weeks. I just had to focus on one thing at a time, and the next hurdle was getting through seeing our families this morning.

Rafael looked at me. "The doctor from the clinic is dead. We killed him last night." His voice had an edge to it.

I bit my lower lip, not knowing what to say to that. It was a bit like a cat bringing its owner a dead bird. Was the owner supposed to be repulsed by the deadly act, or was she pleased that the cat cared enough about her to bring such a gift?

"People will be expecting me to make a quick appearance before breakfast to confirm to our fathers that you were a virgin for me last night. Although it's basically a charade given that they both know what happened to you. But I don't want to give people any opportunity to start any unnecessary gossip."

I nodded. Although it would just be our closest family members at the breakfast this morning, other wedding guests had stayed the night at the hotel and would still be milling around. Rafael needed to make everything look as normal as possible, so as not to raise any suspicions.

"I'll just be a few minutes."

I remained seated and watched him leave.

I knew I should start to shower and dress, but I had no energy and my limbs felt heavy.

I jumped when I heard a sharp knock at the bedroom door.

I froze.

I wasn't expecting anyone.

There was another hard rap.

I bolted to my feet.

I mentally shook myself. I couldn't spend my life being afraid each time I heard a knock at the door. Anyway, Emanuel would be downstairs right now talking to Rafael.

I slowly padded across the room in my bare feet and pulled the door open.

The air rushed from my lungs in a small cry...

Emanuel was standing on the other side.

I grabbed the door and slammed it shut.

His foot wedged in the gap to stop it closing.

And he pushed his way forward.

"Jessica..." he rasped.

A violent shudder ran through me. "W-Why are...you here?" I croaked, tightening the belt of my robe with shaking hands.

"I wanted to see if you enjoyed last night," he smirked. "So, did my son fuck you?"

I felt the blood drain from my face.

"I knew he wouldn't have the balls to do it," he laughed harshly. "You know it's bad luck not to consummate the wedding, don't you?"

I took a step back as he leered at me, panic clawing at my insides.

"And a tight little pussy like yours needs to be fucked regularly to break you in."

Bile rushed up my throat. "Please—"

The door was still ajar.

It creaked as someone pushed it open.

I willed it to be someone who could help me...

Because I knew I couldn't never go through the same thing again.

My mother-in-law, Ortensia, bustled in.

"Oh, Emanuel, she exclaimed. "I thought you'd be downstairs. I passed Rafael on the way here and he said he was meeting you."

Emanuel gave me a dark look before turning to his wife. "I thought we were meeting here. I'll head downstairs."

I held my breath as he left, and once he was gone, I slumped onto the couch.

"I just thought I'd check to see that you're alright," my mother-in-law said in a kindly voice.

I clasped my hands tightly in my lap to stop them from shaking. It felt strange thinking that I had a mother-in-law now...as well as a monster for a father-in-law. How much did she know about what had happened with Emanuel?

Gazing at my red eyes, she put her hand gently to my cheek. "There dear, you have done your duty and done your family proud."

I blushed bright red and tears pricked the back of my eyes, but I knew this was only the start. I would have to face the rest of our families soon.

She left me to it and quietly clicked the door shut behind her.

Shame flooded my entire being and my tears fell. Had my father been right when he said I attracted these sorts of situations? Was it my fault in some way?

A few minutes later, I was still sat in the same place when Rafael returned.

I averted my eyes so that he wouldn't detect my fresh tears.

But he strode over to me. "Jessica," he said. "You're shaking."

I couldn't speak.

He knelt on the floor beside me. "What's happened?" he said softly.

I continued staring down at my hands.

"Did somebody say something to you?"

I looked up and gave the smallest nod.

Rafael briefly closed his eyes. "Was it my father?"

I took a deep breath. "Yes," I whispered. "He came here when you were gone. Ortensia arrived before he could do anything..."

His gaze flicked to my arm and I looked down to see a finger-shaped bruise forming.

"Did he do that?"

I nodded.

He took in a deep breath as he clenched his jaw. "I'm so sorry, Jessica," he said in a harsh whisper, surprising me with his words.

"What do you mean?"

"You're mine to protect and mine to keep safe. I should never have left you here alone. I swear that bastard will never touch you again, not as long as I'm alive."

Tears threatened again and I didn't know why. Why did he feel that he had to keep me safe? I was already damaged goods—nothing could change that. I wasn't deserving of his care or protection.

His mouth was set in a grim line. "I'll cancel the breakfast with our families. You're in no fit state to face anyone, let alone my father again."

"No, please don't do that." My words came out in a rush. "You said yourself that we have to keep everything as normal as possible while other people are around, so that no one suspects anything is wrong. I have to keep what happened a secret..."

Rafael said nothing for a few moments and I could tell he didn't want me to have to go through seeing Emanuel again. "Only if you're absolutely sure?"

"I'm sure," I tried to say as firmly as possible. I didn't know if I was still in shock, but I knew I had to do this.

"You should get ready now," he said gently. "We'll stay downstairs for as short a time as possible."

"Okay." It would be relatively easy for me to act like the blushing bride today. I was mortified—not because of my wedding night, but because of the secret I was keeping.

I was terrified someone outside our two families might find out the truth—might find out that I had not been pure for Rafael and that we hadn't consummated our marriage. Would someone check our bedlinen after we had left the room? My body quaked at the thought.

"Don't worry about seeing our families downstairs. I'll be by your side the whole time. We'll just keep conversation as brief and general as possible."

I nodded, although I couldn't help but worry about all the questions everyone would ask.

I got dressed in a new pale pink shift dress and brushed out my hair.

"You look pretty in your dress."

I blushed, not used to having a man comment on my appearance. "I, rather than my mother, chose it. That's why it's not outrageous or garish." I had definitely not bought it from Signora Demonte's boutique.

Rafael stared at me. "The color suits you."

"I wish I hadn't let my mother persuade me to buy the matching heeled pumps. My feet are still aching from yesterday and I really could have done with wearing some lower heels today." I was babbling—as if he would care about my footwear or aching feet. But I was trying to think about these trivial things in an attempt to stop my mind repeatedly running over what had just happened with Emanuel.

As we made our way downstairs, I wobbled on my heels and Rafael grabbed my hand to steady me.

I startled at his touch and then steeled myself as I allowed him to help me down the stairs. His hand felt warm and strong wrapped around mine.

When we reached the private dining room where our immediate families would be waiting for us, he was still holding my hand. "I'm going to keep holding your hand if that's okay with you? That way, you can just squeeze my hand if you need a break or anything else. I'm here for you."

I nodded.

His words and the feeling of his grasp reassured me to an extent, but my legs still felt shaky as we walked into the room and all eyes turned to us.

I felt a crimson tide surge up my cheeks. Even though it was just our closest relations here, rather than the whole of the Società like yesterday, I still felt like I was drowning.

My mother rushed straight over to me. "Jessica! How was last night?"

She had no tact—I thought she would have realized that I wouldn't want to talk about last night. No doubt she would even ask me how big Rafael's penis was. I prayed she'd at least wait for him to move away before asking anything like that.

She tried to drag me away from Rafael so that she could interrogate me in private. "Rafael, I know you will have business to discuss with the men. You can leave Jessica with me."

"No, Casmundina. I have no business this morning.

When my mother saw that Rafael wasn't going to let go of my hand, she pursed her lips. She wasn't put off that easily. "I hope Jessica satisfied you in the bedroom?"

She had the subtlety of an elephant.

Rafael, to his credit, did not respond and instead stared at her with a penetrating look until she felt uncomfortable enough to look away, swiftly excusing herself and scuttling off to find my father.

Gabriel carried over two cups of coffee and handed one to each of us. As he handed over my cup, he looked carefully at me; however, I averted my gaze. He was a Santino man and one day he would be Capo of the Società.

Everyone knew that Gabriel was already heavily involved in managing Società affairs, and he was already seen as a brutal and ruthless leader. I knew I would be avoiding him as much as possible. I shivered as thoughts about the Santino family ran through my mind.

"Are you cold?" questioned Rafael, looking down at me.

I shrugged. "A bit," I fibbed, as he pulled me closer into his side.

Rafael, true to his word, did not leave my side, and he shielded me from any further prying from our families. Thankfully, Emanuel did not come near me, probably because Rafael was glued to my side.

Finally, it was time to leave and both families, including Emanuel, gathered around Rafael's black SUV to wave us off.

As I sank against the luxurious leather seat, I thanked God that the wedding was finished.

But I had the feeling that my problems with Emanuel weren't yet over...

CHAPTER 9

JESSICA

When we reached the mansion Rafael shared with Gabriel, I looked curiously at the house that I was seeing for the first time. I had been to his parents' home a few times for Società functions, but Rafael and Gabriel had moved out from their family home and instead bought this mansion a few years ago.

Rafael showed me around downstairs, and as we walked around in silence, I was struck by how untidy and dusty it was. They obviously were leading a bachelor lifestyle here.

The mansion was quite different from how I had expected. I had imagined a hotel-style interior with clean, modern lines and a masculine edge. Instead, the house had a rustic feel, similar to a lodge, with lots of wood, comfy couches, and soft rugs. We could have been by a lake or in the countryside, especially with the green views surrounding the house.

There was wood paneling in the den, with more wood running from floor-to-ceiling in the stairwell.

As Rafael led me upstairs toward the bedrooms, I felt my heartbeat quicken. He walked past an open door and gestured into the bedroom. "That's Gabriel's room."

Then he showed me into another bedroom. I looked around myself, noticing that it was as untidy and dusty as downstairs. "This is my room. It will be your room too, from now on."

I don't know what I had expected—perhaps separate rooms, or at least separate beds.

My breathing became shallow as he carried on. "My soldiers monitor the CCTV in the common areas like the hallways, stairs, and garages. I don't want them gossiping that we have separate rooms, so we will be in the same bedroom as anyone would expect of a normal husband and wife."

I knew how the Società liked nothing more than a piece of juicy gossip, and a newlywed couple already leading separate lives would give the gossips a field day.

At that moment, Rafael's cell phone rang and he took the call while I awkwardly stood next to him. I looked around the room to give myself something to do, but my eyes kept returning to one place: the huge bed.

After the short call, Rafael turned to me. "Look, I know it's bad timing, but I have to go with Gabriel to visit one of our clubs to sort out an issue. You can settle in. You should unpack your things."

"Um, okay."

"There's no maid to help you unpack. We don't have a housekeeper or maid at the moment. The last housekeeper we employed stole from us, so Gabriel got rid of her."

I knew Gabriel would have done more than just fire her, but I didn't ask for details—I didn't need to. I knew what happened to anyone who betrayed the Società.

"You can find a new one for us. You can telephone my mother—she's bound to know of someone and if she doesn't, she'll know who to ask."

I quaked inwardly at the thought of having to telephone his parents' home.

Now that I was married, I was expected to go to my mother-in-law when I needed something rather than to my own mother. It was thought to be disrespectful not to defer to my mother-in-law on all relevant matters now that I was part of the Santino family.

After Rafael had gone, I was left by myself in the house.

As I looked around the bedroom, I knew I needed to stay busy to keep my mind off what would happen tonight in this room. Rafael had spared me last night, but I knew he wouldn't carry on showing me mercy.

It was only early afternoon and I didn't know when Rafael or Gabriel would be back. I sank down on the couch in the corner and my mind started going at a hundred miles an hour—everything replaying in my mind again and again.

After twenty minutes, I still hadn't moved from that spot.

And as my gaze fell on the bed again, I made up my mind.

I knew what I had to do.

Collecting my purse and making sure I had my cell, I left the house and walked up to the soldier guarding the gate.

I stopped a few feet from him, not wanting to get too close.

"I need someone to drive me to visit my mother please," I said as firmly as I could.

"I'll call a soldier to take you. It'll just be a couple of minutes, ma'am.'

I nodded and then walked a few meters away. Just being near an unknown man was making me shaky.

When a black SUV pulled up, the soldier driving it jumped out and opened the back door for me. I carefully got in, making sure to stay as far away from him as possible.

It was only a twenty minute drive to my parents' mansion. And during that time, I kept thinking about what I needed to do.

When we arrived, I sat rooted to my seat until the soldier opened the door.

Reluctantly stepping out, the mansion's front door opened instantly and I came face-to-face with my mother.

Her eyebrows shot up. "Jessica, what are you doing here? Shouldn't you be at Rafael's home?"

I swallowed the lump in my throat. "I need to talk to you and Father."

Her brows puckered together but she led me down the hallway to his office.

"Cecilio, Jessica is here. She wants to talk to us."

I slowly stepped into the office, my nerves making me more wobbly in my high heels than usual. I sat on the edge of one of the leather wingback chairs in front of my father's desk.

"What is it?" my father demanded, clearly irritated that he was being interrupted.

"I think..." But the rest of my words wouldn't come out.

"Spit it out, Jessica," my father said tersely. "I don't have all day."

"You need to annul my marriage," I blurted out.

I heard my mother suck in a breath.

"What the hell are you talking about?" my father growled.

What happened this morning with Emanuel came tumbling out. And my parents sat silently while I relived the incident.

"I'm not safe around him. I can't stay in that family," I croaked.

"Have you lost your goddamn mind, Jessica?" my father yelled, making me quake as I briefly shut my eyes.

But I had to go on. "An annulment is possible because I didn't consummate my marriage last night..."

"What the hell are you talking about now?" he snapped.

"I-I didn't sleep with Rafael last night," I whispered. "That means we can annul the marriage..."

My mother interrupted. "Did he want sex with you?"

I nodded. "But I didn't let it happen... I couldn't."

"You're determined to make a fool of me," my father bellowed. "You act like a fucking slut with his father, but then you refuse your husband his marital rights? You know what they call girls like you? *A fucking cocktease.*"

I felt like I'd been punched in the stomach. I couldn't believe my own father would talk to me like this.

"There will be no annulment!"

"I can't stay there," I sobbed. "I can never sleep with Rafael—and he won't want a wife who can't do that with him."

"You will go back to Rafael's mansion immediately, and you'll fucking open your legs whenever and wherever he wants!" my father bellowed. Do you understand me, you stupid girl? I will not let you shame me! I'll fucking hold you down myself if I need to so that your husband can fuck you!"

I tasted bile rise up in my throat.

"Now get out and get back to your husband immediately!"

Stumbling out of the office, I slowly made my way to the powder room, and there, I sobbed my heart out. I couldn't be the wife Rafael needed.

But I knew I had no choice but to return. My parents were unwilling to help me. I wished my sister, Juliana, was still here—she would have helped.

Splashing cold water on my face, I took my sunglasses and hid my red eyes behind them.

Stepping out of the powder room, my mother was nowhere in sight. I knew I was a huge disappointment to her. I walked to the front door and let myself out. Climbing back into the SUV, I asked the soldier to take me back to Rafael's mansion.

Once back there, I knew I couldn't keep crying.

There was no way out of this marriage for me.

What I needed was to keep busy so that I wouldn't think about what I would have to do in Rafael's bed tonight.

Rafael had spared me last night, but I knew he wouldn't carry on showing me mercy.

It was only early afternoon and I didn't know when Rafael or Gabriel would be back. Would the men be expecting me to prepare dinner for them given that there was no housekeeper? I didn't want to anger Rafael in any way before tonight...

I kicked off my pale pink suede pumps and stripped off my shift dress.

My luggage had already been brought here and I found it lined up in the walk-in closet.

I opened one of the cases and found some gray jeans and a black t-shirt to change into.

My mother would have a fit if she saw me—it would be another disappointment to add to the rest of the list. She had purchased a multitude of 'Stepford Wife' outfits for me to wear in my new role as Mrs. Rafael Santino.

The dresses, skirts, and blouses chosen by her were too formal for me. The dark colors of the jeans and t-shirt were more suitable for doing the housework, I justified to myself—although I knew that there was also another reason I was drawn to these clothes.

Since the attack, I felt a need to wear clothes that would not draw attention to myself or my body. Dark, boring colors made me stand out less. I wanted to be inconspicuous. And being in a strange house made this feeling inside of me more acute.

I decided to go downstairs and check out the food situation. I found that there was hardly any fresh food in the fridge.

Taking a deep breath, I picked up the phone and telephoned the local grocery store that delivered to my mother's house. It was owned by a Società family, and although it was run as a front for laundering money, it had good stock and could be trusted to deliver to our homes. I placed an order and knew it would arrive within the hour.

While I waited for the grocery delivery, I had another look around downstairs. I had to find something to keep me busy...

The formal dining room didn't look like it was used often, and it was dustier than the kitchen. I decided we would eat tonight around the table in the smaller breakfast room which was next door to the kitchen. After hunting out some cleaning supplies, I set to work in the kitchen and breakfast room.

The soldiers at the gate took the delivery of the groceries and two of them carried them up to the house. I felt uncomfortable being by myself in the house and letting these two Santino soldiers come in, and I breathed a sigh of relief when they left and I could close the door behind them.

Before I started preparing dinner, I thought about the herb garden I had seen outside from the bedroom window. I decided to spare a few minutes to have a look at it and, surprisingly, I found it was better looked after than the house. I picked some fresh basil, bay leaves, and thyme. There were also strawberries growing in the garden and I picked some of those as well.

As I gathered what I needed, I reminded myself that cooking soothed me. I needed to throw myself into my new duties to keep my mind off everything else.

Back in the kitchen, I removed a whole chicken from the groceries and started to prepare it. I rubbed olive oil over it and sprinkled it with salt, before adding the herbs that I had collected from the garden and covering the top of the chicken with slices of Parma ham.

After I had put it in the oven, I set to work on parboiling some potatoes, which I would add to the roasting tray later. I picked out the vegetables I had ordered, washing and chopping some carrots and green vegetables, which I set aside to steam later.

I didn't know whether the men would expect dessert, so I washed the strawberries and left them in a bowl. If anyone wanted dessert, I would serve them with the cream and sugar that had also been delivered from the store.

Now that the dinner was in the oven, I decided to get to work on cleaning this bachelor pad. There was far too much work for me to accomplish in an afternoon, so I decided to focus on finishing the kitchen before moving onto Rafael's bedroom. His adjoining bathroom was remarkably clean, so at least that was something.

I stripped the bed in Rafael's bedroom and bundled up the sheets, taking them down to the laundry room, where I was dismayed to find a huge pile of unwashed laundry. I didn't have the time to do anything about it now, so I added the sheets to the heap.

I found the linen cupboard and selected some clean sheets and re-made the bed. The sheets were high quality Egyptian cotton and I ran my hand over their smoothness as I finished making the bed. I then set to work dusting, polishing, and vacuuming the bedroom, before giving the adjoining bathroom a once-over for the sake of completeness.

By the time I was finished in the bedroom, the chicken was almost done. I wasn't sure what time the men would be home and I hoped that the meat wouldn't get overdone and dry while I waited for them. I wondered whether I should call Rafael on his cell phone but then decided against it. I wanted to delay Rafael's return as much as possible.

Not long later, Rafael and Gabriel arrived home and I heard them as they made their way to the kitchen.

"Hi." I nervously wiped my hands against my gray jeans. "Are you ready for dinner? I've made roast chicken." I hoped that my cooking would help put Rafael in a good mood.

Gabriel scowled. "We have Italian food on Mondays—specifically spaghetti and meatballs." His tone was abrupt. I got the feeling that I had done something wrong.

"Oh...I wasn't sure what the arrangements would be for dinner, so I went ahead and cooked something..."

Gabriel opened the top drawer next to the range cooker. "All the take-out menus are kept in here. We always have meatballs on Mondays. You just have to dial the number."

"I didn't know..."

Gabriel looked darkly at me. "I don't know how long you're planning on sticking around, but changing our food is not the way to endear yourself to your fellow housemates."

"I'm sorry—"

"It's fine," Rafael said tersely. "We'll have the chicken today." I sensed that he also wasn't happy. Maybe he preferred spaghetti meatballs as well?

Gabriel walked over to where I was standing next to the chicken and came to a stop right beside me. He picked up the carving knife, and my body instantly recoiled.

"Really?" he growled. "If I wanted to kill you, Jessica, I have plenty of sharper knives than this old carving knife."

I felt my cheeks pale.

As he started carving the meat, I slowly inched away a few steps, hoping he wouldn't notice. Although it was evening now, he still looked fresh and composed, his tie fully knotted and the creases in his dark suit still sharp. Tiredness didn't mar his features and I was reminded that he was a deadly machine.

He put some chicken on a plate and added potatoes and vegetables. "I've got work to do. I'll eat in the office. Rafael, come in when you get a chance and we can go over business." As he walked past me on his way out of the kitchen, he came so near to me that I gasped and took a swift step backward. He glowered at me but didn't say anything more.

Rafael and I were alone in the kitchen. I stood in the middle of the room. "I don't think he likes me," I murmured.

"He'll get used to you. You're family now. Sometimes he forgets that he's talking to his family rather than one of his men."

I worried my lower lip, not sure that Rafael really wanted to eat the chicken. Judging by his expression, the answer was in the negative. "Um, do you want me to order Italian instead?"

"This will be fine."

He reached for two more plates and filled them with food for us both before carrying them through the adjoining door to the breakfast room. "Bring cutlery," he instructed me.

He set down the plates on the table, and we sat down opposite each other and ate in an uncomfortable silence.

I wondered if I should ask how his day had been, as this was how my mother always started a conversation at dinner at home. I started to open my mouth, but then shut it again, deciding it might be better not to speak to Rafael right now.

I didn't want to annoy him, especially given what was going to happen later between us in the bedroom. I tried to keep my mind off the latter, but it was impossible and I was only able to pick at my food.

Once we had eaten, I started to clear the dishes.

"Leave that. It's time for bed." It wasn't a request—it was an order. He took my hand and tugged me up the stairs to his bedroom.

CHAPTER 10

JESSICA

Once we reached the bedroom, I grabbed my nightdress and bolted into the bathroom to change into it there. The nightdress was another one of my mother's purchases—it was silk, trimmed with lace, and came to mid-thigh level. Luckily, it had a matching robe which would cover up a bit more of my body.

After securely tying the belt of the robe, I opened the bathroom door and found Rafael undressed to his boxer briefs.

I walked quickly across the bedroom, averting my eyes from him and quickly getting under the covers. Not that the covers would save me from him tonight.

Rafael walked into the bathroom and I heard the shower running, giving me a few more precious minutes to prepare myself for what was to come. I would have to bear his touch and the invasion of his body into mine. My blood ran cold, and my stomach twisted.

Then I told myself that this was probably how all Mafia brides felt when it was their first time with their new husband. But I knew I wasn't just worried about the awkwardness of having sex with a virtual stranger.

I was petrified that it would remind me of what had happened at the clinic, that I wouldn't be able to stand Rafael's touch after what I had been through—and that Rafael would punish me for not fulfilling my marital duty.

It was hopeless whatever I chose: Either endure my husband's attentions and have the memories from the clinic come flooding back to terrorize me, or refuse my husband and have to bear whatever harsh punishment he inflicted upon me.

I had tried so hard to keep the memories of the clinic from consuming me whole. But tonight, I knew that barrier would come crashing down. And I felt sick to my stomach thinking about it.

The bathroom door opened, and I felt the small hairs on the back of my neck rise.

I instinctively shrank back as he walked toward the bed. The blue in his irises seemed even darker than usual, making his eyes flash ominously as he locked his gaze on me.

As he got closer, I tried to press myself further against the headboard. I prayed that he would at least be gentle with me, that I wouldn't face the same violence as last time. If I didn't fight him, then perhaps he would go easier on me.

I inhaled a breath, yet it felt like my lungs weren't working and I couldn't get enough oxygen.

He came and kneeled on the side of the bed. He was so near that I could feel the heat rolling off his body. "You're shaking," he said.

Did he get off on my terror? "I..." But I couldn't say anything. I couldn't force out the words past the lump in my throat. I tried to look away from his piercing stare.

"Look at me." His voice was deep and commanding.

But I couldn't. I was frozen as I felt terror spike in my veins, sending needles of fear shooting across my skin. I cringed back from his hands as he took hold of my face and forced me to look at him. His hands felt hot, like they were burning my ice-cold skin.

"Please don't." I whispered.

"What's going on?"

I swallowed and tried to speak, but all that came out was a small squeak from the back of my throat.

He lifted his arm, and my muscles froze rigid as I screwed my eyes shut.

"Hey, you think I'm going to strike you? I would never do that." Instead, he stroked my cheek. "Jessica, you don't have to be afraid of me."

But his touch was too much for me. "Yes, I do! You're a Santino, aren't you?"

"What do you mean?"

"You're all the same—monsters."

He looked at me carefully. "Do you think that I am going to force you tonight?"

"Aren't you?"

"That wasn't my intention, no. I thought you understood—we will share a bedroom for appearances' sake. You are mine now, but we will have a marriage in name only."

Surprise took the place of some of my fear.

"Come, sleep now." With that, he untied my robe and carefully pushed it off my shoulders before removing it completely. The movement of the silky fabric over my skin felt like a caress, and a shiver ran through my body. He gently pushed me back against the mattress. "Lie down," he commanded.

I obeyed his instruction, confused and my mind struggling to understand what was going on.

He cocked his head to one side and frowned. "Sorry. Perhaps I shouldn't have just touched you..."

"No. It's fine. Just as long as there are no sudden movements. I'm fine as long as I know someone is going to touch me before they actually do it."

He nodded.

"What about...children? You'll need an heir." I knew one of my main duties as his wife was to provide him with a bloodline to carry on the Santino name. That was non-negotiable.

"There's always IVF, but we don't need to think about that just now." He was so close that I could feel his warm breath against my skin as he spoke. "Just know that I'll never force myself on you. You have nothing to worry about in that regard."

I didn't know this man—*my husband*—but this wasn't what I thought would happen tonight. I felt tears of relief spring to my eyes, and I tried to gulp them back, but one slid down my cold cheek.

"Hey, it's okay." He wiped the tear away with the pad of his thumb. He frowned at me. "I thought you understood—I'll never force you and I don't expect us to share a bed."

"You aren't sleeping in the bed?"

"No. You can have the bed, Jessica. I'll sleep on the couch."

I suddenly felt like I could breathe again. I then looked at the small couch set at the end of the bed, and I knew he would struggle to fit his tall frame on it. "Your bed's huge...I don't mind us sharing, as long as you keep to your side," I said tentatively.

He regarded me for a few, long seconds. "Okay."

As he climbed into the bed, I thought about how tonight would be the first time that I would share a bed with a man. Despite it being my suggestion, I still felt nerves quivering in my stomach.

I felt his muscular body stretch out next to me, his size and body heat quickly taking over the bed. Oh God, why had I even suggested this?

Rafael looked across at me. "Do you want me to put a pillow between us?"

"Um...I trust you," I replied somewhat unconvincingly.

"Thanks for the vote of confidence," he said dryly. "You know this will only work if we trust each other, right?"

"It's just that you must have...physical urges. All men do." My cheeks were burning, and I wished he would switch the lights off already.

"As do all women," he responded unhelpfully.

"I just meant..." My voice trailed off. This was too embarrassing to talk about with a virtual stranger.

"If you're worried I'll jump you during the night, you don't need to be concerned."

"You can sleep with other women." My words rushed out. "I won't object to that."

He looked at me carefully. Then without another word, he switched off his nightstand lamp, plunging us into an uneasy darkness.

It was odd being in bed with a stranger and I found it hard to fall asleep. I consciously tried not to move around too much because I didn't want to disturb Rafael. All the time, my mind kept running over the last few weeks. Finally, after a long time, I drifted off to sleep.

***

In the morning, when I woke up, Rafael was already gone.

I headed into the bathroom, undressed, and got into the shower, letting the hot water soothe my weary body. I stood under the hot spray for a long time, before eventually turning it off and reaching for a towel to dry myself.

Once I was dry, I wrapped the towel around the top of my breasts and left my wet hair tumbling over my shoulders.

As I walked back into the bedroom, Rafael opened the door from the hallway.

"Oh, my!" I jumped out of my skin. "I thought you'd gone to work."

He had a sheen of sweat over his face and obviously had just either been to the gym or for a run. His damp t-shirt was clinging to his muscles, and I couldn't help my eyes traveling down to his shorts where I noticed his strong thighs and tanned legs. I flushed as I realized that I had been staring at him.

"Sorry, I just came for a shower after my run. Don't worry, I'll shower in the guest room."

"No, it's fine. I've finished." I hurriedly turned away from him. "The bathroom's all yours."

While he showered, I got dressed in another pair of dark jeans and a charcoal top.

Rafael came back with a towel wrapped around his waist, smelling of soap and a hint of cologne. Despite the size of the room, his presence felt overwhelming. Before he could drop his towel to get dressed, I scurried into the bathroom with my hairbrush and closed the door behind me.

I combed out my wet, tangled hair in there, taking my time. I wasn't sure how long to give him to dress, so I lingered for as long as possible.

When I finally came out of the bathroom, I found Rafael had left and there was a note next to my pillow. "Here's my mother's telephone number. Call her about finding a housekeeper and with your questions. I'll be home at 7 p.m."

I went downstairs to an empty house and made some toast and coffee. I was glad that I was by myself because, this way, I didn't have to worry that I'd be in anyone's way. While I ate, I decided on what I would do today. My parents made it clear yesterday that there was no way out of this marriage for me, so I knew I had to get on with things.

And I felt a little calmer now that I knew Rafael wouldn't expect me to have sex with him. I knew I just had to keep as busy as possible and not think about what had happened. I had to block it out and start afresh. That was the only way I would be able to stay sane.

First on the list was tackling the huge pile of laundry. I put one load in the wash and then rang the grocery store to order some ingredients for tonight's dinner. As Gabriel and Rafael had seemed put out by the lack of Italian food last night, I would cook spaghetti meatballs tonight.

After I had put in my order, I set to work on dusting, polishing, vacuuming, and mopping the drawing room, entrance foyer, hallway, stairs, and landing. I would ask Gabriel tonight if he minded me going into his bedroom and then I could clean his room too.

Throughout the day, I worked my way through the huge amount of laundry, so that by the early evening all the clothes and sheets had been put through the washer and dryer and I could iron the clean clothes.

It was strange being in this house. It was my home now, however, everything felt alien. All the small noises in the house made me jump, yet the silence was just as oppressive. I was used to having my family around me during the day and my mother's housekeeper and maids bustling around the place.

When the men arrived home, I was in the kitchen, checking whether the spaghetti was cooked. Rafael had phoned ahead to let me know what time to expect them home.

I poked my head into the hallway and saw Rafael head into the office with some papers. Gabriel was walking toward the kitchen.

As he strode into the room, he looked to where I was standing in front of the cooker before glancing around and taking in the dinner preparations. "What's the meaning of this?"

I jumped at Gabriel's tone. "I'm sorry that dinner isn't quite ready, but it will only be another couple of minutes until I can serve it up."

"That's not what I'm talking about. What have you been doing all day?"

"I...I've tried to do as much of the cleaning today as I could, but I only finished the drawing room, foyer, stairs, and hallways. I'll do more tomorrow. But I did manage to clear all the laundry and iron your and Rafael's shirts."

"My brother didn't marry you to gain a woman to skivvy around the house. You're supposed to be his wife, not our maid."

"I-I don't mind, honestly. I enjoy housework and cooking, and it gives me something to do—"

"Rafael told me he gave you clear instructions to find a new housekeeper and left you our mother's telephone number so that you could call for her help. We did not ask you to cook and clean for us."

I was bewildered by his words and frightened by his harsh tone. The fear made nausea swirl in my stomach.

Rafael came into the kitchen. I could feel tears threatening, so I quickly turned away and fiddled with the handle of the pan.

"Hey, Jessica." He looked from me to Gabriel. "What's going on?"

"Nothing," I said quickly. "I just have to strain the spaghetti and then everything will be ready."

He gave me a questioning look but, thankfully, didn't probe any further.

Once I'd got all the food onto the table, I stepped away. "I'm not hungry. I'm going to head up to bed."

I turned and fled up the stairs, holding back my tears until I reached the bedroom.

Everything I did lately kept going wrong—my engagement, seeing Juliana, even just cooking dinner. I must be cursed, I thought, as a wet trail ran down my cold cheeks.

People being angry at me was frightening. Their anger meant that things were slipping out of my control, and that feeling made my chest constrict and my breaths painful. I tried to shake the dread that had settled over me, but it was like a fog, heavy and all-consuming.

I knew I wouldn't be able to do anything else tonight, so I undressed for bed.

CHAPTER 11

RAFAEL

As Jessica wasn't hungry, Gabriel and I sat down to eat.

Since yesterday, I hadn't stopped blaming myself for my father getting to Jessica again.

How could I have been so fucking stupid?

Even if I'd thought he'd never have the arrogance to try something like that again, I should still have had more protection in place for her.

Since I'd brought Jessica here yesterday, I'd double-checked all the mansion's security arrangements. I'd also given the gate soldiers strict instructions to call me or Gabriel for authorization before letting anyone into the grounds, including my father and any other Società men. Jessica would be safe here and I wouldn't let anything else happen to her.

As we dished up, I looked at Gabriel, who was still wearing his suit jacket and tie.

"It was hot as hell out there today." We were in L.A. and it was the middle of summer. "You know, it wouldn't kill you to go tie-less just for one day."

He frowned at me. "No, it won't. But I might just kill you for *not* wearing a tie." I knew he was kidding—Mafia humor. He was obsessive about dressing smart, while I always wore a suit but usually didn't bother with the tie, particularly on days like today when it was so hot.

"What did you say to Jessica before?" I got the sense that he might have said something to upset her.

Once he'd repeated what he'd said, my suspicion was confirmed. "I still don't get why she didn't want to eat with us," Gabriel commented.

"She's scared of you," I explained, spearing another meatball with my fork.

"Good," he said in a matter-of-fact tone. "I'll make a good Capo, then."

I sighed, exasperated at my brother. "She's a member of this family now and I don't want her to be scared of any of us. Christ, Gabriel, not everything's about fucking work. I feel sorry for the girl you marry someday."

"She'll cope. She'll have to—just as Jessica needs to."

It was hard getting through to my brother sometimes, but I needed him to understand where I was coming from. "I want her to be happy here. This is her home as well now."

"Fine. I'll try not to make any more jokes about knives," he replied, referring to his comment from when he was carving the roast chicken last night.

"I'd appreciate that," I said dryly, as we ate.

I felt bad that Jessica was upset by what Gabriel had said to her. I was still feeling guilty about last night, about how Jessica had thought I was going to have sex with her. I should have clarified things on our wedding night, or at the very least before I went to work yesterday afternoon. Instead, she'd probably been worrying the whole time about what I was going to do to her.

I had no idea of how to handle her and this situation.

Although Jessica had given me permission to sleep with other women, the truth was that I wouldn't. Now that I was married to Jessica, I didn't want to be with other women. It didn't feel right.

I couldn't stop thinking about how she'd suffered at the hands of my father. And no matter how much I wanted to, I couldn't change what had happened.

JESSICA

It took ages to fall asleep tonight. I don't remember Rafael coming to bed, so he must have still been working in the office.

I must have been tired though, and I drifted off and fell into a world full of darkness and shadows, where Emanuel was lurking everywhere and trying to chase me. I ran as fast as I could, trying to escape him, but it was no good and I felt his cold fingers reach out to grab me. As his hands touched me, I screamed out.

"Wake up, Jessica!"

My eyes flew open and I jumped as I saw Rafael next to me. "It's okay, it's just a bad dream," he said quietly.

I let out a sob and threw myself into his arms, needing to feel something solid and real, needing to get rid of the feel of Emanuel's cold hands on me. "It felt so real," I cried.

Rafael was silent for a moment. "Were you dreaming about the attack?"

I nodded into the darkness.

"It's okay, I'll never let anything like that happen to you ever again, I promise you," he murmured, stroking my hair back from my forehead.

I clung to Rafael, seeking comfort from his body. I could feel the bare skin of his chest under my wet cheek and the roughness of his chest hair under my fingers.

"If anyone ever touches you again, I'll start a fucking war," he said in a low voice. "No one will ever hurt you again—because I'm going to take care of you from now on."

I didn't want to lower my defenses around this man—because I didn't know what to expect of him. He was a Made Man and violence ran through his entire being. What if, one day, he showed that side of himself to me? What if he couldn't restrain the brutality within him and hurt me?

I knew those were things which could easily happen.

Tonight, however, I didn't want to let go of him. I suppressed my thoughts and fears, instead letting his body warm the chill in my limbs.

And when I fell asleep this time, I was still in his arms, relishing the feel of being curled up against his chest.

RAFAEL

The following day, I got up early for a run like I normally did. I was pulling on a pair of shorts over my briefs when Jessica turned over, her dark hair tussled from her sleep.

"Morning," she murmured. Her eyes ran down my body to my shorts. "Where are you going?"

"For a run."

She pushed herself into a sitting position and rubbed the sleep from her eyes.

I raised an eyebrow. "Do you want to come? I saw you unpacked some running gear into the closet."

"It would be good to get out of the house." She gave me a shy smile as she pushed her hair off her face. "I won't be as fast as you, but I promise not to get in the way."

"It'll be nice to have a running buddy. I'll meet you downstairs in ten minutes."

I waited for Jessica in the kitchen, and a few minutes later she came down. It was already warm at this hour, and it was going to be a hot day; however, despite this, she had dressed in sweatpants and a black oversized t-shirt. "I'm ready."

"I normally run around our estate, if that's okay with you?"

"Sure, I don't want to put you out or be in the way."

We set off at a gentle jog and I ran at a slower pace than normal so that Jessica could keep pace with me. I knew she said she didn't want to put me out, but I wanted to stay by her side.

The sun had come up, and I noticed that the morning light caught the chestnut highlights in Jessica's dark hair, giving it a luxurious vibrancy as we jogged.

"Are those stables?" asked Jessica, as we stopped for a breather near some outbuildings.

"Yes. We have quite a bit of land here and keep some horses. Here, I'll show you," I said, taking her hand and leading her into the stables.

"This one's a beauty," she said, stroking a gleaming black stallion. There were five horses here in total.

"That's Storm. You can ride any of the horses here except for Storm—he's Gabriel's favorite and the one he always rides. Do you ride?"

"Yes, but I'm not that good. I was seven years old when my parents moved to their current house, and I was really excited because there was a small block of stables at the side of the house. I thought that I could ask for a horse for my birthday and then I could ride every day. My father, however, decided to convert the block into his interrogation rooms, so that was the end of that dream. I guess having to choose between horses or a torture room, a Made Man would decide on a torture room every time."

I chuckled and then asked her something I'd been wondering. "Where did you learn to cook?"

Jessica looked surprised at my question, probably due to my reaction when I came home last night, making me feel even more guilty. "Um, I've always liked cooking, although my mother didn't like me spending too much time with the servants. But I still went to the kitchen to help our housekeeper, Elsie—my mother rarely goes into the kitchen, so I usually didn't get found out by her."

"The housekeeper taught you to cook?"

"Yes. When Jake and Juliana were both at school, I was at home alone for another year before I was old enough to start kindergarten. Without Juliana by my side, I used to follow Elsie around while she cleaned the house and cooked our meals. Once I started school, I carried on helping her sometimes because I enjoyed it, and over the years I got quite good at cooking."

"Gabriel told me what he said to you last night. I'm sorry, he shouldn't have snapped at you yesterday, Jessica."

She bit down on her lower lip. "I don't want to impose myself in your home. Just tell me what you want me to do as your wife, and I'll try my best to fulfill your expectations," she said quietly.

I was realizing that Jessica was very sensitive, which I supposed was understandable after what she'd been through. Gabriel and I weren't the most empathetic of guys, but we would have to try harder to take her vulnerabilities into consideration.

"It's your home too now, and I want you to feel comfortable in it. Yesterday you caught him at a bad moment. He was preoccupied with work issues—he's obsessed with work and lets it take him over at times. But that's no excuse for the way he spoke to you, and I've asked him to be more respectful around you."

We left the stables and carried on with our run, neither of us saying anything for the next couple of minutes.

Finally, I broke the silence, needing to get something off my chest. "I've been so angry about what my father did to you—angry about failing to protect you and angry that I haven't been able to get vengeance for you yet. Believe me when I tell you that he will pay. I can never make up to you for what he did, but know that you are safe now and I will look after you from now on. You have my word on that."

"Thank you," she whispered.

"You don't have to thank me for looking after you. That's my job as your husband."

Somehow, it was easier to talk while we were jogging together. We had talked very briefly after her nightmare last night. I didn't want to make her feel uncomfortable by bringing up the attack again, but there was no easy way to mention it and I needed her to know that she was safe with me.

Once the contract had been signed, Jessica had been mine. I should have seen that she was protected; I should have made sure that nothing happened to her. I had lost control of the situation, and I knew she would never be able to forgive me for not looking after her.

All I could do now was to take care of her and make sure nothing like that ever happened again. I would do whatever was required to prevent harm to her.

"By the way, your meatballs last night were amazing. Gabriel even said they were better than the takeout we normally get, which is saying something given that he has insisted on takeout from that same restaurant every Monday since we moved into this house. He said you can cook them every week for our Monday Port-Mortem."

Jessica paled. "Your Monday *Port-Mortem*? I'm not sure I want to be part of whatever that is."

I grinned. "Don't worry, there are no dead bodies. It's just what we call our Monday night meetings over dinner. We go over what targets we've dealt with over the past week and run through the priorities for the coming week."

"*Dealt with?*" asked Jessica, visibly swallowing.

"Yes, dealt with. Some are operational targets we need to achieve, while others are targets of the human sort that we need to eliminate."

"My father never talked about killing at the dinner table..."

"Things are a bit different around here. I guess we've gotten used to being two guys living by ourselves, and we talk shop whenever we can."

"Why do you have to have such a morbid name for it? Surely it puts you off your food?"

"Not really. It's just what we started calling it. It's no more morbid than anything else we do in our world." I shrugged. "What else would you have us call it?"

"Um, how about 'Meatball Mondays'?" she suggested.

I laughed out loud at that. "That could be kind of catchy, however, it doesn't have the same ring to it. Anyhow, the Monday Post-Mortem is here to stay. We have to celebrate the small wins as well as the big wins, and what better way than with our favorite meal."

"Celebrating the killing of others is wrong."

I suddenly became serious. "If we don't kill them, they'll kill us. It's the way it works, and I have no qualms about protecting the organization and those I love."

We stopped for a water break, and I handed Jessica a bottle. She thirstily gulped down some water as she smoothed back wavy tendrils of hair that had escaped from her ponytail and fallen on her face.

"How long have you and Gabriel lived here now?" asked Jessica, unsubtly changing the subject to something less deadly.

"I was nineteen and Gabriel was twenty when we bought this place. We wanted to move out of our parents' home and decided to get a place together."

"Your estate is really peaceful."

"That's why we chose it. My father likes living in the city, but Gabriel and I are more comfortable on the outskirts."

Jessica drank more of her water.

"I meant it, Jessica, when I said before that you need to be able to tell me the truth about how you're feeling. You are my priority now and I will do everything in my power to keep you safe."

"I don't know what to make of you," she blurted out. "I mean, you're a born killer, yet you say you won't hurt me."

"Why is that so hard to understand?"

"You've been cheated out of your rightful entitlement—a pure virgin for your wife. You were angry that my family didn't tell you."

I looked her over. She was attractive with her glowing eyes and a lithe body. Even with the cover of her baggy clothes, I knew from the figure-hugging dress she wore to our engagement party that she had an attractive body with a nice ass, small waist, and high breasts. I sighed. She hadn't deserved any of what had happened. "You're right, I was angry—angry that I didn't protect you. I still am. But you are not responsible for what happened."

She nodded, but I could see she still had her doubts.

JESSICA

While we took a water break during our run, I thought about what Rafael had said. Although he said that looking after me was just part of his job as my husband, I was glad for his protection. Knowing he had my back made me feel a little safer.

As we were drinking our water, I could see that Rafael wanted to say something else to me.

"My mother has invited us and Gabriel to dinner at the end of this month for my father's birthday. I have to attend, but you can skip this dinner and I'll just say that you're not feeling well."

I was confused about Rafael's apparent desire to protect me—Made Men weren't known for their compassion toward their wives. "I won't be able to use that excuse every time I need to go to something where your father is in attendance. Maybe I should just go?"

"You don't have to. I know how difficult it will be for you."

I thought for a few minutes and then steeled myself. Rafael had made sure that I was safe since that awful morning at the hotel. "I have to face your father at some point, and the more I avoid him, the more he'll know how much he's affected me and is still affecting me."

Despite my words, Rafael's concern for me warmed the cold pit inside my stomach. I hadn't expected him to act like this, and I felt surprised by him and confused by my own reaction toward him.

When we got back to the house after our jog, Rafael passed a second water bottle as we stood and did our stretches. I drank what I wanted and then handed the bottle back to him, watching the strong muscles in his neck as he gulped down the remaining water.

I couldn't help but stare, flushing as I caught his gaze—he knew I had been watching him. His expression was intense and unnerving. But instead of darting my eyes away, I kept looking at him, taking him in.

Very slowly, he stepped toward me.

He brought his hand up and unhurriedly stroked my cheek. Upon his touch, I felt a quiver run through me. "I've been wanting to do this," he murmured.

He carefully took me into his arms and bent his head to mine. I watched the blue in his irises flash with something I couldn't put a name on.

He brushed his lips against mine, tenderly taking his time and making no demands of me.

His lips caressed mine and I felt my eyes close as the sensation from his mouth rippled through my body. But the sensation wasn't fear—it was something else.

I lost myself to the kiss and to him. And when he pulled away, I found myself breathless and disorientated.

"Anything more than that will need to come from you," he said in a low voice.

I swallowed hard, confused by what had just happened—what I had just let happen. "I can't do...anything else with you."

"You feel like that now, and you may never change your mind, and that's alright. But you may also one day want to change your mind. I'll wait for however long you need me to."

I shook my head. "I won't change..."

"Shhh," he soothed, taking me into his arms and pulling me against his chest. "You're safe with me. I won't ever touch you unless you ask me to." I let him hold me, his touch making me feel heady. "I know I mentioned satisfying my needs elsewhere. But the truth is, I don't want to, and I won't be doing that."

"I'm glad," I whispered, realizing that even though I wasn't going to sleep with him, I didn't want him to be with anyone else.

When he let go of me, I finished the rest of my stretches before going inside and up to our bedroom to shower.

I didn't understand why Rafael was showing kindness toward me. I'd rarely had dealings with men outside my own family, so I couldn't draw on previous experience. I'd been sent to an all-girls convent school where we'd been taught by nuns, so I hadn't mixed with boys much while growing up.

The only men I really knew were Made Men, and the one thing they all had in common was cruelty.

CHAPTER 12

JESSICA

That afternoon, my mind wandered back to earlier.

Rafael's kiss had been gentle—unlike what I would have expected from a man like him.

I enjoyed working out with Rafael today. Doing something normal with him made him feel more human to me.

His body was like a machine—refined to perfection. Although no matter how beautiful his body was, I could never forget that his was a soul that fed on violence.

I knew that Rafael thought of me as sullied. Who would want someone like me for a wife, especially in the Mafia world where virginity was the prize awarded to a husband when he married?

Nothing was going to change Rafael's view of me after what had happened, and I just had to get used to that.

He had accepted me as his wife and not insisted on an annulment, and I had to be thankful for that. If it had gotten out what had happened, the further shame I would have faced would have been unbearable.

That my honor had been taken before my wedding day would mean humiliation, pitying looks, and salacious gossip. I shuddered just thinking of it. And I would be blamed for what had happened; they would say that I led Emanuel on, that I was a tease.

I couldn't blame Rafael for feeling the way he did. All these men were brought up knowing that one day they would have an arranged marriage to cement a bond with a fellow family. And their reward for that arranged marriage was a pure, untouched virgin.

Of course, before marriage, the men would play around with other girls and sow their wild oats. But those girls weren't suitable to be their wives or the mothers of their future children, not in this world where discretion and duty were key. Not many women could understand those duties, not unless they had been born into and brought up in this world. That was why it was so important that we married one of our own.

Today I cleaned the office, but I didn't go into Gabriel's bedroom because I would ask him before going into his private quarters.

The office had two desks in it, and I assumed that one was for each brother. I thought about how they did everything together. They had moved out of their parents' home and moved into a place of their own together. They worked together and they lived together.

The Società was their sole desire in life. They both knew that they wouldn't marry for love; instead, they would marry a Società daughter who would support them in their work and give them the heirs they needed to succeed in this world.

For a Made Man not to have a son was unthinkable. He needed a male heir to take over his position within the Società.

Within the organization, family was key. We couldn't trust outsiders or bring them into our world. Instead, we bred the future generations—the future Made Men and the future Mafia princesses who would marry them and produce their babies. And so, our dynasty continued.

The Mafia's obsessive focus on family was a big reason why we were so successful. Our marriages cemented the bonds between the families and guaranteed a line of future generations to carry on our great organization.

***

That evening, when Gabriel and Rafael returned home, they both headed straight for their office first.

I was checking on dinner when I heard my name hollered from down the hallway. "Jessica!"

I headed to the door but before I could get there, Gabriel stormed to the kitchen. "Have you been in my office today?"

My body tensed at his expression. "Yes, um, I thought I would tidy it up for you. But I didn't move anything. I just dusted, cleaned, and polished around things. And it looks better—"

"You shouldn't go in there without my permission."

"I...I didn't go into your bedroom." I couldn't stop my voice from shaking. "I thought I would ask you about your private quarters before going in there. But I didn't think you'd mind about the office." I saw Rafael come up behind his brother, frowning as he listened to our conversation.

"The office *is* one of my private areas. Stay out of there from now on—"

"Gabriel," growled Rafael in warning, as he walked into the kitchen. "Don't speak to Jessica like that." His tone silenced Gabriel, who glared at me once more before stalking to the office.

"Sorry about my brother—he's an asshole sometimes," said Rafael, touching me lightly on my arm.

I was taken aback by Gabriel's words and felt tears sting the back of my eyes. I knew he disliked me. Not only was I a constant reminder of Juliana, but I was also the reason he had gotten shot just before my wedding. And he wasn't going to forgive me for either of those things.

I would have to tread more carefully around him. I now knew that the office the brothers shared was off-limits. He and Rafael were at work most of the time anyway. When he was home, it was a big house and I would avoid him as much as possible.

RAFAEL

The next day, I was sparring with Gabriel in our home workout studio.

"Get your head in the game," snarled Gabriel, as he landed a shot on my upper cheek, causing blood to pour out from the resulting cut. "There's no point training with you if you don't even attempt to put up a decent fight."

My brother was right—I was distracted by thoughts of Jessica and getting revenge against my father. This was something that was constantly on my mind, my bitterness eating away inside me.

Just then, Jessica came into the studio, carrying various cleaning supplies. She stopped dead in her tracks when she saw blood running down my face and Gabriel wiping his bloody knuckles against the bottom of his sweat-drenched white t-shirt.

She made a small indistinguishable noise before trying to clear her throat. "I...uh..." she mumbled, her huge gray eyes unblinking and wary and her breaths coming too quickly. I could see something was affecting her, but I wasn't sure if it was the pouring blood or the bare-faced aggression emanating from my brother who was in full attack mode.

"What is it?" snapped Gabriel, throwing a hostile glare in Jessica's direction as she cowered against the door, her eyes fixed on him as if she feared he'd pounce on her if she let her defenses down.

Gabriel hated being interrupted while he was working, and training was work to him. He treated his body like a machine and honed every inch to perfection.

"N-Nothing," she stammered as she rushed out of the room, almost tripping over her own feet.

"What the hell?" He glared after her. "I hardly said a word to her."

"That's the point."

"You've lost me there, little brother."

I raised an eyebrow at him. "You hardly say a word to her unless it's to snarl at her."

"What else do you want me to say to her? She's obviously scared of me and I can't change that." Gabriel enjoyed invoking fear in others and the hold it gave him over people—he enjoyed it probably too much, meaning that he would make a good, ruthless Capo when the time came.

"You're a man. She's likely scared of most men after what's happened to her," I pointed out.

"Maybe she would benefit from learning some self-defense."

"Meaning?" I barked at my brother.

"Meaning, I'm the least of her worries. I've noticed she gets antsy whenever people come to the house, even when it's just the guards bringing up the groceries that have been delivered. Maybe some defense skills would help give her some more confidence."

I silently berated myself for not noticing that the guards bringing the deliveries had bothered Jessica. I would have to do something about that. "I'll look into it. Until then, Gabriel, cut her some slack."

"It grates on my nerves the way she scurries around the place like a little mouse," he said through gritted teeth.

"You'll survive," I drawled. "Can you try to keep your pained outrage to a minimum?"

Gabriel wiped the sweat from his face.

"Anyway, where else do you expect my wife to live? She's mine now. It's her home now as well and I want her to be happy here." My voice was steely. "After what our father did, that's the least we can do for her."

Gabriel didn't reply. As far as he was concerned, if it wasn't about work, he wasn't interested in talking about it.

I walked up to my brother. "You need to be gentler with Jessica." My tone made it clear that this was non-negotiable for me.

"I shouldn't have snapped at her last night," Gabriel conceded.

"She was only cleaning to try and help."

"I get it," Gabriel responded testily. "I'll apologize to her."

I stared at my older brother for a long moment. "You know, you just need to get over Juliana."

"What the fuck are you talking about now?" Gabriel's mood had been very volatile since the incident involving Juliana where he'd been shot.

"You heard." I took a long look at him. "You offered your help to her, and she didn't take her."

"She couldn't take it—because of that madman."

"Whatever. She knows we're here if she comes back and that we'll protect her. But you can't keep taking out your frustrations on everyone around you. Especially not Jessica—she doesn't deserve that, especially after what she's been through with our family."

"I know, man." He paused. "I'm sorry." My brother didn't apologize to many people, but I knew he was genuine, and that meant a lot to me.

"You know, Gabriel, I would put my life on the line for you," I said quietly.

"And I'd do the same for you—I've always kept you and our siblings safe, and I always will." Not many people felt safe around Gabriel, but he was right when he said that me and our siblings had nothing to worry about when he was around. And that couldn't be said for all Capos and Capos-to-be. Too many Mafia families were rife with infighting and familial murder, and I knew I was lucky to have a brother whom I could trust and rely upon.

"I want you to look out for Jess in the same way—she's one of us now. And she's important to me." And I surprised myself by realizing that she was.

Gabriel gave a look of surprise. "Don't tell me that you're falling in love with her?"

"She's my wife now and my responsibility. I won't let anyone think that I don't protect what is mine."

"If it's that important to you, then you know I'll look out for her too. You have my word on that."

I nodded my gratitude, and he nodded back at me. I knew my brother wouldn't go back on his word to me. He might be cold and heartless, but he was loyal.

"Our house was a bit of a mess and particularly the office," I pointed out.

"Hell, you've made your point, Rafael. You can stop trying to make me feel guilty—you know it won't work on me. Though I'll admit the office looks better now, even compared to when we had help around the house. What are we doing about getting a replacement housekeeper?"

"What, you mean after you killed the last one?"

"She stole from us. She knew the consequences. I thought you said Jessica would find us a new housekeeper?"

"Jessica likes doing housework and cooking. She's a bit of a homebody and she says it keeps her busy and keeps her mind off things. If she wants to do it, then I'll let her. I've told her I've got no problem getting a new housekeeper, but she seems to want to do it herself."

"That's not something I'd expect from a Mafia princess," remarked Gabriel.

"Yeah, but then I guess she's not really a typical Mafia princess."

And, for some reason, that thought made me glad.

***

After finishing up our training, I went to the bedroom to shower and change. Jessica was in there, making the bed, her eyes red. She had obviously been crying.

She tensed slightly as she heard my approach, but then relaxed once she saw it was just me.

"I know you've had an awful time the last couple of months, but eventually you will learn to trust a man again."

She shook her head. "I don't think I can."

"You can always trust me, I promise you that."

She wiped the tears away from her face with trembling hands.

"And you don't have to be afraid of Gabriel. He's my family, and he's your family now. He won't hurt you."

"The best reassurance you can give me is that he's family?" Her voice moved from upset to anger. "Family ties don't make a difference in our world. Just look at my family—my parents still gave me to a Santino man, even after your father raped me."

"That was different—"

"How? Because your father is our Capo and therefore can do what he wants? Remember that Gabriel will be Capo one day too."

"He's not like my father. My father is a psychopath and he manipulates people. Gabriel would never betray me or you like that, I swear."

Jessica broke down again. I took her in my arms and thankfully she didn't fight me. "I'm here for you. We'll take baby steps, and I'll take each and every one of those steps with you. We'll get through this together."

"I don't know who I can trust anymore," she sobbed. "Nothing's straightforward now. It's not just me doubting all men, I doubt myself all the time now—am I too naïve, was I too gullible?"

"Stop, Jess," I said gently. "Stop blaming yourself. You weren't to blame for what happened. I can't ever make it up to you for what's happened but know that I'll never stop trying. No one will ever hurt you again."

"You can't protect me from your father."

"Yes, I can."

"You can't, Rafael. He's Capo—no one can stop him if he wants to do something."

CHAPTER 13

JESSICA

The next day, Rafael was working from home, and just before lunch, I was about to go into the office to ask him something.

The door was slightly ajar, and I heard not just his voice but also the deep timbre of other male voices.

I recoiled—he definitely wasn't talking to Gabriel. I knew he must have some of his men in with him.

I started to breathe too fast but I still couldn't get enough oxygen into my lungs.

I knew it was irrational—because nothing could happen to me while Rafael was in the house. But I couldn't stop the fear from crawling under every inch of my skin.

I heard Rafael's speak. "These are the immediate enhancements I require to all security measures around our whole estate."

"We'll get on it straightaway," another man replied.

"I want everything completed in the next 24 hours," Rafael said tersely. "I don't care if you have to work around the clock—just get it done."

"Is there a reason for this?" a second man asked. "Is there intel about a new threat?"

"No."

The ensuing silence gave me the sense that the men were confused about his orders.

"Boss, it's just that the estate is already superbly protected…"

"There's no new intel," Rafael responded. "But I have Jessica here now—and I need to make sure that *my wife* is protected in every way possible. I'm not leaving anything to chance, not when it comes to her."

There was something about the way he said 'my wife'—something that made a warmth suffuse my entire body, making my nerve-endings tingle and my heart beat just a little too fast.

Did he actually want me as his wife?

Did he really want me here?

I turned around and headed to the kitchen. But I found it hard to concentrate on anything else as his words kept running through my head…

***

Over the next few weeks, Rafael and I started to go on a run together every morning.

We hadn't kissed again, but I hadn't expected us to. During our runs, however, I sometimes found my eyes drifting over Rafael's body. He looked good in his workout gear, his strong physique gleaming with sweat. His proximity always seemed to overwhelm me and made it hard to concentrate.

I enjoyed the peace of the early morning and the calm that seemed to be in him during this time—he was more relaxed than when he was in full work mode and somehow easier to talk to.

The other aspect I enjoyed of living here was the presence of the horses.

Today I walked up to the stables in the afternoon and had sugar lumps ready in my pockets for the horses. I think I enjoyed feeding them even more than they enjoyed it. They were peaceful creatures, serene and calming. And I needed calm in my life after the last few months.

As soon as I got near, I heard a couple of whinnies from the horses as they sensed my approach. As I entered the stables, I saw Storm's black ears prick up in delight. I gave a sugar lump to each horse, patting each one as I passed them, finally reaching Storm at the end.

For him, as always, I had saved two sugar lumps. He wolfed down the sugar and I laughed at the feel of his soft nose as he nuzzled against my hand.

"So that's why Storm's always fucking snaffling around my pockets now whenever I come to ride him."

I jumped as I heard a low voice come from behind me and spun around to find Gabriel glaring at me. "I...sorry...I was just giving him a sugar lump."

"Or three?" he questioned harshly.

"Well, maybe two—but they were only small ones..." My voice trailed off.

Rafael had warned me to stay away from Storm, that he was Gabriel's favorite, but I hadn't been able to resist.

"I'm sorry. I'll stay away from Storm from now on."

Gabriel regarded me with his cold stare, sending a shiver through me. I quickly looked away, self-conscious under his scrutiny. "No. He likes you. He doesn't like many people. And I don't always get down to see him every day when I'm too busy with work."

"So, y-you don't mind...?" I tried to stop my voice from shaking but failed miserably. Most men scared me, and Gabriel's mere presence was enough to send a shard of ice to my chest.

"Why would I?"

Because you're a cold-hearted control freak, I thought to myself, but I didn't dare to say those words out loud as I valued my life too much.

Gabriel took a step closer to Storm and me, making me recoil.

"You have to stop doing that," he said in a hard tone.

"Doing what?"

"Jumping out of your skin every time I come near you."

"Well, I wouldn't if you weren't so scary all the time," I countered testily, slapping my hand over my mouth when I remembered who I was talking to.

He laughed out loud. "That's better. Say what you think to me instead of being a quiet little mouse who scurries around the place, afraid of disturbing anyone."

"I am *not* a mouse," I retorted, irritated at his characterization of me.

"Then stop acting like one. You are Rafael's wife now. You need to exude strength and confidence, then people will respect you."

"That's easy for you to say."

His voice softened very slightly. "I'm sorry I snapped at you."

"You and your family can trust me," I said quickly. "I would never snoop, and I would never betray you."

"Not even after what my father did to you?" he asked, his eyebrows raised in question.

My cheeks heated. "Rafael protected me and my reputation after that happened. I won't ever forget that."

"Good. Anyhow, I apologize for what I've said. I'm not used to having to carefully choose my words. I say what I think."

"I can tell."

"I know it's been difficult for you, but you are under our protection now. Nothing will happen to you—I promise you that."

I nodded, but I still didn't know how I could suddenly stop being so afraid all the time.

Sensing my doubts, Gabriel carried on. "We all have scars. You have to fight your weaknesses. In our world—the Mafia world—life is harsh, and it will devour you if you let it."

"I'll try," I said as firmly as I could. From the few things my own brother had told me, training for the Società initiation was pretty tough for the men, and I doubted a man like Emanuel would have spared his sons. "And thank you."

"For what?"

"For what you just said. And for letting me spend time with Storm—he really is a beauty,"

"Just don't go spoiling him with those sugar lumps," he said tersely. "He'll expect that every day otherwise."

And just like that, he was back to the brusque, standoffish man I usually encountered each day. I now knew, however, in that cold heart of his was something a little bit like humanity.

RAFAEL

The following week arrived and along with it came my father's birthday dinner.

When we reached my parents' home that evening, I turned off the ignition and looked at Jessica.

"Are you sure you want to do this?" I asked quietly.

She nodded in response.

"Okay. But know that nothing will happen to you tonight."

She nodded again, although this time it was more hesitant.

I got out of the car and walked around to her side, opening the passenger door and offering her my hand. She gratefully accepted it, and I helped her out of the car as she tried not to step on the hem of her long plum-colored dress.

She often wore shades of purple, although normally more of a paler shade which she called 'lilac'. She'd told me on one of our runs that it was her favorite color. She often painted her nails that color, and although she didn't wear much make-up normally, she had a lilac eyeshadow which really brought out the silver tones in her pretty gray eyes. Her favorite purse was also made from a soft, lilac leather.

Once Jess had exited the car and straightened her dress, I took her hand firmly in mine. I felt her shiver slightly under my touch, but then she tightened her fingers around mine.

We walked to the door, where my mother stepped out to greet us. "There you are, Rafael. We were wondering what had held you up—you've missed the drinks. We were just going through to the dining room for the meal."

"Sorry, Mother, I had some business to take care of." That was a fib. I had purposely timed our arrival to miss the drinks and thus minimize the time Jessica would have to spend with my family tonight.

"Jessica, dear, you look beautiful. I hope my son realizes what a lucky man he is."

"That I do," I chuckled, noting the look of confusion on Jessica's face as I spoke.

The presence of the twins ensured that conversation during the meal was flowing and therefore no one seemed to notice that Jessica was quiet.

No one, that is, apart from my father.

"So, Jessica, how are you finding married life?" said my father loudly, his lewd tone making her pale.

Jessica visibly swallowed. "It's fine, thank you."

"Come now, surely you can share more details than that?" he continued, openly leering at her.

I clenched my fists under the table.

"When will you be breeding an heir for my son? You know what is expected of you, don't you? And I'm sure my son is enjoying having a nubile young girl in his bed." He laughed a cruel laugh, and Jessica looked away, red rapidly rising over her pale cheeks.

"That's enough, Father," I snarled.

Gabriel quickly changed the subject to a business matter. I reached under the table for Jessica's small, cold hand and gave it a squeeze. She gave me a small smile to let me know that she was alright—well, as alright as anyone could be in such a situation.

The meal continued and my father said nothing more to Jessica.

After the main meal had been consumed, Jessica excused herself to go to the powder room.

A couple of minutes later, my father stood up. "I'm going to get another couple of bottles from the wine cellar..."

JESSICA

In the hallway, I asked the maid the way to the powder room.

She directed me through a door to another very long hallway. "Keep going down that hallway. Once you pass the library, then the powder room is the fourth door on the left."

The mansion was enormous, I thought as I walked down the hallway. This part of the mansion also felt colder for some reason.

Suddenly the lights blacked out.

I stopped in my tracks and my eyes darted upward.

The lights must be operated by motion sensors, I thought.

I took a few steps in the darkness, but the lights didn't come back on.

My pulse began to beat too quickly.

It must be a power cut, I told myself.

The hallway was pitch black.

I carefully started walking forward again.

Wobbling on my heels, I reached out a hand to the wall to steady myself.

I thought I heard a sound from behind me.

I spun my head around.

It was too dark to see anything.

My step quickened.

Had I already passed the library?

I wasn't sure. The darkness was disorientating me.

I tried the next door on my left.

It was locked.

I thought I heard another sound.

Swiveling my head around, I squinted my eyes.

I still couldn't make anything out...

Then someone cleared their throat.

The blood roared in my ears.

I needed to find the powder room and quick. It would have a lock.

I broke into a run.

Stumbling on the hem of my long dress, I righted my body.

And I jumped as I heard a voice rasping right next me.

As my eyes grew accustomed to the dark, I saw him.

Emanuel...

His lips pulled up into an evil smile.

"Jessica, I've been wondering when I'd get you to myself..."

RAFAEL

My father clearly had drunk too much tonight. He was much too fond of his alcohol.

I excused myself from the table and followed him.

He did not make for the wine cellar and instead headed in the opposite direction.

I started to quicken my step.

The lights blinked off.

Without a pause, I broke into a run.

As my eyes got used to the dark in the next few seconds, I saw Jessica ahead and my father right behind her.

Jessica stumbled.

My father shot out a hand to grab her. "Jessica, I've been wondering when I'd get you to myself..."

Before he could touch her, I slammed him into the opposite wall, its surface thudding with the sound of the harsh impact of his body into its unforgiving solidness. "Don't you dare touch her!"

"You think you can stop me?" he slurred. "I'm Capo. She has to do whatever I tell her to, including fucking spreading her legs."

The lights flicked back on.

Gabriel was hot on my heels, and he took Jessica's arm and led her away. "Come on, Jessica, let's get you somewhere where you can sit down." She was as pale as a sheet and looked like she might pass out.

The blood was drumming in my ears, beating so intensely that it seemed to echo around my entire body.

For my father to think that he could attack my wife while I was in the same house showed how arrogant he was and how sloppy he'd become. I grabbed him by the collar and dragged him to his office, his drunkenness making it easier than it should have been.

He stumbled in my hold but I didn't slow down or loosen my grip.

Once we were in his office, I shoved him onto his desk.

A groan of pain escaped his lips as his spine connected with the wooden surface at an unnatural angle, jarring his body.

He tried to scramble back up but I rammed him back onto the desk and then tightened a grip around his throat.

His fingers clawed at my wrist, trying to prize my grasp from his oxygen supply as his face started to go red.

"You shouldn't have ever touched Jessica," I snarled. I'd wanted to do this for so long, to steal every last breath from his lungs and squeeze every last drop of blood from his body.

Every inch of my skin prickled with adrenaline. How I'd longed to take my fury out on this pathetic man who preyed on the innocent.

His pupils were dilated with terror. He knew he was no match for my rage, not in his current state.

"Look, Rafael—" he rasped.

"Shut your fucking mouth!" I wanted to beat him bloody and wanted to slam my fists repeatedly into his face and body.

"Don't...let the little whore get between us..."

"Don't you dare talk about her like that," I roared. "What man forces himself upon an innocent, powerless woman?"

"She's a part of our world, and she knows...what sort of men we are..." He struggled to force his words out.

"No, the fuck she didn't know! Not until you put your slimy, disgusting hands on her."

He'd become complacent since my wedding, thinking that he'd got away with what he'd done. It made this all the more satisfying—he hadn't seen this coming, the arrogant prick.

I pulled a pair of pliers from my pocket and then a knife from my holster.

I saw the panic in his eyes as I slowly set them on the desk out of his reach, letting the ruthless metal of the sharp knife blade glint under the electric light.

I brought the pliers next to his face while keeping hold of his throat with my other hand. "Should I start with your fingernails or teeth?" My voice dripped with my dark intentions.

"How dare you t-threaten me like this," he said hoarsely, trying to exert his authority but unable to prevent the break in his voice.

"Or should I start with my knife? Do you want me to cut out your tongue or hack off your dick first?"

This time he didn't even try to mask his fear.

"What do you...want?" He had to push his words out against the grip of my hand around his neck. "More money? I can give you however...much you need."

A harsh laugh escaped my mouth. "I've got more money than I'll ever need. No, what I want is to see you suffer."

I delighted in seeing the slick of sweat over his face as he scrambled under me. But what I really wanted were his screams.

"I'm your f-father..."

"You're nothing to me. And Mother will be better off without you. You're a pathetic piece of shit. I want to gut you like a pig and see your blood pool on the floor."

I grabbed his chin and dug my fingers in, forcing his jaw open. "This is what it feels like to be powerless, to be someone's victim..."

I grabbed his tongue and his eyes almost popped out of his head as he waited for me to slice it off.

He tried to get more words out to plead with me.

But I didn't let him say anything else.

I was playing a game with him though. As much as I longed to and as much as he deserved it, I couldn't use the pliers or knife on him today. I couldn't leave their harsh marks on him.

Not if I wanted Gabriel to become Capo and the Santino family name to stay strong—and I needed both those things as they were my guarantee of keeping Jessica and her secret safe. I would have the power to get rid of anyone who jeopardized her safety or threatened to reveal what had happened to her, and no one would dare question me as long as the Santinos remained at the head of the Società.

Instead, I pulled from my pocket a pill and jabbed it down his throat with my fingers, causing him to splutter as he tried to draw a deep breath while attempting simultaneously to keep the tablet from going down his throat.

I'd obtained the pill from a clandestine contact and had been carrying it with me every day since I'd found out about Jessica's rape. Once it took effect it would simulate a heart attack, leaving no traces behind. It would look like natural causes.

He continued to struggle under me, not even bothering to hide his terror now. This was the end of this life.

"How I would have loved to have tortured you to death," I spat out, as I watched his face pale as the pill started to slow his heart.

I knew his vision was starting to blur as the pill worked to deprive his brain of oxygen. His limbs quivered, and he could no longer talk or pathetically beg as the life was sucked out of him.

I watched his face with satisfaction as his skin turned blue, his body grew limp, and his mouth began to froth.

I had been waiting for this opportunity to present itself. That came tonight when my father had dismissed the soldiers who usually kept a very close guard around him, and they had retired to the guard room beside the front gates. He obviously thought that he didn't need their protection given that he had three of his sons in his house tonight. That he thought he was safe around me was arrogant beyond belief.

He grew more desperate, weakly clutching at his throat and chest, reaching out with his hand to plead with me as the life ebbed from his body.

And vengeance flew through my body as I watched him take his very last breath.

As I looked at his lifeless body, I recited the words every Made Man said upon a death: "Santa Maria, Madre di Dio, prega per noi peccatori, adesso e nell'ora della nostra morte."

I thought about the meaning of the words: "Holy Mary, Mother of God, pray for us sinners now and at the hour of our death." He would need every bit of this prayer where he was going: straight to Hell.

I called my mother to the drawing room and broke the news to her. "It looks like our father has had a heart attack. You should call the doctor, but he's already dead."

She had been in this life long enough to know not to ask questions. I doubted my mother would miss him—he had been a cruel husband to her.

I hoped that now I would be able to manage the anger that had been racing though my body and burning me alive since the night I'd found out what he'd done to Jessica.

My need for revenge had come second to the need of keeping Jessica's secret safe from the rest of the Società. The Società was an incestuous tangle of relationships between the different families. If my father had come to an obviously violent end, there would be no way to hide that fact—not from the household staff, the soldiers guarding the property, or the doctor who worked for us.

And then we ran the risk that eventually people would find out the reason why I had done it. And I wouldn't risk Jessica's rape being found out and gossiped about. I wouldn't do that to Jess—she meant too much to me.

JESSICA

I let Gabriel lead me to the sitting room and collapsed into an armchair. My hands were trembling, and my breaths were coming too quickly.

"I-I'm okay," I stammered.

"You will be. Rafael is ending his life right now. After today, Emanuel Santino will never be able to hurt you again."

That news made a numbness spread over me. I didn't know if I should feel elated or sad that another person's life was ending as we spoke. I couldn't really process it all right at this moment. "You should get back to your mother...you don't need to stay with me."

"I'm staying. You shouldn't be alone right now."

"No, really. I know you don't like me—you don't have to stay here with me, I'll be fine."

Gabriel frowned at me. "Why do you think I don't like you?"

The shock coursing through my body made me less diplomatic than usual. "I know I probably remind you...a little of my sister. And even if I don't, I was the reason you got shot just before my wedding."

"You're not responsible for what happened that day."

"The only reason Juliana was here was to see me. If she hadn't come to see me, you wouldn't have been shot."

"I don't blame you. It was just a gunshot wound—I've had worse," he responded.

"I'm still sorry."

He paused. "I know I've been a little short with you at times. You're right, having you around does remind me—not of Juliana herself, but of our failure to protect her." He sighed. "It's just frustrating that we haven't been able to help her—it makes me so angry."

I looked at Gabriel and saw the pain on his face. "You really like her, huh?" I said softly.

"I know in our world we're not supposed to fall in love with people, but I wish there was more I could do to help her. She doesn't deserve what's happened to her. She doesn't deserve any of it."

I nodded. Because he was right—Juliana didn't deserve what had happened to her, but there was nothing we could do to help her.

"I've also been angry that we weren't able to protect you, Jessica."

"Me?" I blurted out.

"You've been ours to protect since you signed the contract. That was when you became a Santino. We should have done more to look after you. We failed you. Now that I am Capo, I will make sure that no one harms you ever again."

He was right—he was the new Capo now.

"I told Juliana before her wedding that I would always be here for her if she ever needed anything. The same goes for you. You are my sister-in-law now—you are my family."

I was stunned at his words, both about me and about Juliana. Perhaps he had more humanity in him than I'd given him credit for.

CHAPTER 14

RAFAEL

After informing my mother that my father was dead, I took Jessica home.

Gabriel stayed behind to deal with the aftermath. We had been flawless in our execution—no one would ever find out that our father's death was deliberate.

As far as everyone was concerned, it was a heart attack that had taken him. There was nothing to suggest otherwise, nothing to trace back to the small pill I had forced down his throat.

Tonight Gabriel became Capo—the boss of the Società Mafia. And I became his Consigliere, his chief adviser and second-in-command. We had taken over power of the Società and tomorrow we would get to work.

Cecilio Bonardi was still an Underboss and I hoped he wouldn't let us down. If he did, we would deal with him too. Nothing and nobody was going to get in our way now.

That night, as Jessica lay in bed, I stripped off my clothes. I could see her carefully watching me, with a small frown across her brow, as her eyes took in my body from head to toe.

I climbed into bed. Before I turned off the lamp on the nightstand, I turned to her. "Are you alright? Do you want me to sleep in a guest room tonight?"

"Why would I want that?"

"I know that tonight couldn't have been easy for you—with my father, the violence, and everything."

"You're my avenging angel," she said quietly.

"I'll never be an angel, but I'll always protect what's mine."

Jessica turned to me, a pink tinge highlighting her cheeks. "I want you…"

I stilled, not quite believing what she's just said.

I didn't want to take advantage of her. In the morning, she might regret asking me to do this.

But my mind was in turmoil after the events of tonight. She had looked beautiful tonight—she was always beautiful in my eyes. "I'd like nothing more than to kiss you right now. But are you sure?"

She nodded.

I smoothed the waves back from her forehead before lowering my hands and running them gently down her arms.

I looked into her eyes and saw apprehension there. But there was also something else that hadn't been there before—there was curiosity and, more than that, there was desire.

She wanted this. She wanted me.

And that thought made me even more eager for her body.

But I would take it slow. After what had happened to her, I wouldn't rush her. "I won't do anything you don't want me to do."

She looked at me with her wide gray eyes. She didn't say anything.

"You just have to tell me to stop, okay?"

"Okay," she whispered.

I had to be sure that she understood this. "I've got no expectations of you. I won't make you do anything you're not comfortable with. You can always tell me to stop. And I will stop—no matter how much I want you. I'll always stop if you tell me to."

As I spoke, I saw the frown disappear from her brow. And I knew that she understood me.

She was lying down on the bed against the pillows. I raised myself on one arm above her and stroked her dark glossy waves back from her face. "You're beautiful," I said in a low voice as I took her in.

Bending my head down to her face, I pressed my mouth against hers—my lips firm but undemanding, wanting her to know how much I desired her.

I didn't, however, want my desire to frighten her. I needed to take it slow with her.

I found her attractive and she was the only one I wanted. I toyed with her mouth, letting her know this, using my lips and tongue to arouse her desire for me.

As she laid under me, I felt her breath quicken and she willingly accepted my tongue into her mouth, enjoying its caresses. She breathed a soft moan and I felt her raise herself up slightly toward me, pressing her mouth against mine.

Kissing her, I skimmed my hands down her arms and over her hips and felt her shiver under me. I could see she was affected by my touch as I ran a trail of small kisses from her mouth, down her neck and to the soft skin above the swell of her breasts.

I wanted to strip off her silky nightdress.

It was similar to all the other nightdresses she had worn since we'd been married—a flimsy sheath of fabric teasing me with a glimpse of her slender shoulders underneath its spaghetti straps, arousing me with the way the smooth fabric clung to her high breasts and emphasized her taut nipples.

The short hem skimmed the top of her shapely thighs and the secret place at their apex.

I needed to expose her naked body to me.

Pressing my lips to her chest, I kissed her fabric-covered breasts and stomach, all the while using my hands to caress the bare skin of her arms and legs. I wanted her used to having my touch on her bare skin before I took more.

Soon she was squirming with need beneath me, the movement of her hips making the silky fabric ride up and give me a glimpse of her matching panties.

I exhaled sharply when I saw the pale silk was darkened. Fuck, she was wet. She was aroused and wanted this too.

I wanted to rip her panties off and fuck her hard like I'd been wanting to do for so long now.

I willed myself to show restraint and take my time, not frightening her before she was ready to fully give herself to me. Moving back up her body, I met her mouth again. And then I lifted my weight slightly off of her. "Turn over," I instructed.

"Wh-What are you doing?" she stammered.

"I want to kiss every inch of your body, worship every curve and dip."

She slowly turned onto her stomach.

I ran my hands over her hair, massaging her scalp with my fingers, planting kisses down the back of her neck and trailing them down her spine, my lips leaving small moist marks on her nightdress.

My eyes were drawn to the curve of her ass and as I ran more kisses there, I could smell the arousal coming from her wet panties.

I slowly lifted the hem of her nightdress, revealing those panties and running my nose against her wetness, inhaling her desire.

I worked my way back up her body, over her spine and her shoulders, to her face. She was still on her stomach, her head turned to the side with her face against the pillow, and I could see her expression as I stroked her, her lips parted as her pink tongue moistened her full lips.

Moving my mouth over the shell of her ear, I gently caressed it with my tongue, causing her to quiver under me. "I want to pull the straps down of your nightdress," I whispered into her ear. "Down your shoulders and all the way down your arms. I want to see the flawless skin of your back."

Her breathing quickened.

"As I pull it down all the way, I'll see your back. And then as I pull it down your legs, I'll see your thighs... will you let me do that?"

She gave me a nod, her eyes glazing over.

"No," I said harshly. "I need you to look me in the eye and tell me you want me to do it."

Jessica looked at me in confusion. "I don't understand..."

"I won't do anything unless you explicitly tell me you want it. You have to be sure."

She looked at me, her eyes wide. "I want it," she said quietly.

I held her gaze, and as she continued looking at me, I knew she wanted this. I dipped my head back down to hers, kissing her harder than before as I started to slide the thin straps down her arms.

Her eyes remained fully open, her breaths coming out unevenly.

But she didn't stop me.

I slid the silk all the way off her body as she laid under me, her skin naked apart from the small panties. They were the only barrier now preventing my cock from invading her pussy. I moved my lips over each bump of her spine, teasing her bare skin with my tongue as she closed her eyes.

"I want to kiss your nakedness, with my lips leaving my wet saliva on you, marking you as mine," I growled.

"I want that too," she whispered, looking at me.

I felt a surge of triumph. I hadn't had to coax the words out of her. She'd come right out and said she wanted it. She wanted me.

She still lay on her stomach and I covered her flawless skin with my harsh kisses, my breath rasping as I moved down her body. And as my face moved over her ass, I kissed her rounded cheeks and the musky smell of her arousal enticed me.

Working my way down the back of her thighs and the back of her knees, I gently splayed her legs with my hands so that I could run my tongue up the insides of her thighs until I reached their apex where her scent met me.

And as my tongue flicked over the dampness, I heard a sharp intake of breath from her.

I wanted to tear her panties off, tear down that barrier between my mouth and her pussy. But I wouldn't do it without her permission.

I slowly moved back up to her face, her head still to the side upon the pillow and her eyes tightly closed. Her breaths were coming in small gasps.

I kissed her throat at the base, making her moan. "Please…" She raised herself on her forearms, pressing her neck toward my lips. "Please, I need you."

"No, first I want to see all of you. I want to turn you over and run my tongue over your stomach, breasts, and nipples…"

"Yes," she breathed.

I flipped her over and met her gaze, her pupils dilated. I brushed my lips against the side of her neck as my hands played with her sensitive breasts, catching the heavy orbs in my hands.

I tongued the valley between her breasts, licking and kissing around her globes, before feasting on her nipples and enjoying her small cries as she arched her back, pushing her nipples more into my mouth.

And then I kissed her lips again, watching her eyes drift shut as my hand trailed over her stomach to the space between her thighs.

I stroked her panties, fondling her pussy lips through the fabric and feeling their slickness.

"I want to take your panties off. I want my tongue between your legs, licking your clit, feasting on your pussy..."

She nodded, her eyes tightly shut.

"No," I said, my voice severe with need. "You know what you have to say. I told you that any more would have to come from you."

She barely opened her eyes. "Yes," she breathed. "I want this."

I felt my balls tighten as I kissed her hard. I slid the silk panties down her legs and then used my hands to part her thighs so that my fingers could delve into her wet folds and tease her pussy and its erect bud.

She was soaked with need and her glistening labia enticed me.

I lowered my lips to her clit, latching onto it and sucking hard. At the first stroke of my tongue against her clit, she moaned loudly and I couldn't stop my tongue from lapping at her juices, teasing her entrance and sucking on her labia.

Fuck, she liked my mouth on her pussy and her wet lips were so sweet as I flicked my tongue over her entrance. As her moans became more intense, she whispered, "Are you going to...?"

I knew what she was asking—she wanted to know if I would penetrate her. "This is just about you and your pleasure."

She grasped the sheets tightly beneath her, her moans becoming more intense until she cried out loudly, her inner muscles spasming. She looked up in shock.

I raised my head and met her eyes. "Are you okay?"

She didn't say anything but then she laughed out loud. "That was…unbelievable."

I tugged her onto my chest, holding her and stroking her until her breathing slowed down. She raised her head slightly and looked at me. "What about you…?"

"I'll take care of myself in a minute. I just want to make sure you're okay first."

"Yes, I am," she said sleepily. "For the first time in a long time, I'm more than okay."

I left her to go into the bathroom and took care of myself in the shower. Then, a few minutes later, I returned to cuddle her in bed as I watched her fall asleep in my arms, a small smile on her face.

CHAPTER 15

RAFAEL

The next morning, I lay in bed watching Jessica, enjoying her serene expression, enjoying the peacefulness on her face while it lasted—because when she woke up, she might regret what had happened last night.

She stirred in my arms, her eyes drifting open.

"Hey," I said quietly. I was on edge. Before yesterday, I could never have believed that she would want an intimate relationship with me. And today, in the cold light of a new day, I was apprehensive that she would regret her actions.

"Good morning," she murmured.

"And is it a good morning?" I inquired.

I was rewarded as her soft gray eyes lit up. "Yes, it is," she smiled.

I exhaled a sigh of relief—my patience had been worth it, and I was pleased I had been able to give her pleasure.

Sometimes during the day when she thought I wasn't watching her, I would see a frown cross her features. And I knew she was thinking about the attack.

I hated that. My father could still get to her through her memories. And although I had killed him now, those memories would last forever in her mind. I wished that I could kill those memories too, but I knew that wasn't possible.

JESSICA

I didn't know what made me want to be close with Rafael last night of all nights.

Maybe I had been seduced by his power and aroused by his violence—perhaps I was going to make a better Mafia wife than I thought.

I could never forget that he was a Made Man and that his life was all about violence and hurting people. But, at the same time, something about him enthralled me, making me want to run my fingers over his strong physique and feel his electrifying touch in return.

When we went running together, I couldn't help my eyes from drifting to his body and my mind wandering to thoughts about what it would be like to make love with him.

He had stuck to his promise of not touching me until I had asked him to, and that made me feel like perhaps I could trust him. I knew that if he wanted to, he could easily overpower me and force me to submit to him, but so far, he had stayed true to his word.

Whenever he ran his gaze silently over me, brushed lightly against me in bed, or put his hand against the small of my back, I would feel my skin prickle with acute awareness and my core tighten with a longing for more.

I don't know what was making me feel this way, but I did know that I wanted more from Rafael and I didn't want to hold back any longer.

RAFAEL

The next day, we had to go and choose a casket for our father's funeral. Our mother had left it to us since she didn't feel up to leaving the house. Her widowed sister had moved in with her, so she wasn't by herself, plus all the Società wives had rallied around her.

Our mother wanted all her children involved in the decisions regarding the funeral. Therefore, today Gabriel and I drove over to the funeral parlor, picking up Nate and Nancia on the way.

"It's bad enough you drag me to training all the time," muttered Nate, dragging his hand through his blond-bronze hair. Our youngest brother was dressed in jeans, a white t-shirt, and a leather jacket. "Now you're dragging me here as well."

"Shut it," snapped Gabriel at our youngest brother, clearly not wanting to deal with his teenage surliness today. "And where the hell is your tie?" he asked as he ran his gaze over Nate's casual clothes, clearly thinking they weren't appropriate for such a somber occasion. Nate had the whole moody, laid-back attitude that girls seemed to love, and his good looks only served to add to that.

As we walked into the funeral parlor, we were greeted by a scrawny kid who looked like he was barely out of high school. He was in dire need of a decent haircut and a suit that fitted him properly. "How can I help you? Are you looking for anything in particular?" he asked.

"Well, Simon," said Nate, peering at the boy's name badge, "obviously we're looking for something to put a *dead body in*."

Simon visibly gulped.

"We're here to look for a casket for our father," said Gabriel, glaring at Nate.

"And do you have any model in mind?"

"What would you recommend?" asked Nancia politely, deferring to the expertise of the salesman.

"This is one of our most popular models," said Simon, gesturing with his hands to an oak casket which had an image of angels etched onto its wood casing.

"And one of the most expensive models," added Nate pointedly. He was well aware of how cruel our father had been, and like me and Gabriel, he wasn't grieving the death of our father.

"And that's a popular choice? Why would people want pictures on the casket?" asked Nancia, her brow slightly furrowing in concentration. She had never chosen a casket before, and this was all new to her.

"Yes, it is popular. People like the comfort of knowing that their cherished family member is going to a better place once they pass through the pearly gates."

"The pearly gates? Christ, he needs to improve his sales spiel," muttered Gabriel under his breath.

"Our father definitely won't be seeing any angels before he burns in hell," drawled Nate.

Simon could only manage a squeak in response, and Gabriel huffed as he started to lose patience. He didn't have much patience at the best of times, and I knew that he was irritated this visit was taking him away from business matters he needed to deal with.

"You're not one of the funeral parlor employees we usually deal with," I said to Simon. "We know them all quite well, given how often we're here."

"You come here often?" said Simon in a high-pitched voice as his eyes widened.

This kid must be new, I thought. "Yeah, we're here all the time. How long have you worked here?" I inquired.

"It's my f-first week," he stammered, losing more confidence the longer he dealt with us.

"Don't worry, your advice is really helpful to us," reassured Nancia, smiling at him. Trust her to feel sympathy for *Sensitive Simon* here. He needed to toughen up if he was going to work for an undertaker whose main client was the Mafia.

"We don't want anything that's going to cost extra," declared Nate.

An old lady, who appeared to be looking for a casket for her recently-deceased husband, shot us a dirty look while also tightening her grip on her purse and hugging it into her body—she obviously thought we were the sort of people who weren't to be trusted.

"What's your cheapest model?" Nate said loudly.

"For fuck's sake, Nate," snapped Gabriel, finally losing his temper. "Can you try to act like a son in mourning for just a few fucking minutes? Our father has just died, Mother is beyond upset, and everyone in the Società will be attending this fucking funeral."

What my eldest brother really meant, but couldn't say in front of the twins, was that we had to seem like a family in mourning. We didn't want any suspicions raised as to the possibility that our father's death wasn't from natural causes. We had to keep the truth quiet in order to protect Jess.

"It's not as if we can't afford it," added Gabriel, unclenching his fists and trying to calm down.

"It's not as if he was a good man," retorted Nate.

"Look, Nate, this isn't the time or place for you to object about what we do in our business," I said in a quiet voice.

I turned to Simon, who was quietly edging away.

"Er...do you want me to get my manager to assist you?" he suggested in a hopeful tone, clearly keen to offload our dysfunctional family onto someone else.

"Yes," said Gabriel tersely.

"No," I said forcefully at the same time. "We'll take whatever is your most popular model. And you're not paying for it, Nate, so stop whining about the cost," I said before he could make another inappropriate comment.

Simon's eyes darted from me to Nate and then to Gabriel. And, having second thoughts, he scuttled away to get his manager after all.

Nancia gave a final sympathetic smile to Simon.

And Nate, upon seeing this, rolled his eyes. Nancia always had a thing for the weakest person or underdog in a situation, and she obviously thought we were being too hard on Sensitive Simon.

***

The funeral took place later that week, and it was a grand affair as befitted the former Capo of the Società.

Mother was pleased with the arrangements we had made and particularly liked the casket we had chosen, including the engravings. The funeral passed without any suspicions being raised as to the circumstances surrounding my father's death and the events preceding it.

Once the day was finally over, I breathed a sigh of relief. No one had appeared suspicious, meaning that I could stop worrying that someone would find out Jessica's secret.

CHAPTER 16

JESSICA

After breakfast, Rafael and Gabriel were getting ready to leave when the perimeter soldiers rang to say someone was making their way up to the house.

"The soldiers report that Jacob and Casmundina Bonardi have just arrived," Rafael said to Gabriel.

Rafael turned to me as I stood at the sink and stacked the dishwasher. "Did you invite your brother and mother over this morning?"

I dried my wet hands. "No, I didn't. And they didn't say they were coming over."

Just then, the doorbell rang, and Gabriel answered it. A minute later, my mother came bustling into our kitchen, followed by Jacob.

My mother was wearing a green rhinestone-encrusted skirt and matching jacket. As if that wasn't bad enough, the rest of her outfit—blouse, shoes, and purse—were also a sparkly green. She always said she had to maintain standards as the wife of a Società Underboss, but today she looked like a Christmas tree to me.

"This is a surprise, Casmundina, and at such an early hour. We weren't expecting you," Rafael said drily, reluctantly accepting a double kiss from my mother before subtly wiping the wet marks from his cheeks.

"Rafael, Gabriel, so wonderful to see you," gushed my mother.

She also gave me a kiss, although she frowned as her eyes took in my dark jeans and oversized khaki top. "What are you wearing, Jessica? Hardly an appropriate outfit for a Santino wife, I would have thought." Before I could respond, she changed the subject. "I can't wait to see the house—obviously I've never been here before. Well, aren't you going to show me around?" she demanded.

I felt embarrassment suffuse my cheeks at the blatant busybody that was my mother.

Jacob, however, wasted no time on greetings or pleasantries. "Last night my parents told me what happened to Jessica before the wedding—what your father did," Jacob snarled.

"We've dealt with it," Rafael replied in a steely voice, looking him square in the eye.

"Once the engagement contract was signed, she became yours. That meant you were supposed to protect her," Jacob spat before turning to me. "Jess, you don't have to stay here in this house."

"This does not concern you." Rafael's voice was pure ice. "She is a Santino now and my wife."

"She's my sister and your family has dishonored her. Like hell it doesn't concern me!"

"Watch your tone—don't forget I'm a Santino," warned Rafael.

"And we rule the Società," added Gabriel, his tone severe.

Jacob looked at them fiercely. "I don't give a fuck what your last name is. The Santinos and the Società failed to protect Jess, just like they failed to protect my other sister." Jacob reached for his revolver.

"Jake, no!" I cried, my hands flying to my chest.

As soon as Jacob drew his gun, Gabriel pulled his weapon too and aimed it at my brother.

"Why didn't you protect Jess before the wedding? Once she was engaged to you, she was your responsibility," thundered Jacob.

"Dear God," I whispered, my eyes fixed on his revolver which was pointed at Rafael. "Jake...it doesn't matter now."

"How can you say it doesn't matter? They should have protected you. I should have protected you." Jacob raked his free hand through his hair. He looked awful, guilt eating away at his conscience. "It will always matter, Jess. You don't have to stay in this marriage. You know that, don't you?"

"Mother, do something," I pleaded to my mother, who stood beside us looking at her nails.

"What do you want me to do?" she asked in a bored tone.

"But why did you come here today if it wasn't to help calm Jake and avert a crisis?" I asked desperately. Crisis was an understatement when describing the potential fallout from today if shots were fired. I looked at my mother imploringly.

"Jacob said he was coming over and I thought I would get a ride with him." She then adopted her martyred tone. "What else am I supposed to do but come here if my own daughter doesn't bother to visit me? I can't believe I've raised such self-centered daughters—first Juliana, now you."

"Look, Jacob, lower your weapon and we'll talk about this in the office, away from the women," gritted out Rafael, eyeballing my brother and his weapon.

When my brother didn't respond, I walked over to him slowly.

"Don't, Jessica," growled Rafael.

"He's my brother!" I wouldn't abandon him, no matter what.

I reached his side and could see the pain burning in his eyes—pain for me, pain for Juliana, and pain for what had become of us all.

I hesitated, apprehension making my movements stall.

But then put my hand gently on his arm, guiding him to lower it.

He didn't fight me, nor did he take his eyes off Rafael. Gabriel lowered his gun too but kept it drawn and at his side as he led the men into the office.

I was left with my mother. "You know, Jessica, you haven't attended a single one of my wives' coffee mornings since your wedding."

"Mother, I haven't really felt like attending social functions."

"Nonsense. This is your time to shine and show everyone your triumph. Becoming a Santino wife is one of the most coveted positions for a woman in the Società. You should be relishing your new position."

What had happened had hardly felt like a triumph. My mother, however, was oblivious to my feelings as always.

"Your mother-in-law, Ortensia, never has time to attend my events. However, Jessica, you are a Santino now—think of the status it would elevate my coffee mornings to if I was to have a Santino wife in attendance!"

Jesus, I couldn't believe my mother. Here was my older brother threatening to shoot my husband and start a civil war within the Società, yet all my mother was concerned about was being crowned 'Queen of the Mafia Coffee Morning Circuit.'

I sat with my mother in the drawing room, serving her tea and listening to her rabbit on about domestic matters and the latest gossip. I kept looking anxiously at the door to the office and listening out for any raised voices.

"Do you like my new outfit, Jessica?"

"Um, it's a bit...different from your usual choices."

"I am now the mother of a Santino wife and I have a Santino as my son-in-law, so I have to dress accordingly. This outfit is more suited to my new status."

She was talking like I had married into royalty—God give me strength.

RAFAEL

In the office, none of us sat down. We stood glaring at each other.

"You were supposed to look after her, not let your father have her," Jacob spat at me.

I struggled to keep my tone calm. "I didn't let my father do anything. I had no fucking idea what he had planned."

"Why the hell weren't you at the doctor's clinic to protect her?" he questioned hostilely.

I swallowed my anger. "I didn't even know there was an appointment scheduled. My mother took care of that side of things."

Jacob looked exhausted, unshaven, and with dark circles under his eyes as if he hadn't slept all night after finding out what had happened to Jessica. "Fuck, now your mother was in on it as well? Christ, your family is beyond twisted."

"Of course my mother wasn't in on it," I retorted. "None of us had any idea."

"It was your job to have some fucking idea," Jacob shouted. "She was your fiancée, which made her your responsibility to protect and look after."

"And where the hell were you?" I snapped as guilt needled at me, making me want to lash out at somebody else.

"Do you think I would just let this happen to my own sister? You signed the contract. She was your responsibility," he said cuttingly.

I gave a harsh laugh, even though his words had riled me. "Just admit it, Jacob. You failed her as much as I did."

Jacob lunged for me, his eyes wild, but Gabriel intercepted him and held him back as he struggled to get out of his hold. "Get the fuck in control of yourself," ordered Gabriel. "I understand you're upset but this isn't the way to handle things," he growled.

"Upset? You think I'm upset?" He shook his head, closing his eyes for a moment. "That doesn't even begin to describe it. How would you feel if Nancia had been defiled before marriage?"

I would kill anyone who touched Nancia before her marriage, and we all knew that. "Look, Jacob, it's done now and we've dealt with the issue. My father is no longer here to prey on Jessica or any other woman in the Società."

Jacob's eyes reflected a hunger for revenge—a feeling I knew too well. "If your father was still here, I'd kill him with my bare hands, Capo or not," he said furiously.

"It's over now, Jacob," reiterated Gabriel.

"It's over? Are you fucking kidding me?" Jacob leaned over the desk, bracing his arms over the tabletop as if trying to keep himself upright under the weight of his burden. "Of course it isn't over. She's still married to you and has to share your bed every night," he said, stabbing his finger toward me. "What sort of sick man would force a woman to share his bed after what his father had done to her?"

I clenched my fists and strode toward Jacob, Gabriel grabbing my arm to stop me. "How I act with my wife is none of your fucking business," I said, my voice dangerously low. "I've never forced Jessica to do anything, nor will I."

Jacob straightened up. "Oh, so you're telling me that you asked her on your wedding night if she wanted to sleep in your bed with you?

Because I don't seem to remember you asking her that when you took her up to your bedroom while your men made their sleazy comments about what you were going to do to her."

"That was just drunken banter that every couple gets before their wedding night," I said dismissively. "I've never disrespected Jessica, and you would do well to remember your place."

Jacob was breathing hard and gritted his teeth. "But how many of your men already knew about what had happened? And what about your two soldiers who drove Jessica to the clinic, the ones who were in charge of her protection that day?"

"They've been eliminated and as far as we know, they didn't tell anyone about what happened that day."

"They were supposed to look after her that day, not hand her on a silver platter to your perverted father."

"Tell me, Jacob," I said slowly. "Why the hell weren't you or your men protecting your sister that day?"

"Because you told my mother that your soldiers would protect her at the clinic," he yelled.

"I didn't tell your mother anything. It was all my father's doing. When will you get that through your thick skull? Do you really think I would let anyone do that to any woman, let alone my own wife-to-be? Anyhow, it's over now and there's nothing any of us can do to change the past."

"Of course it isn't over. Do you think it's over for my sister? You're still married to Jess. You're still forcing her to share your bed. It won't be over until the marriage is annulled."

"What sort of message do you think that would send to the rest of the Società?" said Gabriel.

"All you care about is your reputation—the reputation of your precious Santino family."

"No, you're wrong there," I cut in. "All I care about is *Jessica's* reputation. If we go for an annulment, everyone will talk and probably speculate that she was damaged goods."

"Don't you fucking dare talk about my little sister like that!"

"It's the truth, though," Gabriel commented. "That's the exact phrase people in the Mafia world like to use, and we won't be able to stop them. You know that an annulment would only be sought if the girl wasn't a virgin. What sort of life would that leave for Jessica? I doubt your parents will take her back."

"I'll look after her. I'll take care of her," said Jacob obstinately, his hands shoved in his pockets. "I'll get my own place and she can live with me."

"And when you get married one day—what will your future wife think about your sister with her sullied reputation living in your home?" Gabriel questioned, thinking about the reality of such a situation.

"She'll do whatever I tell her to do, including having Jess live with us," he snapped in a cold voice.

I narrowed my gaze at my brother-in-law. "Jessica is mine now, and we won't be getting an annulment."

Jacob just continued to stare at me, looking like he would like nothing more than to kill me at this very moment.

I sighed, running my hand over my chin. "I know what's happened is fucked up. But I swear to you on my honor that Jessica won't be hurt like that ever again."

"She didn't deserve to be hurt like that in the first place," he murmured, his body slumping in despair.

"I know," I said quietly. "That we can both agree on."

When it was clear that there was nothing more either of us could say, Gabriel suggested we get back to the women.

Before we left the office, Gabriel looked at Jacob. "Jacob," said Gabriel coldly. "You will never speak like that to me or my Consigliere, or raise a gun to us, ever again. I don't give a shit what the reason is. I won't tolerate that sort of behavior or disrespect from any of my men. Am I making myself clear?"

Jacob looked him hard in the eye and nodded once. "Understood, Capo," he growled, before striding out of the room without a backward glance.

JESSICA

At last, the office door finally opened, and the men stepped out. Jacob still didn't look happy, but he was somewhat calmer compared to when he had arrived.

"Come, Mother, we're leaving. I have business to attend to. Jess, I'll call you later," said Jacob, obviously wanting to talk to me in private.

"But we've only just gotten here!" Mother was oblivious to everyone's eagerness to end this visit and I had to practically push her toward the door as she continued rabbiting on about her coffee mornings. "I really must insist that you make an effort to attend my next coffee morning, Jessica. It's the least you can do for me. You will be the guest of honor."

Jacob finally managed to get her out of the house and Gabriel shut the door after them. "That woman is fucking irritating," he muttered.

"Yep, she sure is," Rafael agreed. "Gabriel, why don't you go to the club without me. I'll follow once I've talked with Jessica."

"Is everything okay?" I asked Rafael.

"Yes, it is now. Your brother is understandably upset after finding out about what happened to you. I assured him neither Gabriel nor I had any knowledge of it before the wedding and that we have dealt with it."

"I'm sorry he acted like that."

"Gabriel warned him not to speak to either of us or raise a gun at us like that ever again. Once your father dies, he is supposed to take over and become an Underboss. But brother-in-law or not, I won't accept that sort of behavior from any of our men, nor will Gabriel."

"He was worried about me," I said in defense of my brother.

"I know. That's why I let it go this time. For you. Because I care about you, Jessica."

***

That afternoon, Jacob called me.

"I've spoken with our parents and I'm sorry, but they won't have you back in their home. I've thought about it though, and I could get a house and you could live there with me."

"You know that wouldn't work, Jake. Rafael would hunt you down for taking me away from him. But thank you and please don't worry—he's not that bad."

"Not that bad? You are my sister and you deserve the best, not the son of a monster."

"He's nothing like Emanuel. He's treated me well so far."

"For fuck's sake, Jess. I can't believe this has happened to you. First Juliana's life was fucked up and now yours. I'm so sorry, I should have protected you better—both of you." His voice was more distraught than I'd ever heard of him.

"You didn't know what Emanuel would do. No one could have guessed, not even his sons."

Jacob blaming himself was self-destructive. Emanuel had already destroyed part of me. I didn't want the effects of his actions to destroy part of Jacob too.

"Jake, you've always been there for Juliana and me. You've been the best big brother I could have asked for. You've never let me down and I know you never will."

We talked for ages, but nothing I said could convince him that he hadn't let me down.

"Damn it, Jake, you can't blame yourself. Please don't do this to yourself."

"Don't curse," said Jacob automatically.

I gave a small smile. "So, I'm old enough to be married off, but I'm still not old enough to curse?"

"You'll never be old enough to curse." Jacob was suddenly more serious. "Whatever happens, you'll always be my baby sister, and I'll always be here for you if you need protection—you just have to say the word."

I told him how grateful I was for his support. But deep down, I knew that no member of the Santino family would ever let someone else tell them what to do. They ruled the Società and did as they pleased in this city.

CHAPTER 17

RAFAEL

The following day I had an early start scheduled, so I delayed my run with Jess until the evening. After a long day of dealing with business headaches and trouble from the Russian Bratva, I was glad to finally get home.

During our run the next day, I couldn't keep my eyes off Jessica's body. Despite her dark sweatpants and navy-blue t-shirt, I couldn't help my mind conjuring up images of her tight ass and her enticing breasts, and I found my memory replaying the sounds of her crying out as I had sucked her ripe nipples a week ago.

As she ran, I let the memories from that night replay in my mind, and I found myself wanting to wrap my body around hers and thrust hard inside her until I was spent.

"Are you checking me out?" she giggled, catching my eye.

"No more than you've been checking me out the last couple of weeks."

She flushed as she laughed. "I hoped you wouldn't notice that."

"I'm trained to notice everything. And I definitely would notice someone watching me."

At the end of our run, we did our final stretches and finished the last of the water. I watched as a bead of perspiration rolled down her neck and disappeared into the v-neck of her t-shirt, knowing that it would drip down to between her breasts.

How I would love for my tongue to lash between her breasts, licking up that bead and dampening her sensitive skin with my saliva.

We headed into the house. Normally, Jessica would prepare breakfast while I showered and then we would eat together. But today when she headed to the kitchen, I caught her hand and pulled her toward me. "Why don't you join me in the shower today?"

She hesitated for a second before smiling shyly at me. "Okay."

We went upstairs to our bathroom and both started undressing. "You're pretty hot in your workout gear," I said in a low voice.

She darted a look at me.

When she didn't say anything, I added, "I won't do anything you don't want, okay?"

"Okay," she said.

I stepped into the shower, giving her some space to finish undressing. Once she was naked, I looked at her appraisingly and reached to pull her into the shower, tugging her under the hot spray with me.

We let the hot water run over our bodies and I could see her looking at my cock, which was rock hard. After washing her body and mine, I held her in my arms and pressed my lips to hers, kissing her like I'd been wanting to kiss her all throughout our run.

As we kissed, I began to caress her pussy very lightly, just skimming my fingertips over her sensitive bud.

She closed her eyes and gave in to the sensations while I watched her face.

Even under the water of the shower, I could feel her slickness as I manipulated her clit, her body responding to me beautifully.

She bit her lip and leaned her small hands against my strong arms, steadying herself as her arousal started to weaken her limbs.

As her breaths turned into pants, I slowed down and led her out of the shower, but I didn't bother to dry her.

I tugged her back to the bedroom and gently guided her to lie down on the bed.

She lay on her back, her lightly tanned body stretched out and glowing against the white sheets. I took in her beauty, and it took my breath away.

She looked up at me expectantly. I've moved myself above her and dipped my head to that tender spot at the base of her throat, kissing her gently, making love to her skin.

I let my tongue travel down the valley between her succulent breasts before taking one of her erect nipples in my mouth, enjoying its hardness against my tongue.

As I sucked on it, she moaned, and the sound made my dick even stiffer. Just as before, I didn't rush her and I lavished attention on her body, raining kisses on her lips and across her sensitive skin.

Just occasionally I flicked my fingers over her swollen clit, knowing that was where she wanted to be touched but denying her the pressure she wanted there for now.

"I won't do anything more unless you ask me to." I wouldn't force anything on her, no matter how much I wanted her.

She opened her eyes, and I could see her pupils dilated in her shimmering gray irises. "I want you," she whispered.

"What do you want from me?"

"I want you to make love to me."

I paused. "Are you sure?" I had to be certain. She had to be certain.

"Yes, I've never been more sure of anything."

I felt something surge through me at the implication in her words that she trusted me. That was what I had wanted all along—for her to trust me and for her to open up to me.

I went back to her body, working my way down to her beautiful legs, licking the soft skin between her thighs from where I could see her pussy lips gleaming with arousal.

Christ, she was so responsive. I ran my nose along her pussy, inhaling her sexy scent before latching my tongue onto her clit, making her moan in pleasure.

It didn't take long for my tongue to draw her near climax, but before she could tumble into that abyss, I withdrew my tongue from her clit and went back to gently toying with her labia.

She was squirming under me and eventually I dipped my tongue to lap at her entrance, alternatively circling her swollen bud.

I knew she was ready for more and I looked into her eyes. "I want to put my finger in you slowly." When she frowned slightly, I explained. "I want to stretch your muscles with my fingers first. It will make it easier for you to accept my cock."

"Okay."

I went back to stroking her body and licking her silky folds, enjoying the taste of her on my tongue. And as her pleasure heightened, I moistened my index finger with my saliva and pushed the tip of it into her tight channel.

She tensed slightly. "You can tell me to stop whenever you want." My voice was husky with need.

Upon hearing my reassuring words, she laid back with my finger inside her and let me continue tonguing her clit.

As she relaxed, I slowly moved the tip of my finger in and out of her pussy. And each time I inserted my digit just a little bit deeper inside her tight channel.

She was so tight. I couldn't wait to have her muscles clenching around my dick and making me come.

I turned to her breasts and started tugging her nipples again—she loved having her nipples played with.

By now, my index finger was all the way inside her, moving in and out slowly. The next time my finger penetrated her, I added a second finger.

"What are you doing?" A hint of anxiety crept into her voice.

"I'm adding a second finger. More fingers together will mimic the size of my cock better and stretch you to accommodate it. Does that sound okay to you?"

She thought about it for a moment and then nodded. "I trust you."

I slowly pushed the second finger in more deeply, carefully listening to her breathing and watching her face.

And eventually I had two thick fingers thrusting in and out of her heavenly pussy, before I added a third digit.

"I like you like this," I growled, the friction of my digits inside her pussy stimulating its nerve endings and causing copious slick juices to coat my fingers.

As I plunged my thick fingers into her, she started moving her hips to meet them and to deepen their penetration.

And that was when I knew she was ready for my dick.

As I kissed her neck, she tentatively reached for my hardness, running her fingers up and down my shaft.

"I need it harder," I said in a hoarse voice, and she dutifully obliged. My eyes focused on the beautiful girl before me as she ran her hands along my dick and I found it hard to hold back. I had never held back with a woman—I just took what I wanted.

But with Jessica, it was different.

I was different.

I parted her thighs and rested my body between her spread legs, lining up my erection with her entrance.

I then lowered my mouth to hers, seducing her with my lips as I ran the tip of my cock up and down her pussy lips until she was raising her hips and trying to increase the friction between the head of my cock and her clit.

I pressed the head of my cock gently against her entrance, kissing her mouth and playing with her nipples up same time. I felt her tense up. "Easy. I've got all the time in the world."

I continued kissing her and playing with her hard nipples until her tension eased, and then I pushed just the head of my cock inside her.

She gave a small cry as I entered her and I held myself still, taking my weight onto my arms above her. It was killing me, but I did it for her.

"Let me know when you want me to continue," I said, my gaze fixed on her wide eyes and her gasping mouth.

Once she had adjusted to my penetration of her, she gave a small nod and raised her head up to kiss me. She was so very responsive and I gradually eased myself into her inch by inch until my erection was all the way in and fully sheathed in her pussy.

Fuck, she was so tight, so exquisite.

I stayed like that for a minute, letting her stretch to accommodate my size, just kissing and caressing her.

Then I eased my cock out of her pussy and as I thrust back in slowly, she moaned, the sound going straight to my dick. And as I penetrated her again and again, I could see her desire being ignited.

I moved in and out of her, massaging her tight insides with my cock each time I thrust into her, relishing her muscles quivering around my girth.

As I could see her reaching her peak and feel her muscles tightening, I sped up my thrusts, finally letting go and plunging deep inside her like I had been longing to do.

My balls slapped against her pussy as I thrust as deep as I could, each thrust eliciting a deep moan from her, her muscles gripping my cock and bringing me so near to coming.

I held myself back as her moans grew louder and her pants more urgent, using my cock to push her over the edge until she cried out loudly in ecstasy. Her cheeks flushed and her lips parted.

Christ, she looked so sexy.

At last I gave myself up to my orgasm, thrusting hard inside her pulsating pussy and letting her squeeze my dick so tight until I spurted thick, white cum inside her as she tried to get her breath back.

After I had drained every last drop of my cum into her, I stayed inside her as I drew her into my arms and pulled her head down onto my chest. "Are you okay?"

"Yes," she breathed.

I hugged her even more tightly. She had given another part of herself to me today, and it warmed my heart. I was a cold-blooded killer and killing was my religion, so much so that I'd never thought that I could feel like this about anyone in my life.

***

The next morning, I watched Jessica as she slept in my arms. I could never tire of looking at her.

As she opened her eyes, she murmured, "Hi."

"Hey there. How are you?"

"Great," she replied, and I felt my heart fill with relief. It wasn't just about sex. I could get that easily enough at one of our clubs. There was something about her that made me want to get close to her and make her mine.

"I'm glad to hear that. Are you in pain? I can get you a painkiller from the bathroom if you want?"

"No, I'm fine, but..." She went quiet and didn't finish her sentence.

"You can talk to me, Jessica, about anything, I mean that."

Jessica licked her dry lips. "I'm not on the pill," she said quietly.

I frowned. "I thought you got contraception from the doctor?"

"I did. I started to take it, but then I stopped. Just getting those pills out every day brought back memories I didn't want to think about. So I stopped taking them after a bit."

"Don't worry, it's not a problem. I'll get you the morning-after pill."

"No, I'm fine."

"You don't want it?" I couldn't keep the surprise from my voice.

"No." Her voice was firmer now. "I stopped taking the pill because of the memories, but I didn't start taking it again once we were married because I want children."

"You do?"

"Yes, I do. I've always wanted children. I know I'm still young, but I want to be a hands-on mom and be able to do things with my children. I know a lot of Società wives have nannies, but that's not me. I want to be different from my own mother. I want to be closer to my children. I love children."

I was taken aback. "You know, you don't have to have children this way. Even if you want children and I need an heir, I don't want you to feel you have to have sex with me to produce our children—there are other ways to achieve that like IVF. I don't want you to have to do something you're not comfortable doing."

She smiled her sweet smile. "Getting pregnant this way is just fine with me. I enjoyed it and I think I'm looking forward to getting some more practice in," she giggled, blushing at the same time. "But what about you? Would you be okay about trying for a baby already?"

A huge grin spread across my face. "I'd like nothing more. I'm already twenty-five and I want children. If you don't want to take the pill, I'm fine with that. And when we have a baby, I'll be more than happy with that as well."

I was stunned. Maybe I had been wrong—perhaps we would be able to move past what had happened before the wedding, and perhaps Jess would be able to forgive me for not protecting her. I had thought that when the time came to needing to produce an heir, we would have to go through complicated IVF procedures and all the stress that would entail and all the memories that it might dredge up for Jessica.

As I looked at her, I thought that she really was a remarkable woman. And I knew how lucky I was to have her as my wife.

CHAPTER 18

RAFAEL

At work the next day, my phone rang. I looked down at the screen to see that it was Jacob. I sighed. I wasn't his favorite person right now and I wasn't in the mood to speak to my new brother-in-law.

I hit the call button. "Jacob, what do you need?" I said tersely, not bothering with pleasantries.

"I can't get hold of Gabriel. I need one of you to come down to the Matrix," he said, referring to one of our nightclubs.

"What's it about?"

"I'd rather not say over the phone."

What was this, a game of twenty fucking questions? "Is it about the business?" We had to be careful what we said over the phone as the Feds were always wire-tapping us.

"No, it's not business. There's a woman here to see Gabriel."

"I'm not my brother's fucking keeper," I snapped. If Gabriel was having issues with one of his many women and they were now turning up at the club, it had nothing to do with me.

"You'll want to hear this," replied Jacob sharply. "And it's better she doesn't hang around, trust me. You'll agree once you hear what she has to say."

"For fuck's sake, I'm in the middle of something here. Let me wrap it up and I'll be with you in thirty." I disconnected the call. I had a busy day ahead of me, and a cozy discussion with my brother-in-law and one of Gabriel's floozies was the last thing I needed.

When I walked into the Matrix a while later, I saw Gabriel standing in the middle of the main floor talking with Jacob.

"You could have told me you no longer needed me," I said curtly to Jacob. He was obviously trying to deliberately needle me. He was still pissed off about the situation with Jessica and he was still pissed off with me.

"Gabriel just got here two minutes ago. Anyhow, I think you should hear this too, given that it affects you and probably my sister as well."

I couldn't give a shit about what my brother did in his love life, and I couldn't see how it affected Jess or me. But I was here now. "Where is this woman?"

"I put her in the office. She's here with her daughter." Her daughter? I hoped that Gabriel hadn't got one of them pregnant.

When we walked into the office, I was taken aback to see an extremely thin, worn-out woman sitting in one of the chairs in front of the desk. She was thin and pale. In the corner of the room hovered a teenage girl, who I presumed must be the daughter.

"I'm told you need to see me," said Gabriel, getting right to the point. He sat down in the chair behind the desk, while I stood next to him and Jacob leaned against the window with one hand in his pocket.

"Hello, Gabriel," said the older woman.

"Have we met before?" my brother asked her.

"Yes, we have, but it was many years ago."

Gabriel frowned as he concentrated on her face. "You do look familiar somehow," he said slowly. "But I'm sorry, I don't recall."

The woman gave a small laugh. "I didn't expect you to. You were just a young boy back then. And I look very different from how I looked then. My parents were Luigi and Giuseppina Pugliesi."

The room fell silent for a few long moments. "You're Carmela Pugliesi?" I asked, vaguely remembering the girl who had been promised to the Greco family as part of a deal for an alliance—an alliance, if I remembered correctly, fell apart after a matter of months.

"Yes, I am. Well, I was until I became Carmela Greco." According to the gossip at the time, she had been thrown out by her husband less than a year after her marriage because she had cheated on him.

"That's why you look familiar," stated Gabriel. "You look like your father."

"Yes, everyone always did say that I took after him."

"You don't look well, Carmela," said Gabriel, stating what was obvious to all of us.

"I'm not. My heart is failing, and the doctors can do no more for me. I was born with a defect and have had surgery, but my heart can't take the strain any longer. I am on the list for a heart transplant, but I'm far down the list and it's too late now—my heart won't hold out much longer."

"I'm sorry to hear that," replied Gabriel quietly.

"You're probably wondering why I'm here today. This is Arabella," she said, gesturing to the girl with her. "She is my only child...and she is your half-sister."

I shot a look toward the young girl who had moved out from the shadow of the back wall and now hovered protectively by her mother's side. I looked at her properly for the first time since I'd entered the room. She had black hair and blue eyes, eyes which were so like Nancia's—exactly the same shape and exactly the same shade of the dark blue.

"Mom," exclaimed the girl. "You said we were coming here because you needed to see an old family friend. You didn't say we were going to see *them*."

"Sweetheart, I knew you wouldn't bring me here today if I told you the truth."

She looked back at my brother and me. "Once I pass, Bella will have no family left except for you. I know your father is dead now and so she'll be safe to come here if she ever needs help."

"Mom, no, you know I'll be able to manage by myself. I've taken care of us for the last year, haven't I?"

"It's not that, sweetheart. You know that." She looked back at us. "My husband threw me out just after Bella was born. It was obvious that she wasn't his daughter because she had been born too early. We had only been married for six months by then." She looked us straight in the eye. "Your father raped me before I was married."

After a moment of stunned silence, Gabriel found his voice. "Did your husband demand a paternity test?"

Carmela gave a harsh laugh. "He didn't have to. I told him the truth. I knew better than to lie to him. He was a brutal husband even before he discovered Bella wasn't his."

"What happened then?" I asked.

"He threw me out. The alliance between him and the Società had already broken down a couple of months earlier. I came back to my parents, but they refused to take me in. I told them I had been raped and by whom, but that made no difference to them. I'd conceived a child out of wedlock, and I was a disgrace in their eyes."

"What did you do?"

"I had nowhere to live, no job and no qualifications. I sold my wedding and engagement rings and got enough money to pay a deposit and rent on a room in a rundown house. Then I got a job as a waitress in a diner, doing as many shifts as I could—the graveyard shift, double shifts, whatever I could to make ends meet."

"What about Bella?" I asked, looking at the girl and wondering how old she was.

"The other people in the house helped look after Bella. And I looked after their children in return when they were working. We were lucky. It was still hard, but I've never regretted it. We've had a better life than if I had stayed with my husband."

I thought about her parents. They had both since died and Carmela had been their only child. Luigi Pugliesi had been a sanctimonious asshole, so hearing about how he had treated Carmela shouldn't have come as a surprise to me. "It sounded like it was very tough for you," I murmured in sympathy.

Carmela raised her chin up. "We survived. The other families in the house helped and we couldn't have done it without them. No one had much money, and there were plenty of deadbeats and drunks in the neighborhood. But there were just as many good people, all trying to make enough to get by and provide for their families."

"Where are you living?" asked Gabriel.

"We live about two hours from here, outside of L.A."

"How long have the doctors given you?"

"I've not long left. Probably only a few weeks."

"Mom, don't say that," cried the girl. "You're just going through a bad patch. It's always like that after a round of treatments. You have a dip for a while and then you always pick up. You have to," she said in desperation.

"Sweetheart, we both know that's not going to happen this time," she said gently. "And I need to know that you're safe when I'm no longer here."

"Are you worried about your daughter's safety?" I asked, my ears picking up at the hint of terror in Carmela's voice.

"My husband has paid us a visit every few years to see how Bella is getting on."

"You're still married to him?" My voice held surprise at this fact.

"He never got around to divorcing me. I was his second wife. He already had two sons from his first wife, but when she died, I guess he decided he needed another girl to warm his bed. And that's what I was: a girl. I was only sixteen when I was married off to him, a man over twice my age."

"What did he want with Bella?" asked Gabriel, frowning. "He isn't her father, after all."

"He said he still owns her."

"Owns Bella?"

"Yes. Under the engagement contract my parents signed, any children born during the marriage stayed under his sole guardianship. There was no stipulation in the contract about when the child was conceived. The only requirement was that the said child be born while we were married."

"But he didn't take Bella away from you?"

"No, he didn't want to bring her up. But as she became older, he started to take an interest in her. I'm worried about what he might want with her."

"Do you know what he has in mind?"

"No, he hasn't ever shared that with me. The last time he visited was two years ago when Bella was fifteen. So perhaps he is no longer interested in her, but I can't be sure. And I can't go to my grave in peace, knowing that she might be in danger. Once I'm gone, you are the only family she will have left."

"No, Mom, I don't want anything to do with them. I don't want anything to do with the Società. They are the ones who did this to you: that man raped you, then your parents treated you like cattle in one of their business transactions, and finally they disowned you when you asked for their help after I was born. We've managed just fine all these years without their help, and we've taken care of ourselves. I'll never need their help. No one from the Greco family has even asked about me in the last couple of years—they've probably forgotten about me."

"Men like that don't forget, sweetheart. You have been brought up in a different world and you don't understand just how dangerous your stepfather is."

Carmela looked back at us. "Please protect my daughter if she ever needs it. I haven't asked your family for anything over the years, but I ask this one thing from you." Her eyes were imploring us.

"Carmela, you have my word that should Bella ever need anything, we will help her," said Gabriel sincerely.

She nodded. "That's all I ask." She got up to leave.

"Do you need anything else...like money?" I asked clumsily, not knowing how to help this woman the Società had so badly failed.

"We don't need your money," spat Bella. "I'm working. I can support us both."

"You're seventeen. You should be in school," drawled Gabriel.

"Some of us have our priorities straight. My priority is my mom and keeping a roof over our heads. I care about my family—something you probably know nothing about, given how your precious Società treated my mother."

"At least let one of my men drive you home," I said.

"No," hissed Bella. "We'll manage just fine."

"Thank you," said Carmela. "But we have a friend who drove us here and she will drive us home." She may have had a hard life, but I could see she still carried herself with pride.

We stood by awkwardly as Bella helped her mother up and led her out of the room, Carmela leaning heavily against her daughter for support.

Jacob saw them out, leaving me in the office with Gabriel.

"Fuck," I muttered.

"Fuck indeed."

"Do you believe that the girl is our half-sister?" I asked my brother.

"Yes. Did you see her eyes are just like Nancia's?"

"I noticed that too," I commented.

"She's definitely got the Santino look about her. If she didn't, I might doubt her story. But seeing her and knowing already what our father was capable of, the story adds up. Anyhow, I'll get someone on it to check their story and the background details."

"Who will you ask? We need someone discreet."

Gabriel considered this for a few seconds. "I'll get Jacob on it. He's already heard her story and he's got as much interest in keeping this quiet as we have. If it gets out, it will only make things worse for Jessica—because she'll have to hear the endless gossip and speculation about what our father did to Carmela."

***

A few days later, Jacob came to the house to see Gabriel and me.

He had been looking into Carmela and Bella's background. "I broke into their place and got Bella's hairbrush for a DNA sample."

"Christ, we told you to look into Bella, not traumatize her by breaking and entering."

"I was in and out of there without them batting an eyelash." Jacob drawled. "She'll just think that she misplaced the stupid hairbrush. If you're that concerned about it, I'll pay another visit and put the hairbrush back."

"For fuck's sake, you're not going near their place again."

"What did you find?" interjected Gabriel, obviously fed up with our squabbling

"The lab compared Bella's hair with the DNA samples they have on file for the Santinos."

"And?"

"And it's a familial match. She's definitely a Santino." So that was it. Although we had already suspected as much.

"The family priest gave me quite a bit of information on the woman and girl," carried on Jacob. "I had to threaten first to burn down his church, of course, but he came around quickly, especially when I said I'd throw in a sizable donation to the church coffers and his pocket. The good old carrot and stick method—works like a charm every time."

After Jacob had filled us in on what else he had found out, I excused myself as I had some other business to attend to.

As I reached my car, Jacob caught up with me. "Are you going to tell my sister about this?"

"That's my business," I said tersely, not in the mood for Jacob's protective older brother shit right now.

"It is my business if it upsets Jess."

I shot daggers at him with my eyes. "She's my wife. I know how to handle her."

"Yeah, your family sure has enjoyed *handling* her, haven't they?"

My patience snapped and I took a step toward Jacob.

"Jake?" I heard Jessica's voice and turned around to find her standing in the front doorway. "I didn't know you were coming here today."

"I had some business to talk over," he said, walking over to kiss his sister's cheek and give her a hug.

Jessica looked from me to her brother, noting the tension between us. "Do you have time for a coffee?" she asked hesitantly.

Jacob gave her a tender look. "Sure Jess. Coffee sounds good."

Throwing a last glare at me, he headed back inside the house and I left for my meeting.

CHAPTER 19

JESSICA

A couple of weeks later, Rafael and Gabriel's fourteen-year-old siblings, Nancia and Nate, came to stay for a few days.

The twins had a week off school, and while Nancia had some time to relax, Nate's time was mostly going to be taken up with training in preparation for his initiation into the Società. He'd be going to work each day with Rafael and Gabriel, as well as working on his weapon skills.

"What do you think Nancia might like to do today?" I asked Rafael, as I made breakfast and we waited for the twins and Gabriel to come down and join us. "Do you think I should take her shopping? Or perhaps she'd like to go get our nails done?"

"She'll probably like going shopping one day, but she's also quite an outdoors sort of girl. She loves coming here because we have the horses and she can ride. She adores horses and she's always been annoyed that father won't let her have a horse at home and that she has to be driven to a local stable every time she wants to ride. She would much prefer to have her own horse—she even likes doing the mucking out and feeding and all that stuff."

"It's a shame Nate can't spend the day with us too."

"He's got a lot of training to do over the school break. He'll be initiated next year and there's a lot for him to learn in the meantime."

"It'll be nice having another girl to stay and I'm looking forward to us doing stuff together." It would be an opportunity to relax and do some fun things.

It pleased me that I was being accepted into the family and that Rafael wanted me to spend time with his siblings. When he'd first found out about the attack, I'd been afraid that although he said he wouldn't pursue an annulment, he might not want me mixing with his loved ones. I had been worried how my being impure would affect our relationship. I'd always wanted children and I'd been afraid that Rafael might not think I would be fit to be a mother to his children.

However, here we were now, trying for a baby. Things were finally turning around for me, and I still found it hard to believe how well me and Rafael were getting on.

I couldn't wait to have a baby. I knew I shouldn't, but I was already obsessing a little about getting pregnant. I really wanted children and I had read that stress could prevent conception from occurring, and I had definitely been through a lot of stress lately.

I was forcing myself not to think about what had happened and I had even started doing yoga each day in an attempt to ease my anxieties. Having Nancia stay would keep me occupied and hopefully lead to me relaxing a bit more.

That day, I took Nancia to get our nails done and then out for lunch. We had a good time together and I was glad that I was getting on well with one of Rafael's siblings. She was only fourteen years old, and I liked her childlike innocence.

That evening after dinner, we decided to watch a movie in the den.

The guys were already in there sitting on the couches while Nancia and I made popcorn in the kitchen before we joined them. The guys had bottles of beer, but I was avoiding wine and alcohol now that I was hoping to conceive, not that I was much of a drinker, apart from the occasional glass of wine with my dinner.

Nancia sat between Gabriel and Nate on one of the huge couches, while I walked toward Rafael who was on the other couch. As I approached, Rafael reached out his arm, indicating the space next to him.

After hesitating for a moment, I sat down next to him, letting myself press up against him and relax into his embrace. I could sense Gabriel and Nancia watching us, making me blush slightly. So far Rafael and I had not gone out in public much, and even just in front of Gabriel we were very hands-off.

"What are we watching?" I asked, trying to move everyone's focus away from me and onto something else.

Nancia was allowed to choose, and she picked a recent comedy about cops in New York.

I was surprised—I thought she'd choose a girly film about princesses or some suchlike.

"Jeez, Nance, not another cops and robbers movie," groaned Nate. "And you've already watched this one anyway."

"Have you seen this movie, Jessica?" she asked me.

"No, I haven't. In my household, family movie night always consisted of watching The Godfather movies or reruns of The Sopranos."

"That sounds like a typical mobbed-up Italian family," Gabriel laughed. "Nancia is a bit different though—she's obsessed with cops, the FBI and the CIA."

"And horses," chipped in Rafael.

"Yeah, and horses," agreed Gabriel. "We've always said that Nancia's dream job would be as a Mountie in Canada."

"I would love that," enthused Nancia. "I could be a cop and ride a horse all day as well."

"But you don't even live in Canada," pointed out Nate, who was clearly perplexed by his twin's obsessions.

We all laughed.

"Anyway, I'd miss you if you went to Canada," added Nate.

Nancia playfully pushed Nate's shoulder. "Don't worry, I'm not going anywhere without you. I couldn't leave you without your lucky twin."

"Lucky twin?" I asked.

"There's seven minutes between us, and seven is a lucky number. I'm seven minutes younger, so I'm the lucky twin," declared Nancia.

"No, *I'm* the lucky twin—I'm seven minutes older," disagreed Nate.

"That's not how it works, Nate!" exclaimed Nancia.

"Okay, quiet now—both of you. You'll argue about that all night long if we let you," chipped in Gabriel as the movie started.

As we settled back to watch it, Rafael wrapped his hand around mine. I huddled into his embrace, letting myself enjoy his touch.

***

As we got ready for bed that night, I turned to Rafael. "I'm enjoying Nancia and Nate's stay with us." I felt that I was getting closer to Rafael's siblings.

"It's good for you to spend time with them so that you can get to know them. I know Nancia was really excited about having another girl in the family."

"How's Nate's training going?"

Rafael hesitated and then sighed. "He's not particularly keen, but he doesn't say much. Out of the twins, Nancia has always been the more communicative one. Anyhow, that's enough about my siblings. Instead of talking, how about we get in some more baby-making practice?"

And with that, he kissed me passionately and moved his hand inside my nightdress.

RAFAEL

The next morning, as I went to walk into the kitchen for breakfast, I heard Nate and Nancia talking with Jessica.

"I heard Gabriel tell Mother about what happened to you before the wedding...you know, with our father," said Nate. "I just wanted to say we'll always protect you. We've got your back. And you know Rafael will never hurt you, right?"

Sometimes Nate surprised me with his maturity. He was a fourteen-year-old, trying to console my wife who had been raped.

I walked into the room and saw Nancia with her arms around Jess, both with tears in their eyes. They untangled themselves when they saw me and resumed eating, although I could see Jess was affected by the concern the twins had shown her.

I had hoped that Nancia would never find out about what had happened to Jess; however, Nate had overheard Gabriel talking about it and had obviously shared what he knew with his twin sister.

I could tell just by looking at Nancia that she was deeply upset by what she had learned—she was only fourteen and had been shielded all her life, kept in a gilded cage, safe from harm and upset.

When we finished eating, I looked at my watch and told Nate sternly, "You should be at the shooting range by now."

He shrugged as he got up from the table, not particularly excited or unexcited at the prospect, but I couldn't help noticing Nancia frowning at my words as she shot a sympathetic look at her twin.

***

That evening, I came home to find Jess in our bedroom holding a box of tampons and with tears in her eyes.

"Hey, what's going on?" I asked, as I sat next to her on the bed and took her hand.

"I got my period. I'm not pregnant this month."

"Jess," I said gently. "We only just started trying this month. We've got all the time in the world."

"You don't understand," she cried. "I really want a baby."

"I do understand. I want one as well. But it will take however long it takes—we can't rush nature. I don't want you to feel that I'm putting any pressure on you to produce an heir within a certain time period."

"You don't get it," she said more forcefully. "I need to have a baby, someone pure and innocent in my life. Someone not tainted by this violent world that we live in."

"You've got me until then, Jess. I'm always here for you."

"But you're tainted by everything you do. Just like me—I'm tainted too."

I was taken aback by the vehemence in her voice, and it brought my guilt flooding back regarding my failure to protect her from my father. I knew she could never forgive me for not looking after her after she'd become mine through the contract. I deserved to feel guilty, and I felt even worse knowing that my guilt was nothing compared to the pain she'd suffered.

She tried to wipe away her tears with her hands. "A baby will be completely innocent, and I can just enjoy him or her without worrying about anything."

I understood that she had been through a lot lately, and maybe having a baby was her way of coping and moving on, but I was worried by the intensity of her need.

I had hoped that now my father was dead she would be less anxious; however, she had transferred her anxiety to wanting a baby.

Honestly, I just wanted her to be happy, and I felt powerless yet again that I couldn't give her what she needed. I couldn't stand not being in control. Conception was in the hands of fate—and I felt like fucking killing fate right now.

"Look. Jess, you know from your pregnancy research that worrying about getting pregnant is counterproductive and the stress can hold you back. You need to relax more."

"That's easy for you to say! How am I supposed to relax after everything that's happened? I can't stop thinking about it, no matter how much I try not to let those thoughts into my mind. A baby will give me something else to focus on, something to make me happy."

As her voice broke and the tears started falling hard, I took her into my arms and soothed her the best I could. I knew she just wanted something normal and safe, and she thought a baby would give that to her and to us.

I knew from my cousins that when babies didn't come, it could cause all sorts of anguish, and I knew how much Jessica wanted a baby—how much we both wanted a child. I didn't want this to be another thing that could overwhelm her, not after what she'd been through, but I couldn't help feeling a sense of dread about the possibility that falling pregnant might not be as quick as Jess hoped.

CHAPTER 20

JESSICA

The next day, we had just sat down at the table to eat breakfast when Gabriel came in and joined us. "Where's Nate?" he asked, as he helped himself to the scrambled eggs.

We all looked at Nancia, but she just shrugged as she sipped at her orange juice.

Rafael raised an eyebrow in query. "Is he up yet?"

Nancia cleared her throat. "He was already gone this morning when I looked in on him."

"Goddamnit," cursed Gabriel, slamming down the carafe of coffee he was holding. "He knows he's supposed to be working with us today."

"Did he say where he was going?" quizzed Rafael, still looking at Nancia because she was the one out of all of us most likely to know where her twin was.

"No, he didn't tell me," she said, tossing her strawberry-blond hair over her shoulder and setting her mouth in a determined line.

"Nancia," growled Gabriel, a hint of warning in his voice.

"I didn't asked him, alright? I knew you'd try to get it out of me." Her voice was defiant. "Why do you keep forcing him into working with you?"

"Nance, you know it's for his training and that he has to learn these things before he's initiated." Rafael was calmer than his older brother and tried to reason with Nancia in a placatory tone.

"You say it as if he's learning things which will benefit him. Like he really *needs* to learn how to torture and kill people?"

"You know the rules of this life as well as any of us." Gabriel's voice was matter-of-fact, but I could tell that he was trying to keep his anger under control as he spoke to our younger sister. "Nate will be initiated into the Società when he's old enough, and there's no way out of that."

"But you know we don't want him to be initiated!" Although Nancia was angry and arguing, I could see she was also getting upset now, and I suspected her anger was a thin veneer used to disguise her vulnerability. "So why keep on forcing it on him?" I knew Rafael had said that Nate wasn't that keen on his training, but I hadn't known that it was as bad as him not wanting to be initiated—that was disastrous in our world.

"No one in our families has a choice over this, including Nate." Gabriel's voice was hard. "Just because I'm his brother and Capo, that doesn't mean I can give him an out. If anything, it's even more important that he's seen following our rules to set an example to the rest of the Società."

"And what example would that be?" A hint of sarcasm crept into Nancia's voice as she rose to the defense of her twin. "Join your merry band of killers, or be killed yourself?" I could see how Nancia was determined to stand up to her older brothers and do whatever she could to protect her twin brother.

I was getting the distinct impression, however, that it was Nancia, not Nate, who had the problem with Nate being initiated.

Gabriel looked at his sister. "You may not like it, but it's the way it is. Rafael and I have done Nate's training ourselves and we've been way easier on him than if our father had taken charge. Nevertheless, Nate still has certain things he has to learn and there's no easy way around that. You may not like him doing some of those things, but you'll both get used to it—you have to."

Nancia's voice was quieter. "I can't bear to see him do these things." A tear ran silently down her cheek, and although she was talking about Nate suffering, I could see that it was really Nancia who had the issue with it—and it was killing her. They were extremely close, as to be expected for twins, and their bond meant that this was weighing down heavily on Nancia's shoulders.

Gabriel ran his hand through his hair. "He can't keep bailing on us—he's done it too many times recently. If this was any other recruit, he'd have his ass kicked for failing to turn up yet again."

Nancia swiped the tears that had escaped down her cheeks, but somehow I sensed that this was not going to be a quick fix with the twins.

***

Later that day, Nancia and I went shopping at the mall and I let her go on a bit of a spree. She had been really down earlier, worrying about Nate, and I thought this might distract her for a while.

"It's nice having another girl to shop with," commented Nancia. "Nate won't ever come shopping with me—that's the problem of having three brothers. You're lucky, you've got one of each—one brother and one sister."

"Three brothers does sound a bit boisterous."

"Luckily, Nate always sides with me. Otherwise, it would always be three boys against one girl."

I laughed. "Does Nate ever get a choice about whether he wants to take your side or not?"

"Of course he does," said Nancia seriously. "But he always agrees with me because he's my twin and he would do anything for me."

Later that afternoon, we spread out Nancia's purchases and she tried on various items again. "I love this skirt." She twirled in front of the full-length mirror. "But I won't let Gabriel or Rafael see it because they're bound to say it's too short."

"Protective older brothers, huh?"

"Just a bit," she sighed. "At least Nate isn't like that with me yet. Is your older brother the same?"

"Jake? Yes, he is." Thinking about him made a pang of loneliness hit me.

"It's like it goes with the whole Made Man thing. They're over-protective of everyone and everything in their lives." Nancia took off the skirt and swapped it for a pair of capri pants.

"I guess they have to be to an extent, with all the dangers our lifestyle entails."

"I just wish I could have some more freedom. It's so stifling with all the rules. Nate's always being told the things he has to do, like torture and killing; while I'm always being told the things I'm *not* allowed to do, like going out without a guard or being independent in any way. The Mafia world is beyond strange."

"Just enjoy your childhood while it lasts." My voice was wistful.

Nancia stopped preening in front of the mirror. "Jessica, what's it really like?"

"What do you mean?"

"You know, marrying a complete stranger? I can't wait to get married. It'll be like being in a fairytale and everyone will be admiring my ring and beautiful white dress." She smiled, caught up in a girlhood daydream, still very much an innocent at heart.

"I think every young girl thinks that way," I said gently.

"That's what I mean. I have these images in my mind, but then I go to these weddings and watch whoever is the latest bride, and I always end up wondering if it's really as romantic as I think it'll be. What's it like having to marry someone you don't know?"

How could I answer that? Not only had I married a stranger, but my father-in-law had raped me beforehand. I was caught by surprise by Nancia's childlike curiosity, yet I couldn't bring myself to burst her bubble.

"The wedding, the dress, the celebration—it was all wonderful, just like I had always dreamed it would be. Rafael wasn't a complete stranger—I had seen him at Società events and our families know each other. So, although I was a little nervous, it turned out fine."

"Do you love each other?"

"We're…fond of each other. In an arranged marriage, love grows with time."

I couldn't believe I was repeating the empty words I had heard so often parroted by my mother and aunts. Especially when I knew that I was in love with Rafael…and that Rafael couldn't never love me back.

It was like I was on a never-ending rollercoaster. Whenever I thought about Rafael, my heart would soar and I would feel giddy. Then the rollercoaster would swoop downward, and I would remind myself that he would never feel the same way about me, causing a pit of hurt and longing deep inside of me.

I hadn't been a virgin upon our marriage, and thus I was unfit to be his wife.

I tried to convince myself that I should be grateful that he had not sought an annulment and that I had not been humiliated in that way. But the reality was that I wanted more. I wanted a real marriage, with real love.

Being near Rafael made my heart beat faster, my pulse race faster, and my core clench tighter. I had fallen in love with him, the thought unsettling me every time it skittered across my mind—which was all too often.

I knew that arranged marriages in our world were all about forming bonds and producing the next generation of Made Men, but a small part of me had always hoped that I would be one of the lucky women who found love in their marriage.

Rafael had not annulled the marriage after finding out that I wasn't a virgin, but I could no longer feel a sense of gratitude about that. Instead, I felt hurt that I couldn't have the love from him that I so desperately wanted. I knew that was the price I would have to pay for not being a virgin for him.

I told myself that it didn't matter that he didn't love me. What had love given me in life so far? My sister, Juliana, loved me, but this world and its stupid rules meant that she could no longer be part of my life. I assumed my parents loved me—they weren't the sort to tell this to their children—then they had handed me off to a family whose patriarch had raped me.

I told myself that I could manage without Rafael's love. I was old enough to know that love didn't mean that everything would be rosy. Instead, it just brought its own set of complications.

But I also knew that this was why I wanted a baby so desperately: I wanted a baby because he or she would be someone I could love, and someone who would love me back wholly and unconditionally. The baby would know nothing of my shame or dishonor—in its eyes, I would be worthy of love.

"Come on, everyone will be home soon, and I need to get dinner started."

"You're such a great cook. I hope Rafael and Gabriel appreciate how lucky they are. You like cooking for my brothers, don't you?"

I paused for a moment while I considered this. "They're my family now, and they take care of me. I guess cooking and organizing the house is my way of taking care of them."

This whole conversation about my marriage had been painful, so I swiftly changed the subject. "You better put that skirt away before your brothers see how short it is and make you take it back to the store."

***

Gabriel arrived home midway through dinner that evening, which was unusual because it was a Monday and he usually made a big effort to be home on time for the Monday Port-Mortem, given that this meal was in reality a business meeting between the brothers.

I knew that Gabriel had already spoken to Nate earlier in the evening about missing his training today, and although Nate was sullen, Rafael said that the chat seemed to have gone well.

"We were wondering where you'd gotten to," said Rafael, looking carefully at his brother. Even I could tell he was in a vile mood, and it seemed to be about something other than Nate not turning up for his training today. "What's wrong?"

Gabriel clenched his jaw. "Later," he ground out, nodding slightly toward Nancia.

I was used to the brothers talking about work over the dinner table, yet Gabriel not wanting to talk about business matters during the Monday Post-Mortem put me slightly on edge.

Perhaps it was because their younger sister was present? Although it was usual for her to be at these Monday dinners because Nate attended them every week now that he was in training for his initiation, and therefore Nancia usually tagged along with him.

Gabriel sat in his usual spot and Nate passed the large dish of spaghetti to him so that he could serve himself. The rest of the dinner passed with some general talk about work, although it was conspicuous that nothing of any importance was really discussed.

Once everyone had finished their food, Gabriel looked at the twins. "Both of you go and do your homework."

"We're on school break, so don't have homework," responded Nancia in puzzlement.

"Go and watch television then. I need to talk business."

"I should probably stay then," commented Nate.

"No, Nate. This doesn't concern you."

"But I thought now I'm in training, you wanted me at family meetings so that—"

"Just go, both of you, now." Gabriel's voice had risen and the twins looked at each other in alarm. They knew that now was not the time to argue and so Nancia grabbed Nate's hand and together they went to the den.

Gabriel put his head in his hands, and we sat all sat in silence for a minute. Then looked up with pain in his eyes.

"I should go too," I said quietly as I started to gather up the dishes.

Before I could leave the table, however, Gabriel started talking. "Our father has fucked us over again."

"What do you mean?" asked Rafael slowly. I could see the dread in his navy-blue eyes—he knew Gabriel wouldn't be like this unless he was truly worried.

"I was going through his files, and I found this." He pushed a sheaf of papers across the table.

They looked similar to the engagement contract I had signed.

I put the dishes back down on the table. "Is that an engagement contract?" I moved closer to see what the papers said.

"Yes."

"Whose?" asked Rafael, turning the papers around so that he could read them.

"Nancia's," replied Gabriel.

"What?" I felt the blood drain from my face.

"It's for when she turns eighteen," added Gabriel. It wasn't unusual for Mafia families to arrange marriages before their child came of age, and when the child was a minor, a parent would normally sign the engagement contract on their behalf.

"Who is she supposed to marry?" I asked.

"Leoluca Veneti."

"Fuck that," said Rafael, slamming his fist on the table. "That man is an animal."

"Agreed. Our father arranged this just before his death and signed the contract on Nancia's behalf, conveniently forgetting to tell any of us. That bastard only cared about power, and he didn't think twice about signing over his own daughter to that savage."

"What happens now?" I whispered.

Gabriel looked at us. "We forget any supposed alliance with the Veneti family. I'm Capo now and my sister is not marrying that madman under any circumstances. Not when she is eighteen, not ever—even if it means war."

And it would mean war. We all knew that. An engagement contract in the Mafia world was sacrosanct once signed and could not be reversed. Leoluca Veneti would take it as a professional and personal insult that Gabriel did not want his sister marrying into the Veneti family.

She had only been asking me earlier about marriage, unaware that her psychopathic father not only had promised her already but also had given her away to a rival family.

CHAPTER 21

RAFAEL

The next morning, I got up earlier than normal and put on my workout clothes so that I could train with Nate.

As I pulled on my shorts, Jess looked at my body and then reddened when she saw me watching her.

I gave her a grin and she smiled back at me. She was utterly gorgeous in the mornings, her chestnut hair tumbling over her narrow shoulders and her face flushed with sleep. My dick stirred and I wished I could go back to bed, back to my wife.

Kissing her before I reluctantly left, I told her I'd be back in a bit. "Then we've got time to go for a run...or do anything else you want," I growled into her ear, making her shiver and her nipples visibly tighten under her silk chemise. I loved how responsive she was to me.

I headed to the guest room where Nate was sleeping. "Nate, get your lazy ass out of bed now. You missed training yesterday, so you'll be doing double today to make up for it."

"For fuck's sake, it's too fucking early," complained my fourteen-year-old brother.

"Hey, watch your mouth, or I'll leave Gabriel to do your training." That was enough to get Nate to haul his ass out of bed. He knew Gabriel was still pissed with him.

We had decided not to tell the twins yet about the engagement contract our father had signed for Nancia. We needed to work out a plan of action and we wanted that in place before we broke the news to Nancia. This morning, however, I wanted to talk to Nate. Missing work and training was not acceptable, even if he was our brother.

We started with gun practice at the shooting range on our estate. I had to admit that Nate was already a great shot. He still had a bit to learn, but I reckoned he would end up being one of our best weapons handlers.

I addressed my younger brother while we reloaded our guns. "I get you don't like what we do in our line of work. But it's what you've been born into, it's what we've all been born into. None of us have got a choice."

"Yeah, but why can't I just walk away if I want to?" asked Nate.

"Gabriel is Capo and you're his brother, so there will always be a target on your back. Killing you would be a way of getting revenge against the Capo. It's kill or be killed in our business. Anyway, Gabriel needs all the support we can give him—he's our brother and we can't walk away from him because he needs us. Just like he would never walk away from any of us if we needed him."

Nate took a deep breath before speaking. "It's driving me away from Nancia."

"Look, girls are different from us. We shield them from a lot of what goes on in our world, and they don't always get what's at stake and they don't always understand that violence is necessary." I looked hard at him. "You need to keep your home life and work life separate, and not let what's happening at home and with Nancia get in the way of your work and training."

"What, like you did with Jessica, after all that shit happened when you married her?" said Nate with a hint of insolence in his tone as he referred to my need for revenge after my wedding.

"That was different," I gritted out. "Jess is my wife."

"And Nancia is my twin!" he yelled back at me. "You just don't get it. Everything I do affects her. She feels it deeply."

I sighed, rubbing my hand over my unshaven chin. "I don't think she hates you for it," I suggested.

"Have you seen her face when we talk about killing at the Monday Post-Mortems? She's disgusted by what we do." His voice had got quieter, and he was fighting back his emotion.

"What we do is for the business."

"I get that and I understand that, but it's driving me away from her. It's alienating me from her. And I don't know how to get her to come back to me. It's putting up a barrier between us, and there's never been anything like this between us before."

"Maybe it's just the inevitable happening as you both grow up?"

"But I never thought that would happen. I never thought I could lose Nancia. Some days I almost wished I wasn't a twin, that I didn't have a half of me that I could hurt with my actions." Nate looked at me with obvious pain in his eyes. "You know I wouldn't desert Gabriel, but I also need to be there for Nancia—and that's never going to change."

***

A few days later, I was getting dressed in the morning when I saw Jess take out a lilac dress.

She sighed as she took out some skyscraper heels to go with it. "I hate wearing heels," she sighed.

"Is that the outfit you're wearing tonight?" I asked casually. Tonight was a Società dinner and dance.

She nodded. "Unless you would prefer me to wear another one of my dresses?" Uncertainty glazed her soft voice.

I liked the lilac dress but gazed at the other dresses in the closet, wincing when I saw how many of them were colored gold, not to mention the sight of the gold shoes that I had seen her wear previously.

Jessica, noticing my reaction, quickly said, "They're mostly my mother's choices. The lilac dress is one I bought myself."

"You like gold?" I asked.

"What? No, absolutely not."

"But you were wearing gold shoes when we first met."

"You remember that?"

"How could I forget? And a lilac dress—the color was beautiful on you, so I'm glad you're wearing lilac tonight."

She flushed. "I know the dress style is a little plain, but I think I would feel more at ease..."

As her voice trailed off, her last words hit me and I realized she might still feel uncomfortable around other people, so I nodded. I certainly wouldn't be pressuring her into wearing one of the awful look-at-me glitzy dresses chosen by her mother.

***

During the day, I couldn't stop thinking about Jessica and her outfit. I was glad she'd chosen a dress which she would feel comfortable in. I wanted her to feel completely at ease tonight—it was our first big event as a married couple, and I knew she was still nervous that somehow people might discover the awful thing that had happened to her before our marriage.

One thing about her outfit, however, bothered me.

In the late afternoon, on impulse, I picked up my phone and told Nancia's bodyguard to bring my sister to meet me at an exclusive shoe store, before texting Nancia and letting her know that I needed her help.

I was waiting in the store when Nancia arrived, and I breathed a sigh of relief. I wasn't sure who was more nervous—me at having to choose a pair of shoes, or the assistant at seeing an obviously bad guy in her store.

"Thanks for coming, Nancia. You're a lifesaver. I need to pick shoes for Jessica to wear to tonight's dance."

"Got it. You've come to the right person—I love shopping," she said with a grin on her face. "What sort of thing do you think Jess would like?"

"I haven't got a clue," I replied honestly, suddenly wondering what on earth I'd been thinking when I decided to pick out some shoes for my wife.

"Color?"

"Definitely nothing in gold," I clipped.

She quirked an eyebrow at me. "And what sort of heel—stiletto, kitten heel, block heel, wedge…?"

My brow furrowed. "How many different types of heel are there?"

"You'd be surprised," said my younger sister with a smile. "Platform, slingbacks, espadrilles—"

"Okay, okay, I get the idea," I said, running a hand through my sandy hair. "I just need something that looks nice, plus it has to be flat."

"Well, why didn't you say so in the first place," replied Nancia drily, rolling her eyes at me. We browsed the shelves, Nancia with great enthusiasm, me with less so.

Nancia held up a pair of flat shoes with small bows at the front. "What do you think of these ballet flats?"

"Ballet flats?"

"Yes, that's what this style is called."

They looked really nice, but I wasn't entirely sure what I should be looking for. "Are you sure it's not something her mother would pick?"

"No, Mrs. Bonardi definitely wouldn't pick these—because they're tasteful and not tacky."

I smothered a smile. Nancia really shouldn't speak about an Underboss's wife like that, but she was right: Mrs. Bonardi did have a fondness for the tasteless.

I looked at the assistant. "Do these shoes come in lilac?"

"As a matter of fact, you're in luck—they do." We waited while she retrieved a lilac version of the shoes from her storeroom.

When she brought them out, I thought there were perfect—they were a shade similar to Jessica's dress and in an elegant style that I thought would suit her.

"I'll take them," I said without hesitation.

The assistant brought out an ivory box to pack the shoes in, and at the same time, she reached for some pink tissue paper.

"Do you have lilac tissue paper?" I asked on impulse.

She looked up, obviously taken aback that I would be interested in such matters.

"I have some out back. I'll just go get it." She rushed off and came back a minute later with paper in the requested color, before carefully placing the shoes in between the folds. She placed the lid over it and reached for a roll of pink satin ribbon. But then she stopped. "Do you have a preference for the color of the ribbon?"

"The ribbon?" I wondered what she was talking about.

"Yes, we tie a ribbon around the box." Upon seeing my confused expression, she shrugged her shoulders. "The women seem to like that—it makes it look pretty and is more fun to unwrap."

"Lilac," I barked, just wanting to get out of this place.

She reached into a drawer and pulled out some lilac ribbon.

After paying, I gave Nancia a hug outside the store and thanked her for coming before hurrying home to get changed for the dance.

***

When I arrived home, I went straight up to our bedroom and found Jessica already in her lilac dress and the skyscraper heels.

Noticing my gaze upon her, her cheeks tinged pink. "Oh, hi. I was wondering where you'd gotten to?" She wobbled slightly as she turned toward me.

"It won't take me long to get ready. I just need to take a quick shower and then it'll only take me five minutes to get dressed in my tuxedo." I set the box down on the bed and looked at her. "This is for you."

"For me?" Jessica squeaked, her eyes widening. She just stood there, twisting her fingers as if unsure of what she should do next.

"You should open it," I prompted.

"Now?"

"Yeah."

"Okay," she murmured, reaching for the box. She stroked the lilac ribbon before pulling the bow undone and lifting off the lid of the box to reveal the lilac tissue paper. She opened the tissue carefully, as if not wanting to make the paper rustle too much, but her face broke into a smile as soon as the shoes were revealed.

"I thought you might like to wear these tonight."

She stroked the soft leather. "They're my favorite color."

"I know. That's why I chose them. I remember the first time I saw you in lilac—you looked gorgeous."

Jessica blushed at my compliment. "And they're flat. They'll be so much easier to walk in."

"Try them on," I urged.

She removed the skyscraper heels and stepped into the ballet flats. Then she walked across the bedroom without a single wobble. "My mother would never have allowed me to buy flat shoes for tonight. She would say they were too plain and too dowdy."

"Too plain?" The idiosyncrasies of female dressing etiquette were completely beyond me, as demonstrated by my complete bewilderment at the shoe store today.

"Yes. Mother would think that it does not sufficiently scream out my new status as a Santino wife, as the spouse of one of the wealthiest men in the Società. She prefers really high heels and what she calls 'power colors'—colors like gold, red, magenta, orange. She always said as I was already plain, I needed bright colors to improve my appearance."

"You're anything but plain, Jess."

JESSICA

Rafael's words made me blush.

I only had my zipper halfway closed as I couldn't reach the rest. "Could you help me with my zipper?" I asked as I looked at my reflection in the mirror.

Out of the corner of my eye, I saw Rafael move and held my breath as he stepped up behind me, meeting my eyes in the mirror as he towered above me.

Slowly, he moved my dark hair to one side, before bending his head and kissing the nape of my neck, sending a visible shiver through me.

He pulled the zipper up my back and then pressed his lips again to my neck in a more lingering kiss.

He stepped back and looked at me in approval.

I looked at my reflection and my breath caught. I moved my hands over the lilac silk fabric and looked down at my pretty shoes.

"I like this color on you. You look beautiful."

"No, I don't. It's the dress and shoes. They would make anyone look amazing—"

"Say 'thank you', Jessica," he said, interrupting my self-conscious rambling. His voice was commanding, and I felt my core tighten at his authoritative tone.

"Thank you," I said in a breathy voice as he looked at me in a way that made my entire body heat.

I found it hard to believe that Rafael thought me beautiful, especially after I had always been told while growing up that I was plain.

Somehow, wearing this dress and shoes in my favorite color and seeing how Rafael looked at me made me feel attractive for the first time in my life.

When I was ready, we went down to his car.

Even though there was no chance of me wobbling in my new shoes, Rafael took my hand and squeezed it as he held it in his grasp.

And I found myself squeezing his hand in return.

I liked his hand around mine—I liked it when he made me feel safe.

CHAPTER 22

JESSICA

I sat quietly as we drove to the hotel where the evening function was being held. My nerves prevented me from making small talk with Rafael.

This was the first Società event I was attending as Rafael's wife. And since Emanuel's death, I was no longer just the new Santino wife—I was now also the Consigliere's wife. Rafael was now the second most important man in the Società, and that would further increase tonight's interest in me.

As soon as we stepped into the hotel ballroom, I could sense the immediate interest in our arrival.

Very quickly, various Underbosses came up to greet Rafael and engage him in business talk. At the same time, their wives came to kiss my cheek and ask subtle and not-so-subtle questions about how I was finding married life.

I wasn't used to drawing so much attention and I wasn't sure I would ever like it, but I knew it was probably something I would have to get used to as part of my new role as Rafael's wife.

The most surprising thing was that despite my outfit being plainer than most other dresses worn tonight, the lilac dress actually made me feel a little surer of myself somehow. And perhaps if I acted confidently, people wouldn't realize that I was, in fact, a great fraud who had lost her innocence before her wedding day.

After a while, having endured the endless chatter and questions from various other wives, I was beginning to feel a little overwhelmed. Then I felt a touch at my elbow.

I looked around and found myself staring into a striking blue gaze.

"Excuse us, ladies. I'd like to dance with my sister," drawled Jacob.

Of course, none of the women objected. He already carried clear authority in whatever he did, as befitting a future Underboss of the Società.

He led me to the dance floor with a protective hand on my arm, and as we began to dance, I smiled up at him.

"Thank you for saving me from the nosy gossips."

"My pleasure. You looked like you needed it and, anyhow, I wanted to dance with my baby sister tonight."

As I let the music wash over me, I felt a sense of reassurance flow through me. I could be myself with him and didn't have to pretend to be something I was not. I always felt comfortable around Jacob, and I was glad that he was here tonight.

"You look very pretty," remarked Jacob, interrupting my thoughts.

I looked down at myself. "Rafael bought the shoes for me."

Jacob looked intensely into my eyes, and regarding me, he asked, "Is he good to you, Jess?"

I nodded. "Yes, he is."

Jacob let out a sigh of relief. "I'm glad," he breathed into my hair as he drew me closer into his hold.

I was glad as well. Not just for myself, but also for Jacob's sake—because I knew if Rafael ever did anything to me, Jacob would try to kill him, and then Jacob would be killed himself for going against the Consigliere of the Società. The mere thought of that made me shudder.

Jacob looked down at me. "Are you cold?"

"No, I'm okay now that I'm with you."

When the song finished, Rafael approached, giving a piercing look to Jacob and then looking more softly at me.

"Dance with me, Jessica."

I stood on tiptoes to give Jacob a small kiss on his cheek, murmuring, "I'll be okay, Jake."

Jacob gave a small nod to me and then glared at Rafael before stalking off.

I relaxed into Rafael's hold, his embrace making me feel safe despite the acute interest directed toward us by the other people present.

Mafia women had little to fill their days apart from gossip, and a newly married couple was a topic ripe for their curiosity. They would be wondering how I was finding married life and how I was being treated by my husband and my in-laws. They would even speculate how the sex was with my new husband—if he was gentle with me, or if he let his dark side out in the bedroom.

Of course, no one would say anything like that to my face, but I knew that no topic was off-limits for the Mafia wives: I was part of the Società, which meant that my life was not off-limits for their curiosity or for their gossip. It was the same as when Emanuel Santino had thought he could defile me—simply because I was part of the Società and he had been the boss.

As I danced with Rafael, I knew that every nervous glance I gave would have everyone wondering about how Rafael treated me behind closed doors. I was probably failing miserably tonight because I knew that I couldn't carry off the aura of a composed person totally in control of her emotions.

As if sensing my discomfort, Rafael leaned down and said in a low voice into my ear. "You've been amazingly strong tonight. You've been a success."

I looked at him in surprise. "I feel like a complete fraud. I'm just waiting with dread for everyone to find out the real me."

"You are my wife now, Jessica. If anyone ever does or says anything to hurt you ever again, they'll pay for it." He spoke harshly, and I knew he meant every word.

Perhaps he was right. After all, this outfit had made me feel a little less nervous, so maybe being a Santino wife would help me feel more poised and in control over time. Maybe it was a case of fake it until I make it—although I didn't know if I'd ever make it as a confident and self-assured Mafia wife. How could I when I knew that I could never be free from my demons?

At that moment, my mother bustled up to me. "Jessica, what on earth are you wearing?" she inquired abruptly, without any greeting.

"Good evening to you too, Casmundina," sighed Rafael.

"It's a new dress and shoes, Mother."

"I can see that. But it is certainly not one of the dresses I bought for your new role as Rafael's wife. It's incredibly bland. And those shoes! They have no heel, and what on earth are you doing wearing shoes in that awful washed-out color?"

"It's called lilac," interrupted Rafael sharply. "And I bought the shoes for my wife."

"Oh, I see. It's just that in Jessica's new position, everyone will be expecting her to dress a certain way, but I don't think this outfit meets those expectations. I did purchase Jessica a number of suitable dresses and heeled shoes for occasions such as this evening. Did you not see the fuchsia sequined ballgown that I chose for her, with the matching eight inch heels with faux jewels? I would have thought that outfit would have been more suitable—"

"Casmundina, this dress and these shoes are perfect. Jessica looks beautiful. She should wear more lilac. I noticed that you didn't buy anything for her in this color," growled Rafael.

"In lilac?" asked my mother in bafflement.

"Yes, in lilac. It's her favorite color. As her mother, you should have known that." But I knew what he really wanted to say was that, as my mother, she should have known not to let me attend the doctor's clinic alone.

"Yes, well, Jessica has always had a few strange ideas about her outfits. But as you say, you are her husband now. If you don't mind the color and the lack of sophisticated footwear, I suppose it will do."

"I definitely don't mind the color," snapped Rafael. "Now if you'll excuse us, we have to make the rounds," said Rafael in a hard voice, leading me away before my mother could reply, thus sparing me from any further of her opinions.

"Christ, what did I do in a past life to deserve a mother-in-law like her?" he muttered under his breath.

The rest of the night passed without incident. I was glad when we finally reached home and I could relax, although I was a little reluctant to take off my beautiful ballet flats. Placing them in the closet, I realized that I was looking forward to being able to wear them again sometime soon.

"I love my new shoes. I've always wanted ballet flats in lilac."

"You have?"

"Yes, but my mother always thought it an unsuitable color and style."

"Jessica," he said seriously, "if you want something, I need you to tell me."

"It's okay, it's not as if I need any more shoes," I said quickly.

"Jessica," he said a little sternly, "if you ever want anything, I expect you to tell me. You're mine now, and I want to give you whatever will make you happy. Do you understand?"

"Yes," I whispered. He had called me 'his', and his words went straight to my core.

"Good."

After freshening up in the bathroom, I slid between the smooth sheets of the bed straight into Rafael's arms.

RAFAEL

I noticed how Jess had been looking at me while we got ready for bed.

"You look like you want me to fuck you." It wasn't a question because I already knew the answer.

A flush ran up her cheeks as she nodded.

"Okay," I said, prowling to where she lay on the bed. I climbed in next to her and dipped my head toward hers, watching her all the while.

I brushed my lips up against her mouth, enjoying the softness of her lips. She gave a small gasp and as she relaxed under me, I slipped my tongue inside her mouth, caressing her breasts as I toyed with her tongue.

"Are you sure about this?" I murmured between kisses. She had to be sure; I didn't want to ever rush her.

Her pupils were dilated as she opened her eyes and replied. "I want this, please, Rafael." The pleading in her voice made me so hard.

"I'll give you what you need," I growled, "but first I want you to do something for me. I want to see you touch your pussy and make yourself come." I'd been fantasizing about watching her do this but had never asked her until now. This was an image I jerked off to in the shower—an image of her writhing her naked body against my bed, her body eager with arousal and desperate for release.

Her eyes widened with my words, and I could tell she was turned on.

She slowly grasped the hem of her nightdress and pulled it up, first revealing the tops of her curved thighs, then the smooth skin of her belly and the generous curve of her breasts. As she pulled it over her head, the fabric flipped her hair to one side, giving her that just sexy just-got-out-of-bed look.

She leaned back on her arms and settled against the headboard before pushing her panties down her slender legs. Her cheeks were tinged pink, but I could see from her gaze that she was turned on by this—and that pleased me.

"Open your legs for me," I said in a low voice.

She let her legs fall to the sides, giving me that first glimpse of her perfect pink lips, already swollen and peeking out between her narrow strip of dark hair. She bit her lower lip as she brought her hand down her body to play with her sweet pussy.

I watched her as I undid the top couple of buttons on my shirt and then unbuttoned my cuffs.

Her fingers slipped between her labia, and she closed her eyes as she enjoyed the strokes of her slim fingers.

I grabbed the back of my shirt and pulled it over my head swiftly, not wanting to miss a second of the show she was putting on for me. "Use your other hand to spread your pussy lips," I commanded her.

Her other hand reached down between her spread thighs. She used her fingers to hold apart her labia, giving me a better view of where I'd later sink my cock. Her fingers moved to her swollen nub.

"You're not allowed to touch your clit again until I say you can." My words were husky. I wanted her as much on edge as I was. "Do you understand?"

"Yes," she exhaled. It pleased me that she was so willing to please me and that she was putting on this show for me.

I unbuttoned my pants and pushed them down over my thighs, followed by my boxer shorts, my dick springing out from its confines. I was already so hard and eager to take her and make her mine.

I sat down next to her on the side of the bed, resting my hand on her ankle, caressing her skin. I slowly inched my way upward, fondling the smooth skin of her calf.

Her gaze was fixed on my hand and she held her breath as my fingers trailed up to the silky, sensitive skin of her thighs.

I loved that she wasn't hiding her body from me. She was laid back with her legs spread wide open, her wet arousal coating her swollen lips.

I licked my lips as I watched her juices drip like honey—from her pussy, down the crevice between her legs and toward the plump globes of her ass.

"Please, can I touch my clit," she pleaded. I loved that she was submissive in the bedroom. I didn't even have to tell her to beg me.

"No. Not yet." My words were terse.

She mewled in protest but obeyed me.

I fisted my dick in my large palm, wrapping my fingers around my stiffness, resisting the urge to take her right away. My balls ached, and I knew I needed to feel them slapping against her pussy.

She panted as she played with her pussy lips and stroked the sensitive nerve endings at the entrance to her channel. I knew she wanted me to run my tongue along her slit.

But I merely laid my cheek against her inner thigh, watching her. I was so close to her sex; I was sure she could feel my warm breath against her wet flesh. The atmosphere between us was electrifying.

My mouth watered as my eyes drank in the sight of her. I watched as her hips lifted off the mattress and she clenched the muscles in her legs, her eyes glazed over.

I wanted to claim her so badly, but first I wanted to see her get herself off with her own fingers.

As I watched her, my face so close to her core, I inhaled her sexy, musky scent. She was so close to her release and her eyes were shut tightly in concentration.

I watched her for the next couple of minutes before she eventually exclaimed, "I can't!" Her eyes opened, revealing the frustration inside her. I knew that some girls couldn't bring themselves off through masturbation. "Have you ever made yourself come with your own hands?" I asked.

She nodded. "Yes, but not...since the clinic..." Her voice trailed off as a look of pain flitted across the face.

Shit. I didn't want her feeling guilty about enjoying sex or to feel shame when she experienced pleasure. I now felt bad that I had asked her to touch herself in front of me like this.

"Do you want me to do it for you?" I asked.

She nodded, full of trust for me, and I knew I wouldn't let her down.

I moved to sit at the end of the bed, where I could see myself in the full-length mirror on the opposite wall. "Come here," I beckoned.

She got up on her hands and knees and crawled over the mattress to me.

"I want you to sit between my legs, with your back against my chest."

"What are you doing?" There was a small frown between her brows.

"You'll see," I said with a small smile. "It'll be good."

She scooted between my legs and leaned against my chest.

"Open your legs now."

She slowly splayed her legs open, and we both watched our reflection in the mirror opposite.

"You're beautiful, every part of you. I love seeing you all wet and ready for me." As I spoke, I massaged her slick pussy lips, looking at them in the reflection before moving my gaze back up to her face.

She let out small moans as my fingers fondled her slit.

The more aroused she became, the more she writhed against my body, her ass wriggling against my aching hardness. I wanted to lift her ass and impale her on my dick so badly.

"Watch what I'm doing to you," I said harshly. "Your whole body is on display to me. I can see your juices gleaming on your pussy lips and feel your slickness against my fingers. See how beautiful you are?"

Her cheeks blushed but her eyes didn't leave her reflection as she focused on what my fingers were doing to her, her mouth slightly parted and small breaths coming quickly from her.

As I spread her labia and slipped a finger into her tight core, my eyes met hers in the mirror. "Do you like this, Jessica?"

"Yes," she rasped.

I slid my thick finger in and out of her a few times, before penetrating her with a second digit, making her body arch against me.

"Do you like it when I fuck you with my fingers, Jessica?"

"Yes, yes..."

"This is how I'm going to fuck you with my cock," I growled, relishing the feel of her inner muscles gripping my fingers. As those muscles started to tighten even more, it started to become too much for her and she tried to close her legs.

I hooked my legs through hers, anchoring her thighs apart. "No, keep your legs open! I want to see you." I wanted to watch my fingers disappearing inside in her soaking pussy, as I reveled in the wet sounds that were coming from her most private place.

"Please, Raphael—please, I need to come..."

I knew she needed pressure on her clit as well. "No! First, I want to see you play with your tits."

Her hands immediately gripped her full breasts and her fingers tugged at her erect nipples. I couldn't wait to suck on her hard peaks when I took her with my dick.

Finally, I massaged her aching clit. My eyes were burning with desire as I brought her to the brink and watched her full lips part.

Her body bucked against me as I pinched her clit between my finger and thumb, my two fingers still pumping in and out of her pussy.

She screamed out, all the time watching our reflection in the mirror. As she echoed out her cries, she threw her head back against my chest.

I let go of her and pushed her onto her hands and knees. Clamping my hands onto her hips, I pulled her ass up toward me.

Then I grabbed her hair and tugged her head around so that she would see our reflection in the mirror.

Spreading her ass cheeks, I plunged deep into her soaking channel, groaning as I finally felt myself fully sheathed inside her.

My senses were heightened as I looked at the mirror and saw my dick disappearing between her plump ass cheeks again and again. The sight of this, the feel of this, and the sound of my balls slapping against her clit were the most erotic thing I'd ever experienced.

I drove into her relentlessly and heard her scream out for a second time before I exploded deep inside her. I let her clenching muscles wring every last bit of release out of my cock, before pulling out and watching the mixture of her juices and my cum run down her swollen labia.

She was so responsive and so obedient, and I knew that I'd never be able to get enough of her.

"You're beautiful, Jessica," I whispered, as I held her in my arms. "Don't ever forget that."

CHAPTER 23

RAFAEL

I was with Gabriel in the office at Matrix when Jacob came to see us. He had Bella with him. "You have a visitor," he announced.

"Bella," Gabriel greeted, narrowing his gaze as he took in the dark circles under her eyes. "Is your mother alright?"

She shook her head. She cleared her throat and tried to make her voice strong. "She died two days ago."

"I'm very sorry to hear that."

"I don't need your sympathy," she snapped.

Gabriel clenched his jaw. "What can I help you with then? You know, we promised your mother to look out for you. And we'll keep that promise."

She held her head high and looked us in the eye. "I need to borrow some money to pay the bill for the funeral." She was silent for a couple of seconds. "I lost my job two weeks ago—I had to stay home with my mom. The priest at our church had access to a charitable fund which paid for a nurse, but I still couldn't leave my mom, not when she was suffering so much and I knew I only had a short time left with her. The diner couldn't keep my job open for me. So I need to borrow some money to pay for a decent burial." Blinking back a tear, she quickly added. "I'll pay you back as soon as I get a new job."

"Fine," I said before Gabriel could respond. "We've got a job going here for a hostess in the nightclub. You can do that." Matrix was one of our classier establishments—I didn't want her working in any of our seedier joints.

She looked taken aback. "That's not what I was asking. I don't need you to give me a job. I can find my own. You don't have to worry—I'm a hard worker and I'll find a new job quickly and then I can pay you back within a couple of months. I'm not going to disappear without paying you back if that's what you're worried about," she said bitterly.

"I know you won't run off without paying your debt to us—because you'll be right here working for us."

"You're being an asshole," she spat.

"You should watch how you speak to me if you want a favor from me."

"I don't want a favor. I want you to do the decent thing," she hissed.

Gabriel started to speak. "I think we can just—"

I cut Gabriel off. "You can start work next week. That's the deal on the table. Take it or leave."

She considered my offer for a couple of minutes before reluctantly nodding. It was obvious she had no one else to borrow money from.

"Do you have the bill for the funeral with you?"

She nodded and handed it to me. "We'll deal with it. The money will be deducted in installments off your wages. The manager will work it out with you."

"You can just take all my wages."

"No, you'll need some money to live on. The job comes with a place to live too."

"I'm not taking your charity," she said tersely.

"I'm not giving it. The club needs someone living on site to fulfill insurance requirements. The person who did it left last week, so you'll be his replacement. You'll be working as a hostess in the club five evenings a week and you'll sleep here every night. One of my men can help you move your stuff in." I wasn't going to give her an option over this.

"I can manage by myself."

"Just make sure you're here by 6pm tomorrow to start work."

She looked at me as if she wanted to say something. "What is it?"

"I'm a hard worker and I won't do anything dishonest," she said quickly. "I've worked honestly for all the money I've earned so far in my life, and it'll be staying that way." Her voice dripped with disdain, making clear her hatred of us and our way of life.

"Is that all?" I asked.

"No. I may be working for you here, but I don't want anyone knowing our connection," she spat in obvious hatred of us.

"Fine," I gritted out.

She nodded and then walked out of the office.

Gabriel looked at me. "We could have just given her the money. It's not as if we can't afford it. Aren't you the one always telling me that everything isn't about business and money?"

"I know that. But this way we can keep an eye on her, otherwise she'll disappear and we won't see her ever again." Luckily, she didn't know that people like us didn't need insurance and what I'd said about insurance requirements was a lie.

"She'll disappear as soon as she's paid off her debt," Gabriel pointed out.

"We've got a few months until then. And if she's here, we can keep an eye on her."

From the bill for the funeral, I could see the time and date of the service and burial. I knew Gabriel would be reluctant to take time off work to attend, but I asked him anyway if he wanted to go with me. "Do you want to attend the funeral with me?"

"But we're not even related to Carmela," Gabriel complained.

"I know, but we are related to her daughter."

"I wouldn't give one of our men time off to attend a funeral of someone they're not even related to, you know," Gabriel pointed out to me.

"I'll take that as a 'no' then." I sighed. "Fine, I'll go by myself."

A couple of days later, when Bella saw me at the church, her face broke into a look of surprise before swiftly changing to a scowl.

Whatever, I thought. Someone from our family had to attend today and, despite her hostility, I didn't mind it being me.

***

Once it had been confirmed via the DNA test that Bella was our half-sister, and especially now that Bella would also be working in our club and living nearby, I knew I couldn't put off telling Jess any longer. I had to tell her about Bella and what my father had done to Carmela. Gabriel was taking care of telling the twins.

As we lay in bed that night, I held Jess tight against my chest as if my embrace could protect her from anything else bad happening to her.

"I can't believe he did the same thing to someone else," Jess murmured once I had told her the whole story. "What's Bella like?"

"Young and distrustful of us and our ways." There wasn't much else I could say about her since our encounters with her had been brief.

"You should invite her to dinner. We should get to know her."

"I'm not sure she's ready for that yet." I knew that we weren't ready either. "Perhaps we should let her settle into her new place and job first. Also, we've decided not to tell anyone yet about her being related to us."

"Okay," said Jess softly.

Truthfully, I wasn't sure how much Bella would have to do with our family.

***

The next day, Jess and I went for our usual morning run. This had become a habit for us now and it was nice to spend time with Jess before I left to go to work.

For someone with such a delicate figure, she was a lot stronger than she looked. She had good stamina and she was happy to push herself hard. I found our daily runs one of the most peaceful times of my day—a way to calm my soul before the deadly tasks of the day took over.

It was a good way for her to relax too. She had been getting too caught up in wanting a baby, added to which she was worried about the escalation in violence since we had broken Nancia's engagement contract with the Veneti family. As predicted, they had not taken it well and now all gloves were off between our two organizations.

As usual, I handed a bottle of water to Jess and she gulped it down when we stopped for a water break.

A minute later she grimaced and put her hand over her mouth. She swiftly ran a few meters away and was violently sick on the ground, heaving up the contents of her stomach. I immediately went to her and held her hair back from her face and when she was finished, I helped her up.

"Are you okay, Jess?"

"I'm sorry," she gasped.

"Don't apologize. Are you coming down with something?" I put my hand to her forehead and it was clammy, but I couldn't tell if that was from her being unwell or from the exertion of the run.

"I'm not feeling so good."

"Come on, let's sit you down for a few minutes. I've got another bottle of water you can have as well." She used the water to rinse her mouth.

As I ran the pad of my thumb over the small frown between her eyebrows, smoothing the line away, she looked at me with big eyes. "I could be pregnant..."

"It's possible." I replied. "It's also possible that you just have an upset stomach."

Jess's face fell at my words.

"There's only one way to know for sure, Jess. Let's cut our run short, and we can head back to the house so that you can do a pregnancy test." Jess had stocked up on these and they were sitting in the drawer of our bathroom vanity, waiting to be used.

Jessica turned back toward the house and started to run again.

"Hey, let's find out whether you're pregnant or not before we do any more running," I called. "We can walk back for now."

"No, let's run. I want to get back to the house as quickly as possible!" she shouted back over her shoulder as she headed off.

We ran back the normal route to the house and Jessica pushed herself hard. "Slow down, Jess. There's no rush." I could easily keep up with her, but I wanted her to take it easy in case she was, in fact, pregnant.

"I want to find out," she said quickly, anxiety showing across her features.

I wished she wasn't so obsessed with the idea of having a baby. I didn't want her to get her hopes up, especially after her bitter disappointment when her period arrived last month.

When we got to the house, we went straight up to the bedroom. She dashed into our bathroom and grabbed a pregnancy test.

I followed her and put my hands on her arms. "Jess," I said. "I don't want you to be upset if the test says you're not pregnant."

"I know." She gave me a small smile, though I knew she was putting on a brave face. She really wanted this.

"We haven't been trying long, and we've got all the time in the world. I don't want you to feel pressure that you have to get pregnant straight away." I left her in the bathroom to do the test.

A couple of minutes later, she came back out with the white stick.

"How long do we have to wait?" I asked

"It says just a few minutes. And then two lines will come up if I'm pregnant, or one line if I'm not."

We sat next to each other on the couch at the end of our bed, and I held her hand. "You know I love you, no matter what, Jess."

She looked at me in surprise. It was the first time I had told her that I loved her. "I love you too, Rafael."

I was even more surprised than her—that she could love me, a Santino, after what my family had done to her. I wasn't worthy of her love. She was such a kind, strong, compassionate woman. Every time I thought about what she'd been through, guilt ate away at my conscience.

Not many things made me feel guilty in this life, but when it involved those closest to me, then I was just like any other human being—susceptible to my conscience and to morality.

The thought that she loved me back totally consumed me and gave me a feeling that I'd never had before. I knew my parents and siblings loved me, and they would always love me no matter what I did.

But to have this woman, who I'd only met a couple of months ago, put that trust in me by allowing herself to fall in love with me was an indescribable feeling.

Jessica interrupted my thoughts. "Something's appearing." We watched as the test slowly did its thing. I was almost willing it with all my soul to be positive. Ever since Jessica had mentioned wanting a baby, I'd realized how much I wanted one with her—with the woman I loved.

I'd married her because it was expected of me, but now I'd fallen in love with her, and I knew she was the one who could make my life complete. She gave some meaning to my life of violence and death.

"Oh my God, it's two lines!" shrieked Jess.

For a moment, I was stunned. Although I'd been wishing for it and willing for it to happen, the news still astonished me.

For a moment I couldn't do anything, then I stood up and swept Jessica to her feet, lifting her up and whirling her around in my arms. "We're having a baby!" I grinned.

And Jessica laughed her beautiful, soft laugh, and the joy in my heart doubled hearing her. "You better stop spinning me around before I'm sick again," she giggled.

I put her down gently and kissed her passionately.

"Are you okay? How are you feeling? You should sit down—maybe we shouldn't have gone on that run." My words were running together and my mind was all over the place. This was as far from the usual, composed Rafael Santino as I could get.

"I'm fine. I'm just pregnant."

I became serious. "We'll have to stop going for our runs now."

She shook her head. "Exercise is good for pregnant women. We just might have to take it a bit easier later in the pregnancy, but we've got nine months to worry about that."

I put my hand to her stomach, knowing that our baby would be a tiny speck. "Nine months of waiting to meet this baby." Already I was impatient. I still couldn't believe there was another life in her, a life that we had made together. "When can we tell everyone?" I asked.

"They say the pregnancy is generally safe after the first twelve weeks have passed. Hopefully, the sickness will pass by then because I can't imagine feeling like this every day for the next nine months."

"Why don't you take a shower, Jess, and I'll get started on making us breakfast."

"Don't you have to get to work?" Normally I showered while Jess made breakfast, so that I could eat and then head straight off to work.

"There's nothing more important than you right now. You and our baby."

CHAPTER 24

RAFAEL

After the Monday Post-Mortem dinner the following week, Nate and Nancia got up to leave.

"No, don't leave just yet. We need to talk to you, Nancia," Gabriel said.

Nancia sat back down, and Nate automatically sat down as well. Anything that concerned her, concerned him as well. A deep frown marred Nate's forehead—he could already feel it was bad. It was like he had a sixth sense when it came to his twin.

Gabriel frowned. "I've been going through our father's papers. Nancia, it seems that before his death, he promised you in marriage to Leoluca Veneti."

Nancia's blue eyes widened as the words sank in. She had, of course, heard of the Veneti name.

Nate interrupted. "But she was only promised? No contract was signed, so the promise isn't binding," he said, more in hope than anything else.

"The engagement contract was signed. Our father signed it in Nancia's stead," I replied.

"For fuck's sake," exclaimed Nate. "She's not marrying that bastard." And for once, neither Gabriel nor I admonished his bad language.

"We all agree with you on that," responded Gabriel. "We're not going to follow the contract. We're going to tell the Venetis that it's canceled."

"But will they allow you to do that?" said Nancia, finally speaking. She was trying to make her tone strong, even when she was just in front of us, but she couldn't prevent her voice from trembling.

"It doesn't matter whether they want to accept it or not. You're not marrying him. And that's all there is to it," I said firmly.

"However, it will mean tensions will escalate between us and the Venetis," added Gabriel. "And it will probably mean war between our organizations."

"I don't care how many of them we need to kill," growled Nate. "Nancia is my twin, and we have to keep her safe from him."

JESSICA

The next morning, Gabriel and Rafael had left for work while I was having breakfast with the twins.

"I can't believe our father wanted to marry you off to a Veneti," said Nate, still raging about what he learned last night.

Nancia's dark blue eyes were huge on her face. "I'm worried," she said to her twin.

I felt uncomfortable that they were talking about this in front of me, feeling like an intruder in their conversation. When they spoke like this to each other, it was like they shut out the whole world around them. I concentrated intently on eating my cereal and tried to pretend I wasn't listening.

"Don't worry, Nance. I'll never let anyone make you marry someone like that. You're a Mafia princess and you deserve only the best. I would burn down the world before I let anyone undeserving touch you."

Nancia gave a wobbly smile to her twin. "Thanks, Nate."

"But you see now, don't you, why I have to be a Made Man if I'm to protect you from the Venetis?"

"But Gabriel and Rafael can protect me—you don't need to do it too, Nate," pleaded Nancia.

"I'll never leave your protection to anyone else, Nance. You mean too much to me. I'd never be able to live with myself if anything happened to you. I wouldn't want *to live* without you by my side."

Finally accepting the inevitability that Nate would become a Made Man and that there was nothing she could do to change this, Nancia sighed in defeat.

Nate held out his arms, and she huddled in his embrace, letting herself be comforted by her twin.

***

The following day, Rafael took me by the hand and led me upstairs to our bedroom. "I have something for you."

As soon as he opened the door, I saw a pile of ivory boxes, each tied with a beautiful lilac ribbon.

I looked toward Rafael, confusion washing over me.

"You better not have changed your mind about your favorite color."

"It's still lilac," I breathed.

"Good. You'll want to keep all those ribbons then—if you can't find a use for them, I can think of a few things I could do with them," he growled, making my core tighten as I realized he might want to tie me up with them.

"Um, do you want me to open them?"

He nodded, so I untied the first box and pulled out pretty flat sandals in lilac. "Oh, they're gorgeous," I said, a smile lifting the corners of my mouth. After admiring them, I moved on to the next box and found some flat slingbacks in another beautiful shade of lilac. "I love them," I giggled.

As I moved through the boxes, I opened each to find more shoes, all in various shades of lilac. "My mother's not going to be happy," I said, but I couldn't help smiling in delight.

"I don't care about your mother. All I want is for you to be happy."

"You didn't have to buy me so many shoes in an attempt to make me happy, you know."

"I would have bought more if they'd had them, but this was all they had in lilac."

I laughed. "These will keep me going for a while."

"I want to see you happy," he said, suddenly serious. "If it means you wearing shoes and clothes in this color each and every day, I don't care—you look beautiful to me whatever you wear, and you look especially beautiful in lilac."

I let him take me into his arms, and I pulled his head down so that I could kiss him.

Later, having tried on all the new shoes, I put them in my closet.

When I wore lilac clothes or shoes, I no longer felt plain…or maybe I felt prettier because of the way Rafael looked at me now.

I stood back and admired the satisfying new block of color. I found it soothing somehow—it was my happy color, my happy place.

***

A couple of weeks later, I was feeling lousy after vomiting yet again. I had even given up my daily run with Rafael for now. Since the day I'd found out I was pregnant, I'd been sick every morning without fail and then sometimes again later in the day.

"Oh God," I said. "No one told me it would be like this. I knew there might be some morning sickness, but not every single day."

"You're looking pretty worn out, Jess." Rafael looked at me with concern.

"Charming—just what every girl wants to hear from her husband."

"You look as though you've lost weight."

"I wouldn't be surprised if I have. I can hardly keep anything down. Even the smell of food turns my stomach. I'm sorry I haven't been able to cook."

"Me and Gabriel will survive. We lived on takeout before you moved in, and we still have all the menus in the kitchen drawer. Although Gabriel is missing your spaghetti meatballs—he says it's even better than the stuff from his favorite takeout place."

"Don't worry, I'll be back to cooking once this nausea passes."

"No, I don't want you rushing anything. Your health and the baby's health are my priority right now. Gabriel will get used to eating the takeout again. Anyhow, once the baby arrives, you're not going to have as much spare time, so he'll just have to learn to get used to fewer home-cooked meals."

"I should still be able to cook once the baby's here."

"Let's just get through this pregnancy first. I'm not happy about the weight you're losing. It can't be good for the baby. I think we should make another appointment to see the doctor." We'd already had an initial appointment to confirm the pregnancy and our next checkup was for the twelve-week scan.

"All women feel like this, Rafael," I said in an attempt to ease his concern.

"I know, but I'm worried about whether the baby's getting enough nutrients. Maybe the doctor will advise you to take some extra vitamins or something."

"Okay, I'll make an appointment after breakfast, although I don't think I'll be able to manage anything except hot water with lemon." To be honest, I was feeling pretty rough. And if it set Rafael's mind at rest, I was happy to do whatever he wanted.

CHAPTER 25

RAFAEL

I had a meeting with Jacob and a group of our Captains at Matrix. One of Jacob's guys managed the place, and Jacob held a lot of his meetings at the club due to its proximity to the Bonardi mansion. It was a couple of hours before the place opened, so we had the club to ourselves.

I didn't usually come here, so I hadn't seen much of Bella since she had started her new job. I didn't think she wanted much to do with us, given the hostile looks she had bestowed upon me every time I had seen her so far.

I sat down at a table in the empty club with Jacob across from me. He signaled to Bella to bring us over drinks.

I nodded at Bella as I caught her eye. "How is she doing?" I asked Jacob.

"She's as prickly as hell."

I raised an eyebrow at him in question.

He sighed. 'She's a hard worker and the customers like her. She saves her bad attitude for anyone wearing the Società tattoo.'

'Sounds about right,' I muttered, as she came over and put a glass of whiskey down in front of me none-too-gently. Our conversation was interrupted by the arrival of some of the Captains and I swiftly changed the subject.

Once everyone had arrived, we got down to business, namely the issue of recent Bratva attacks on our drug runs. As we talked through options and retaliation plans, Jacob signaled for more drinks to be brought over. We were debating whether to attack an imminent Bratva drug shipment we had received intel about.

Savino Gamberini, a Captain, sat to my left. He was keen to seize the shipment as payback. Some of the other Captains, however, were concerned about hostilities increasing when perhaps we should be trying to get things to simmer down. The less attention we drew to our illegal activities, the better it was for us in terms of avoiding unwanted attention from the DEA and FBI.

Bella came over with a tray of drinks and went around the table, picking up the used glasses and replacing them with new drinks. As she stood by Savino and served him his drink, he grabbed her ass, making her jump and flush bright red before throwing his drink in his face.

Savino smirked at her as he wiped the liquid which was dripping from his face onto the table. "It's a shame to waste good whiskey like that. I'll have to get you to lick it up, or maybe you can make it up to me by licking my dick instead."

"Shut your fucking mouth," I growled. "You better not speak to her like that ever again."

"Why not? She works for us, making her as much as one of our whores as the sluts who work in our whorehouses."

I jerked to my feet, my chair crashing to the ground behind me. "She's my sister, you fucker," I spat out.

The silence in the room was deafening, but all I could hear was heated blood rushing through my veins.

"Your sister?" said Savino in disbelief.

"Yeah, my half-sister," I said, pulling my knife from its sheath.

"I-I didn't know," stuttered Savino, holding his hands up in front of his body as if in surrender. "I apologize—I didn't mean any disrespect."

"But you did disrespect her," I said in a low tone as adrenaline took over my senses.

"I didn't mean—"

I didn't wait for any more of the weasel's words. I grabbed his head and slit his throat from ear to ear.

A strangled cry came from Bella, the only sound in the room apart from the gurgle that came from Savino as his life bled out, seeping into a dark pool of blood around him.

Bella spun around and ran toward the back section for staff.

"Get a clean-up crew in here to deal with this mess," I barked at Jacob as I strode off after her.

I swung open the door to the staff area and saw Bella standing, her arms leaning against a counter to keep her shaking body from collapsing to the floor.

I walked over to her, meeting her eyes and seeing the shock swelling in their depth.

I hesitated only a second and then pulled her into my arms.

"I'm sorry you had to see that," I whispered into her hair. "But no one speaks to you like that ever again."

She broke down into sobs in my arms, and I let her cry for what she had just seen, and perhaps also for her mother—I wasn't sure exactly who her grief was for, but I did know that I had to protect her.

When she had calmed down a little, she pulled away from me, swiping her hand across her eyes. "Your men, they won't tell anyone will they, you know, that I'm your half-sister?"

"It's going to be impossible to keep that secret now that this many people know."

People would easily work out who her father was once they saw her distinctive blue eyes—they were the same stormy dark blue that the rest of the Santinos possessed. And once they found out Carmela was her mother, there would no doubt be speculation whether Carmela had slept with our father willingly or unwillingly.

"I'm sorry I let the cat out of the bag. But it's probably for the best—it's the only way to protect you, Bella."

"I don't want to be known as a Santino," she said resentfully.

"I know, but that's what you are. And too many people knew that even before today—most importantly, your stepfather. It was always going to come out sooner or later. You're family whether you like it or not, and that means we protect you. And you're never going to get rid of us, so stop being so damn hostile all the time."

She sniffed and wiped away another stray tear. "You know that nurse the church paid for...that was you, wasn't it?"

I gave a small nod.

"Thank you," she whispered.

"You don't need to thank me, not ever."

JESSICA

I'd heard about the incident with Bella before Rafael even got home.

"Is it true?" I asked, after recounting a brief summary of what I'd heard.

"More or less," Rafael replied. "How did you hear about it so fast, anyway?"

"It was delivered, with relish, courtesy of my mother."

"Mrs. Bonardi—I should have guessed."

"She was offended that I hadn't told her already and that she had to hear it via the gossip grapevine."

"That sounds like your mother," he said drily.

"I think we should invite Bella over for dinner next week. She must have settled in by now. And if she hasn't, we can see if there's anything we can help with. We can invite her to the Monday Post-Mortem."

"Definitely not," Rafael said forcefully. "Monday dinners are to talk business—she may be family, but we don't know how much we can trust her with such matters yet."

"We'll invite her another night then, say Wednesday."

"No, Jess," he said tersely.

"Why not?" I was taken aback by his vehemence.

"I'm not sure that she likes us, and she's prickly."

It was clear to me that he was trying to find excuses not to invite Bella over. "If she's prickly, it's probably because she's grieving," I pointed out.

"It's more than that. It's just not a good idea to have her over." It was obvious by his tone that he didn't want to discuss it any further, and I dropped the subject.

***

That night, I found it hard to fall asleep for the first time in a long while.

I couldn't stop thinking about what had happened today with Bella.

Rafael wasn't keen on Bella mixing with the family. And I knew the reason why: she was sullied, a product of rape, and thus not worthy of being a part of the Santino family.

The realization hit me hard—*that Rafael saw me in exactly the same way.*

I was also damaged goods; the only difference was that I could give him something, a child to be his heir, and that was why I was still here. If he didn't need an heir, he probably wouldn't want me here, just like he didn't want Bella here.

Rafael had told me that he loved me, but I knew that his love would always be tainted by the knowledge that I had not been pure for him. I knew now that he would never truly love me.

Although he'd told me he'd love me, he'd probably just said that because he thought it was part of what he should say as a husband. Just like he'd said to me at the start of our marriage that looking after me was part of "his job" as my husband. Those were the exact words he'd used.

The only reason he'd married me was because, as a Made Man, he had to marry and produce heirs. Marrying me was part of his job, being my husband was part of his job, and saying he loved me was part of his job.

To love someone, and to know they could never feel the same way about you, was like a punch to the gut—the thought knocked the breath out of me and left a heavy pain in my stomach.

There would always be someone like Bella, or mentions of Emanuel, or something else to remind Rafael of my past. My shame was inescapable.

I knew now, beyond doubt, that I would have to look to our baby for the absolute love I craved.

As I tried to fall asleep, I let myself think about the small life growing inside me, and I was glad that I at least had this baby to look forward to.

***

Two days later, we sat in the consultation room of Dr. Chiara Azzaro. She was the doctor who delivered most of the Società's babies.

I was glad to have the appointment today to take my mind off my relationship with Rafael.

"Morning sickness is common among pregnant women, as you will know," the doctor explained. "When it becomes excessive, however, it is called *hyperemesis gravidarum*."

"How serious is that?" interrupted Rafael tersely.

"Please don't be alarmed at my use of the medical terminology for Jessica's condition. We do need to exercise caution, however, and check that the baby is growing okay and that Jessica isn't getting dehydrated."

"So, the baby's growth can be affected?" questioned Rafael, a deep frown marring his forehead.

I put my hand on top of Rafael's. "If you let the doctor speak, I think she was just getting to that." Rafael was in his Made Man mode, used to issuing dictates and impatient to get answers. However, he needed to step back for a moment and let the doctor do her job, and that included allowing her to explain what was going on.

The doctor smiled at me. She was the OB-GYN used by the women in the Società, so she would be used to dealing with Made Men, yet she still looked grateful for my intervention. Made Men were notoriously demanding and difficult to handle.

"Normally, the baby will take what it needs first from the mother's body, which is probably why Jessica is losing weight. Women often lose weight when they have morning sickness—the body prioritizes the baby's nutrition, therefore the baby will normally still get enough nutrients. However, we will just check on it to make sure everything is going as it should. We'll run bloodwork and also do a scan today."

"We'll get to see the baby?" I asked excitedly. "But the baby hasn't reached twelve weeks yet."

"Yes, we'll be able to see the baby," smiled the doctor. "We have to do the scan slightly different at the pre-twelve-week stage. Instead of using an ultrasound sensor over your stomach, I will have to use an internal probe, however, it won't be painful. The baby will be tiny, although we will be able to see it in the womb."

I looked at Rafael and I could see he was just as eager as me to see our baby. Suddenly my morning sickness was forgotten and I perked up, and although my stomach was fluttering, it was with butterflies of excitement.

My blood was taken and although I normally hated needles, today I was keen to have the blood taken so that we could get to the scan.

Once the blood draws were complete, the doctor asked me to change into a gown behind a screen. I practically ripped my clothes off and flung them to the side as I hurriedly changed into the unbecoming blue paper gown.

Coming out from behind the screen, the doctor asked me to lie back on the examination table and got her equipment ready. As the doctor conducted the scan, Rafael held my hand as we looked in anticipation at the monitor screen.

An image of my womb and the tiny baby moving around in it came up on the monitor. I gasped, lost for words at the sight of the tiny human being growing inside me.

"It's quite active inside you by the look of it," Rafael said, as he looked down and smiled lovingly at me.

I giggled with him as we watched, captivated by the image on the monitor.

My eyes flicked to the doctor, and I noticed she had a serious expression on her face. "What's wrong, doctor?" I tried to keep my voice steady.

"It's nothing to worry about."

Rafael's expression became deadly serious. "Doctor, if there are any issues I want to know—don't sugarcoat it."

Dr. Chiara looked from my file to me. "The baby's fine and is healthy."

I knew there was something wrong. "What is it, doctor? What is it then? Why are you concerned?"

"Perhaps I should speak to Jessica alone," the doctor announced.

"Why?" demanded Rafael.

"Jessica is my patient, and my duty is to her."

"You are a Società doctor," said Rafael in a low voice. "Your duties are to the Santino family and that includes me."

"Mr. Santino, you know as well as I do how the doctor-patient relationship works under law. I really have to insist that I talk to Jessica in private."

"To hell with the law. The Società makes its own rules—including what we do to people who aren't loyal to us."

I intervened then. "Doctor, it's okay. Anything you need to say to me can be said in front of Rafael."

"Mr. and Mrs. Santino, I really would prefer to speak to Jessica—"

"Doctor, please," I said. "I want Rafael to hear whatever you have to say."

The doctor looked doubtfully at me, but she could tell that I wouldn't be persuaded otherwise.

"It's just…" The doctor looked uncomfortable and tailed off.

"For God's sake, doctor, just spit it out." Rafael was almost out of patience.

The doctor looked at me. "You were married eleven weeks ago, correct?"

"Yes, that's right," I answered. "You were at our wedding yourself." Dr. Chiara was always invited to Società weddings, and she loved seeing all the children that she had delivered over the last few years.

"It's just that this baby, this fetus, is fourteen weeks old."

"It can't be," I said in confusion.

"What do you mean, Doctor?" asked Rafael.

Then realization hit me. I felt the blood drain from my face.

I turned to Rafael and saw the exact moment it hit him as well, his eyes registering shock and anger.

The doctor carried on hurriedly. "Sometimes couples anticipate marriage, or the baby comes a bit earlier than expected."

The doctor looked worried for me. I knew she would be wondering if we had indeed anticipated marriage and Rafael was the father, or whether I had slept with someone else without his knowledge.

"But how is that even possible? I had my period a few weeks after our wedding…" My voice drifted off in utter confusion.

"What was the bleeding like, Jessica? Was it as heavy as a normal period?" asked the doctor.

"My periods have always been irregular and on the light side. That period was particularly light, but I thought that was due to the stress

I'd been under before our wedding—stress always seems to affect my cycle."

"The bleeding you had last month is what we call spotting," responded Dr. Chiara. "Between fifteen and twenty-five percent of women spot during their early pregnancy, due to factors such as the implantation of the egg or the changes in the cervix. It's nothing to worry about usually, however it is not a period. So that's why you experienced some light bleeding last month, even though you were already pregnant."

Oh God, this couldn't really be happening. "But I did a pregnancy test last month and it said I wasn't pregnant..."

"Did you do the test as soon as you woke in the morning?"

"No, but that shouldn't matter, surely?" I asked in desperation.

"If you don't test first thing in the morning, it can be harder for the test to detect the HCG hormone, thus giving a negative result when you are, in fact, pregnant." The doctor's tone was sympathetic, yet her words could provide no comfort.

"Doctor, leave us." Rafael's voice was ice cold.

"I'm not sure that's wise," responded the doctor, her eyes darting to Rafael's clenched fists. His whole body was wound up with tension and he looked ready to explode.

"It's okay, doctor. Rafael and I have no secrets." I put my shaky hand on top of Rafael's. "You can leave us, and we'll talk."

Rafael had also noticed the doctor's reluctance to leave me alone with my husband. "Don't worry. She's my wife and she's safe with me. It's too late to protect her now." The doctor was confused by his words. However, she quietly left the room after switching off the monitor.

"Oh my God." As I looked up at Rafael, I couldn't help the horror creeping into my voice. "It's Emanuel's baby." I whispered before breaking down into helpless, gulping sobs.

Rafael took me in his arms and held me tightly, stroking my hair and murmuring comforting words into my hair.

"I never thought...I didn't know." I sobbed into his chest.

"It's not your fault, Jess."

"It is. I should have thought to get the morning-after pill."

"You would have been in shock and not thinking about the pregnancy risk or anything like that. You're not to blame for any of this."

"What do we do now?" I gasped. "I don't know if I can have this baby...but I don't know if I can terminate the pregnancy either."

CHAPTER 26

JESSICA

That evening, in front of the fireplace in the den, we talked about the options of having the baby or not.

Once the options were laid out, Rafael turned to me. "I'll support you in whatever you decide."

"In whatever *I* decide? But we need to make this decision together. What do you think we should do?" Despite the warmth of the open fire, it felt as though icy tentacles were squeezing my body, making it hard to breathe and hard to think.

"If you want to have the baby, I'll be there for you and raise the baby as mine—we'll say the baby was born early and no one has to ever know otherwise. If you prefer to end the pregnancy, I'll be there for you as well and go with you to the doctor."

"What do you think we should do, though?"

"I can't tell you what to do, Jess. It's your body. I have no right to impose my preferences on this situation." His expression was blank, and this was the coldest I'd ever known him to be.

I knew what the options were—I had read the pamphlets the doctor had given us about pregnancy choices. I didn't need him to sound like one of these information guides. I wanted him to hold me, and I needed him to tell me that everything was going to be alright.

He said it was my body and my baby, but our lives were intertwined irrevocably now that we were married. At least that is what I had thought. Maybe he didn't see things the same way as me—maybe he saw this as being my problem and so it was for me to deal with.

We resolved nothing that night, and, having talked in circles and being nowhere nearer a decision, I admitted defeat for the night and dragged my exhausted body upstairs to bed.

There I lay, desperate for sleep and its sweet oblivion, only to have it evade my grasp until the early hours of the morning.

***

Over the next few days, Rafael kept his distance from me.

He didn't even have sex with me at night and I had to pluck up enough courage to ask him to make love to me, but to my utter humiliation he declined, saying that I needed to rest for the sake of the baby.

At night, instead, we kept to our separate sides of the bed, distant from each other physically as well as emotionally.

I began to wonder if he was punishing me. I knew it was my fault for not thinking to take the morning-after pill. How could I have been so stupid? And how could I have been so unlucky to fall pregnant the first time I'd had sex?

I kept trying to talk to him, yet I couldn't get through to him that I genuinely needed his help in making this decision. He watched me closely every time he came into the same room, as if he was trying to get inside my mind to see what I was thinking—and if what I was thinking was the same as what I was telling him to his face.

He kept repeating that he was fine with whatever I chose to do. But I couldn't make a decision without him, since it was something that would affect us both for the rest of our lives.

We had stopped our daily runs each morning, Rafael saying that he didn't think it was a good idea with the pregnancy, despite the doctor clearing me for exercise.

I knew he couldn't bear looking at me now that someone else's baby was inside me.

RAFAEL

When I woke in the morning, I decided to tell Jessica to get dressed in her workout clothes. "Put on your workout clothes and I'll meet you downstairs in five minutes."

I didn't say anything more as I strode out of our bedroom and down the stairs.

I was still so angry with my father. Fury burned a trail through my body during every waking moment, although I was trying hard to stop Jess from sensing my anger. I thought that killing him would make me feel better, but even from the grave he was still able to hurt Jess.

When Jessica arrived downstairs, I opened the door and we headed outside. She started to do the warm-ups we normally did before we went running.

I shook my head. "No," I said.

Her brows knitted together as I took her small hand in mine and paced quickly toward our gym building instead.

We found Gabriel in there, dripping in sweat as he worked out.

"Maybe we should come back later," she suggested tentatively as Gabriel wiped his face with a towel and stared at us.

He prowled toward Jess, stopping right in front of her. "What did you just say?" he demanded in a harsh voice.

I clenched my fists at my sides and took a step nearer to him.

But he held his hand up to me, commanding me to stop.

Jessica cleared her throat. "I meant to say to Rafael...that we should stay and train—because this is my home now too," she squeaked.

"That's better," Gabriel gritted out. "Anyway, I'm done. It's all yours." He turned on his heel and left us.

I don't know what he'd said to her, but I was shocked that she'd actually just stood up for herself.

"Do you want us to use the treadmills today instead of running outside?" asked Jessica, frowning.

"No. I want to teach you some self-defense moves."

"Self-defense?" she said, her voice quivering.

I put my hand against the small of her back, urging her further into the gym area. "Yes. I know you're pregnant, so we won't do anything too physical, but I want to teach you some basic moves."

"For what?" Her voice was wary.

"In case you ever find yourself in a position again where you may need to defend yourself. It'll be useful for you to know a few things."

She looked at the floor and was silent for a while, before finally looking up at me. "You think it was my fault?" she whispered, emotion gleaming in her eyes.

"No." Damn. "That's not what I meant. I just meant it could be helpful. Every woman should know a few basics."

I gave her a moment, and when she had composed herself and was ready, we began. I wasn't going to allow her emotions to prevent her from learning this—I was determined that she wouldn't be so powerless in her life ever again.

I showed her a couple of basic moves and we practiced them side by side, looking at our reflections in the large mirror so that she could copy what I was doing.

I prowled in a circle around her, assessing her moves and using my hands to encourage her body into the correct sequences. "Relax your shoulders," I commanded as I met her eyes in the mirror.

She hesitantly did as I instructed.

"Good girl."

Once I was confident that she had gotten the sequencing moves down, I said, "Let's put what you've learned into practice."

"What does that mean?" she asked in alarm.

"I'm going to come at you and reach out to grab you. I want you to block my hand like I've shown you. Understood?"

She didn't reply.

"Do you understand, Jessica?" My voice was terse. This was important and she needed to get on board with this.

She gave a small nod.

I allowed her a couple of moments and then I approached her slowly, making a gesture as if to grab her.

But she didn't react. She just froze.

I stopped before my hand grabbed her, clenching my jaw. I could see my focus on her was making her nervous, but this was what she needed to be prepared for—this is how she would feel if something ever happened to her again. "Next time, you need to block my arm," I said sternly.

We resumed positions and I swiftly stalked toward her, grabbing at her with my arm.

She stumbled a few steps back, her eyes wide and her lips trembling, before tripping over herself and landing on her butt.

I held out my arm to her and, taking her hand, I hauled her back up. Her eyes were huge on her face.

"You don't have to be scared of me. I'm not going to hurt you—ever. This is just to give you a few skills. Not only that, it will help to build your confidence."

We tried once more, but Jess just stood immobilized and made no attempt to put a fight up.

I tried to bite back my frustration. "What's the matter, Jess?"

She twisted her fingers.

"Tell me."

"It's just that whatever I learn, we both know that I won't ever be able to beat a man." Her voice was quiet.

"I know that. But some of these skills could buy you some time and give you a fighting chance."

She took a sharp breath. "You think...you think I should have fought harder?" A tear rolled down her cheek.

Shit. "That's not what I meant, Jess."

Christ, this wasn't what I'd wanted.

"I want you to have some more confidence in yourself, Jess—some more self-belief."

I filled the couple of steps between us and pulled her in my arms, running my hand over her hair and back, trying to soothe her. Maybe

I was approaching this wrong? Perhaps I should've hired a woman to teach her? Or maybe it just wasn't the right time.

Whatever it was, I knew that she wasn't in the right mindset for this today—and I probably wasn't either. "I think that's enough for today," I said into her dark hair.

"Okay," she replied, her voice wobbly as she untangled herself from my arms before she rushed off back toward the house.

I wondered if I should go after her?

I had the feeling, though, that while she needed comfort, it probably wasn't from me right now.

I also realized that teaching her self-defense today was maybe as much for myself as it was for her—to ease my guilt over the rape.

I knew I could never make up to Jess what my father had done to her. I was giving Jess space, wanting her to make her own decision about the baby. I didn't want her to feel like she had to terminate the pregnancy to appease me.

All I wanted was for her to be happy, and I would be a father to the baby if that was what she wanted. She was the most important person in my life, and I would do anything for her.

So why did it feel like I'd done everything wrong? My allowing her to make up her own mind about the baby was supposed to have made me feel better. Since the day of the scan, however, I felt like everything I did was the wrong thing. I'd been trying to stop Jess from getting hurt any further—by letting her choose what happened next regarding the baby.

This whole situation was fucking messed up, I thought to myself, as I pinched the bridge of my nose and headed for a shower.

CHAPTER 27

JESSICA

That night, I was already in bed when Rafael came in.

As he undressed, I turned over to face him. "Rafael, I want to go see Juliana." I tried to make my voice firm, yet even I could hear the hesitation, fearing Rafael's reaction to my request.

He replied without the slightest pause. "You know that's not possible."

"I need to see my sister."

"Why?"

"So that I can ask for her advice on what I should do about the baby." My muscles were taut with apprehension, waiting to see if I'd be able to convince him to let me go.

"If you need advice from your family, you can speak to your mother here in L.A."

"As if she's a sane person who will give rational advice. Don't forget, she helped my father hide the rape from you—heaven forbid anything stopped my marriage into the great Santino family," I snapped.

"The answer's still no."

I sighed. "Please, Rafael, I really need to do this. I really need to talk to Juliana." Out of my siblings, Jacob was already blaming himself for not protecting me, so talking to him was out of the question—I couldn't bear for him to blame himself any more than he already was. Juliana still didn't know about the rape, and I would have to tell her everything before being able to get her advice, but she was my best option.

"You know it's out of the question. It's far too dangerous for you to go and see your sister in another city. My answer's final." The edge in his voice was unmistakable—he was mad at me. Mad about the baby, and mad about me wanting to see my sister.

Tears of frustration stung the back of my eyes. Rafael was acting like a typical Made Man, issuing his commands and expecting me to obey.

I had hoped he would eventually calm down and we could talk about this more. I felt like this had been made my problem to solve. I knew I was the one having the baby, but I thought we would figure out together what to do.

This isn't how I had imagined my pregnancy would be. I had always imagined being thrilled and excited, looking at baby clothes and booties, decorating a nursery and filling it with stuffed animals. Instead, this pregnancy was something we hardly referred to, and it certainly wasn't a source of excitement or joy.

How could it be, with the knowledge that the father of my baby was my rapist, Emanuel Santino?

How could fate be so cruel to me, to Rafael, and to this baby inside me? What sort of life would this baby have, being the product of an unwanted attack? But it wasn't the baby's fault, so how could anyone blame it or hold it responsible—but then I imagined emotions trumped rationality in circumstances like these.

I tossed and turned the whole night, unable to sleep, trying to decide what to do about the baby. Anxiety was eating me up inside. Of course Rafael wouldn't want to bring up his half-sibling as his child, but I didn't know if I could terminate this pregnancy either. There was a life inside me, a heart beating inside me.

I was lost, and instead of working toward a solution, my thoughts kept wandering further away from reality, to somewhere I could just hide my worries, my hurt and my emotions.

By morning, I was still so unsure—and desperately in need of my older sister's advice. She had always been there for me, someone to lean against and rely upon.

I threw caution to the wind and decided that if Rafael wouldn't let me go see her, I would take matters into my own hands and drive there myself. I would just tell the soldiers at the gate that I was going to my mother's house. By the time they realized I was gone, it would be too late and I would already be well on my way to Chicago.

Now that I had a plan, I quickly showered and got dressed before I could change my mind. I grabbed my car keys from the kitchen and walked into the garage.

A man was leaning against my car.

Rafael.

"Going somewhere?" he said, raising an eyebrow at me. His stance was relaxed; however, I could detect an edge under his calm words.

I looked at his muscled figure, clad in a dress shirt and dark suit for the business he needed to deal with in his day ahead. "I, uh, I thought I'd just go and see my mother."

"So early?"

I took a step backward for some reason. "You did suggest last night that I ask her for her advice."

He prowled closer to me. "And, if I recall correctly, you said she wasn't a sane person who could give you rational advice." I could feel the tension rolling off his body.

"Maybe I changed my mind."

"If you were going to see your mother, for one thing you wouldn't be going so early, and, secondly, you would not be dressed like that." He ran his eyes over my jeans and t-shirt.

"I'm not feeling so good this morning, so I thought my mother would forgive me for not dressing up in my Mafia wife uniform," I snapped, tired from my lack of sleep and nauseous with morning sickness.

"Come on, Jessica," said Rafael tersely. "You're a terrible liar."

I clamped my lips firmly shut. Perhaps it was better not to confirm or deny anything.

"I know you would have fled to Chicago today to see Juliana if I wasn't here right now, standing in your way," he growled.

"If you know how much I need to see her, why won't you let me?" I cried. "Why won't you take me there? If you're with me, you can keep me safe. I just don't understand."

Rafael stood looking down at me, but the hard look in his eyes did not diminish. "You know I can't keep you safe in a city that belongs to another organization."

"I don't need you to keep me safe."

"When will you understand that you are mine to protect now? I can't protect you if I allow you to go to Chicago."

"*Allow?* I'm not a possession you can control, nor am I a pet that you can command and expect obedience from."

"If you ever try to escape again, I won't go so easy on you."

I gaped, not believing what I was hearing from him.

"Now go inside," he barked.

I spun around on my heel, feeling tears threatening, and determined not to cry in front of him.

I knew I wasn't the wife he had expected to get. I had been impure on our wedding night and now I was carrying another's man child—his father's child.

But I couldn't give this baby up. It was innocent, and I couldn't hurt it by terminating the pregnancy.

CHAPTER 28

JESSICA

Over the next week, I knew Rafael was still angry with me.

After what had happened, Rafael took away my cell phone and handed me a replacement. "This is your new cell. It allows you to call me, Gabriel, and the guardhouse."

"So what? You're punishing me now?" I said, in a mixture of surprise and annoyance.

"No. This is just until I know I can trust you again. I can't have you hurt. I can't risk you doing something stupid and getting harmed now that we're at war with the Veneti family."

Over the days that followed, I tried to carry on as normal; however, the tension radiating from him was impossible to ignore.

I carried on with cooking dinner and doing the housework—I felt like it gave me some control by making one place clean and tidy in this messy, screwed-up life of mine. Meals were conducted in silence, and

Gabriel usually ate in the office in order to avoid the strained atmosphere between me and Rafael in the dining room.

I felt I'd been cheated. I'd always wanted a family and to be a mother, and this was how it was happening—under a dark cloud of anger and hurt. Becoming a mother had always been my dream. I thought now that Emanuel was gone forever, I would be able to move on with my life and start putting the past behind me.

But Emanuel was still haunting me from his grave, and he was still hurting me and laughing at me. And not only was he hurting me, but he was hurting Rafael, and he was hurting the life this baby would eventually lead.

I thought that my marriage to Rafael had been growing stronger, but now it was in the worst place it had ever been. And I didn't know if there was any coming back from this.

I kept berating myself. I should have started taking the contraceptive pill or at least taken the morning-after pill. What on earth had I been thinking?

***

A couple of days later, I decided to go for a walk around the grounds.

I'd dressed in white shorts and a lilac top. My shorts were feeling snug, and I knew that I would soon need to think about getting some maternity clothes.

I hadn't been out much since I'd had the baby scan and we'd received the shocking news. But today I decided to change that. I couldn't keep dwelling on all the bad things. That morning, as I had stood in the closet, I'd run my hands over all my lilac shoes and let them soothe my mind and heart before choosing the first ever ballet flats that Rafael had got for me.

I usually loved exploring the grounds and I thought that the fresh air would invigorate me. However, I felt totally lacking in energy today.

After walking for twenty minutes, I decided I'd rather return to the house. I turned to make my way back to the house and there I would go inside and rest for a bit. The thought of a lie down and perhaps a nap sounded appealing right now.

As I walked slowly back to the house, I thought about my bed and curling up in it with a hot water bottle. As I reached the house, I felt a sharp twinge in my abdomen and took a sharp intake of breath. The pain was momentary and once it passed, I continued up the front steps to the doorway, meeting Gabriel who had just exited the door on his way out.

"Hey," I croaked. I was feeling far from sociable, but I didn't want to be rude.

"Jessica?" I heard the alarm in Gabriel's voice and followed his eyes as they moved downward.

Bright red blood stained my white shorts and was spreading fast. "What's happening...?" I gasped, leaning against the wall as I felt pain rip through my body and my legs wobble.

Gabriel was already talking urgently into his phone. Seconds later, the door flew open and Rafael stood in front of us, his face horror-struck as he took in my face and shorts.

"She might be miscarrying," said Gabriel tersely. I couldn't think straight. I felt as if I might pass out.

"It's okay. I've got you, Jess. I'm taking you to the hospital right now." Rafael's voice was gentle as he scooped me up in his arms just as my legs gave way under me.

I've got you. Those were the words he'd said to me when he gave me the engagement ring and I'd wobbled in my heels.

"I can walk. The blood...your suit..." I babbled despite the pain tearing my insides and the fear assaulting my mind.

"Fuck my suit! The only thing that matters right now is you and the baby."

I wanted to insist that I could walk by myself to the car, though in all honesty I wasn't sure if I could.

My stomach was cramping badly, and I thought I was going to throw up. A sweat had broken out on my forehead and fear filled my veins.

"Get in," shouted Gabriel as we reached one of the SUVs parked out front of the house.

Rafael carefully laid me on the back seat and got in next to me while Gabriel took the driver's seat, all the time issuing commands via his cell phone and directing his soldiers to follow us in additional vehicles.

"Christ, there's too much blood." Rafael was worried, and that terrified me.

"I'm scared, Rafael," I said in a small voice, forcing the words out because I was afraid to voice the thoughts running through my mind. What if the baby didn't make it? What if this had all been my fault? Maybe the baby could feel all my stress.

"Once we get to the hospital, the doctors will know what to do," soothed Rafael. "Don't worry—just try to relax."

I could see a black SUV in front of us and I knew that there would be at least one more behind us to provide the necessary security.

Rafael was on the phone with Dr. Chiara, telling her what had happened and instructing her to meet us at the hospital.

The minutes had never moved as slowly as they did now. I willed the car to hurry up, for Gabriel to hurry up, and for my baby to hold on.

I looked down at my shorts. "There's so much blood," I said. I didn't know if it was because my shorts were a light color, but it seemed like way too much blood for the doctor to be able to do anything. *Oh please God, please save my baby*, I whispered in my head.

I was gripping Rafael's hand tight as Gabriel drove at breakneck speed to the hospital. He didn't have to worry about the cops stopping us—they all knew who he was, and they recognized the Società's vehicles. He probably got me to the hospital faster than an ambulance would have.

Rafael's eyes kept darting from my face to my stomach. It was getting hard to keep my eyes open, and even then, the only thing I could look at was all the blood.

I felt like letting my eyes close so that I could be taken into oblivion and away from the pain, but I knew I had to try to stay conscious. "Oh God, there's too much blood," I sobbed.

"Hold on, Jess, just hold on," murmured Rafael, as he smoothed my hair away from my sweaty forehead.

The car lurched as Gabriel slammed on the brakes at the entrance to the hospital and the car doors were ripped open by our soldiers before the vehicle had even stopped.

I clumsily tried to get out of the car, however Rafael swiftly lifted me up in his arms and held me tightly to his chest. "*I've got you, Jess. It's okay.*"

Each time he said those words, I felt reassurance and a warmth wash over me.

A doctor and nurse came running out with a wheelchair, but he ignored them and refused to let me go. "Where's Dr. Chiara?" he demanded.

He was quickly shown the way to her. His presence was commanding—this was a man used to telling people what he wanted and being obeyed. This was one of the few times in my life I was glad to be part of this Mafia life.

After that, everything happened through a disorientating muddle of pain stabbing at my stomach, voices talking over me, and tears blurring my eyes.

I couldn't make sense of much, but the one thing I was sure of was Rafael being at my side and holding my hand tightly, never letting me go.

"I've got you, Jess, just hold on. You and the baby just have to hold on."

I wanted to hold on for him. Not just for the baby, but also for him—for my husband, for the man I loved.

We could make things work with this baby. We just had to get through today, I thought, as everything blurred and went black.

***

Later, when I woke up, I knew the baby was no longer inside me. And I felt an overwhelming sense of loss.

Not just for the baby. But also for what had been taken from me on that day a few months ago at the clinic.

"I'm so sorry, Jess. I'm so very sorry." I looked up at Rafael and saw the anguish in his eyes.

I'd wanted us to plan a life for the three of us together. Now that decision had been taken out of my hands.

I was so numb. I could barely breathe. I gave myself over to my grief and let the tears roll down my face. And the sobs came rushing out of me, while Rafael held me in his arms, whispering to me and stroking my hair.

CHAPTER 29

JESSICA

A few days later, I was at the stables.

The grief inside me was so intense that it physically hurt. The doctor had said that I had done nothing to cause the miscarriage, but I kept wondering if I should have done something differently.

After the miscarriage, I had been avoiding Rafael as much as possible. I had lost the baby, but I couldn't yet face the hurt of losing Rafael. I knew that our marriage was over, but it was as if not talking about it meant that I could delay the inevitable.

I should have never let myself fall in love with him in the first place. A girl like me, who wasn't a virgin for her husband, didn't deserve love.

How could I have been so stupid to think that Rafael could ever really love me? Whatever I did, nothing would ever change my past. I would always be impure in Rafael's eyes. I didn't deserve to be happy with him. He got a bad deal when he married me—no longer a pure virgin, plus pregnant with another man's child.

I loved being with the horses and the stables were one of the places I liked to visit. Whenever I was feeling lonely, I could always come here and find some company amongst the animals.

I was holding out a sugar lump when a voice behind me brought me out of my thoughts. "How's my favorite horse doing today?" Gabriel had come up behind me without me hearing him.

"You shouldn't sneak up on people like that," I murmured.

"I didn't sneak up—you were miles away."

"Storm seems a bit restless today," I said in response to his earlier question.

"He probably senses it in you and it's affecting him."

"You think?" I asked, raising my eyebrows in surprise.

"Horses are very perceptive animals, and Storm is particularly sensitive."

"I wouldn't have imagined you as owning a sensitive animal."

"Just call me the Horse Whisperer," he said as he stroked Storm's muzzle.

I held out my hand to Gabriel, offering him the sugar lumps to feed the horses.

"Thanks," he replied, taking a lump from my palm to feed Storm. He looked at me carefully. "I know things aren't so good with you at the moment, but are you okay?"

"Well, apart from the usual Mob wife problems, I have no energy and my life's a mess."

Gabriel regarded me closely. "You should talk to Rafael."

"He doesn't want to talk to me."

"You should still talk to him. I've said the same to him, that he should talk to you. Nothing will ever get resolved otherwise."

I didn't reply, but in my heart of hearts, I knew he was right.

***

Rafael didn't know how to help me. But one thing he did suggest was that I see my sister.

I jumped at this, desperate to see Juliana again.

Despite our families being enemies, Rafael arranged with Juliana's husband, Marco, that we visit their home.

Rafael was extremely wary of Marco and the other Marchiano brothers, but he was willing to do this for me. And for that, I was grateful to him.

A lot of planning went into this visit, and both Rafael and Marco agreed to put their differences aside for just an afternoon so that Juliana and I could see each other.

Juliana knew about the miscarriage, although I had never told her that the father had been Emanuel—that's something I couldn't admit to her ever. I knew I shouldn't feel ashamed about what had happened, but I did, and I couldn't stop this feeling.

***

Arriving at the Marchiano mansion on the agreed afternoon, I felt a mixture of nerves and excitement.

Juliana's husband, Marco, terrified me the only time I'd met him. And after everything he'd put my sister through, my opinion of him was still the same.

As soon as I saw Juliana, I rushed into her arms and I couldn't hold my tears back. "I'm so glad to see you," I sobbed.

After hugging for what felt like an age, Juliana finally led me to the gardens, and we sat in the sunshine as we talked about everything.

"I'm so sorry about the baby, Jess." She put her hand on mine, and I could see the tears in her eyes.

"It just wasn't meant to be," I said softly.

"Is Rafael good to you?" she asked quietly. Rafael stood a little way away, as did Marco and his brother, Alessio. They were giving us some privacy, but the men were determined to keep us safe. and that meant keeping us in their sights at all times.

I nodded. "He is, but...the baby thing has been hard for both of us."

Juliana nodded as she looked at me with her bright blue eyes. "Jake seems pretty upset by it all too."

"Yeah, he's always there for me, looking out for me. He's a great brother."

"I really miss you and Jake..." Juliana's voice wobbled as she spoke. She'd never wanted to leave Chicago, and the way she'd been ripped away from us had been brutal.

I stole a glance at Marco. He was watching Rafael with narrowed eyes, and his hostility to us sent a shudder through me.

Just then, Juliana's dog came bounding over.

"Mr. Fluffy!" I exclaimed, laughing as the giant bundle of fur jumped up and put his from paws on my lap while licking my face at the same time.

"He still recognizes you," Juliana beamed.

"I've really missed him," I giggled. This was the first time I'd laughed since I'd lost the baby, and something inside me lightened a little. "Does he get on with Marco and his brothers?"

"The men like to pretend that they don't like my dog, but they all have secret soft spot for him."

At that moment, we were interrupted by the arrival of a petite girl with auburn hair.

"Jessica, this is Cate. She's, er, a friend of Alessio's."

She gave me a small smile as I said hi to her.

"I'm just making coffee," Cate said. "Would you girls like some?"

"Sure," replied Juliana. "That would be great. Thanks, Cate."

As the two of them spoke, I couldn't help my eyes running over Cate. She was wearing jeans and a tee, but cuts and bruises were visible on her arms. And even worse, I could see bruising around her neck.

When Cate caught me staring, I quickly looked away, but I couldn't help noticing her flush as her hand went self-consciously around her throat.

Once Cate had gone to the kitchen, Juliana kept her voice low as she explained. "That's the girl I told you about on the phone. Alessio's been keeping her captive here. He says she is a traitor. He even took her to the...garage block."

I paled. I knew from what Juliana and Jake had told me that the garage block was where the Marchiano brothers interrogated and tortured their enemies. *Had Alessio made those marks on her throat and arms?*

My eyes darted up to look at Alessio who was hovering nearby. His dark eyes were intense as they monitored the surroundings. He wore a fitted top, dark denims, and combat boots. He looked like someone who always liked to be in control.

"Alessio comes across as the strong, silent type," Juliana whispered. "But like Marco, he's had a troubled past and has his own demons to deal with."

When Cate came back with the coffee, I saw her shoot a look at Alessio which was a mixture of fear and wariness. She had dark circles under her eyes. I could tell that she'd been through a lot lately, and my heart really went out to her.

We quickly changed the subject. "I still can't believe you're pregnant," I said to Juliana.

"I know it must be hard for you," she said gently.

"Don't be silly," I said quickly. "I want you to be happy, Juliana. And I can see that this baby is something that you want. You really are glowing, and I'm just glad to see you well after everything that's happened. I'm so happy for you—truly, I am. And I get to be an aunt. Which means I get to send lots of presents, and you'll have to send me lots of photos too."

There was a small pause. We both knew that gifts would have to be sent rather than given in person, plus most of what I saw of Juliana's baby would be via photos. Because none of us knew how long our families would remain enemies or how long until I would see my sister again in person.

This knowledge made me want to cram as much into these three hours as I could. I got Juliana to tell me more about her new life here in Chicago, and I told her about Mother, Jake, Nate and Nancia.

"I'm no longer the youngest, not with the twins around," I smiled. "And I like being a sort of big sister to them, especially Nancia. Nancia has always wanted a sister, so she seems happy to have me here."

"I'm glad you have good people around you, Jess."

It was really difficult when it was time to say goodbye. My emotions were still all over the place, but seeing Juliana had definitely been a good thing.

RAFAEL

I could see how much Jess was hurting, but I didn't know how to help her.

One morning in the kitchen as we prepared breakfast together, I turned to her. She was still in her nightclothes, wearing a robe on top, looking listless and distracted.

"How are you doing?" I asked as I used a knife to halve strawberries. Just standing next to her, I could feel a vibe of despondency coming off her, and it made something clench around my heart.

She gave a forced smile. "How are any of us doing?"

"You know, you could talk to someone about the baby...and everything that's happened."

Jess bit her lower lip. "I can't talk about Emanuel. *Omerta* applies, surely?" Omerta was our 'code of silence', preventing us from talking to outsiders about wrongdoings committed within the organization and Mafia.

"Omerta refers to not talking to the authorities about our business matters. What was done to you was not a business matter, and anyhow, you would talk to a therapist, not to the police or authorities."

Jess hesitated before slowly turning to me, a frown marring her brow. "Rafael, I've been thinking, we should start proceedings for annulment."

I froze. "What do you mean, Jessica?" My voice was harsher than I intended.

"I can't go on with this charade, with all the secrets..."

I stared at her, not saying anything, my hand tightening around the knife I was holding.

Her words went on in a rush. "You'll be able to say that you were tricked into the marriage, believing that I was a virgin when I wasn't really one...you can claim fraud."

I raked my hand through my hair and closed my eyes for a moment.

Her voice was barely a whisper now. "I'm living a lie with you—you deserve to be happy with a real wife and a real marriage. I can't give you that. I'm sorry." I could see the huge effort it was taking her to say this to me.

"You don't have anything to be sorry for." My tone was abrupt, and I softened my voice. "Everything's my fault. You were mine once the contract was signed, and I should have protected you. I couldn't even protect you from my own father. I failed you and I'll never stop trying to make that up to you."

"It wasn't your fault, Rafael." I saw a tear slip down her cheek and all I wanted to do was hold her.

"Jess, I don't know what to say or how to make it up to you. I wanted the baby to be your decision—for you to do what you wanted, not what you thought I wanted or the Società would expect of you. I haven't been able to stop thinking about how I've handled it. I see now that we should have made the decision about the baby together; instead, I abandoned you when you needed me most. I'm a complete bastard."

I watched while more tears rolled down her cheeks.

I stepped forward and took her into my embrace. "Christ, you've been so strong through everything. I don't deserve you, Jess. You've made it through the wedding and then coped with the baby news much better than I have."

"Being strong isn't enough though, is it?" she said quietly, her voice echoing the utter defeat inside her.

"What do you mean, Jess?"

"I know you were ashamed of the baby and didn't want anything to do with it."

"Why would you think that?" I asked in genuine surprise.

"How could you be anything else? It's a baby conceived from a rape by your father."

"Jess, the baby was an innocent. I could never have been ashamed of him or her," I said softly.

"But the baby would be just like Bella—and you're ashamed of Bella and didn't want anyone knowing that she was your half-sister. You won't even have her over for dinner."

I ran my hand through my hair. "Jess, I didn't care who knew about Bella being our sister. It was Bella that didn't want us telling people. She wasn't our biggest fan at the start, and she probably still isn't. She disapproves of our criminal lifestyle and our less-than-legal dealings, not to mention being horrified when I knifed a man in front of her."

Jess thought over my words for a while. "I guess our ways might come as a bit of a shock to her if her mom didn't tell her much about us…I suppose she didn't grow up like us."

"If I really hadn't wanted people to know, I would never have said anything the day I killed Savino. But I want people to know who she is because that way she'll get the respect she deserves."

"Does she really not like you that much?" frowned Jess.

"She wasn't brought up in our world and doesn't understand the ways of our life. I've tried to explain to her that she is the same as you and me. She was born into this world by virtue of who her mother, father and stepfather are, and that's something she can never escape—which is why we have to protect her now. Once you are born into the Mafia world, it never lets you go."

"And she'll let you protect her?"

"I've told her she has to, whether she likes it or not. She wants to be able to lead a normal life, but that isn't possible anymore. At least while she works for us at Matrix and lives over the club, we can keep a close eye on her. And about not wanting anything to do with her—I would love it if she'd let us help her more, but she's independent and stubborn. She didn't like me turning up at her mother's funeral. And I had to say the nurse we hired for her mother was paid for via a church fund."

"You got a nurse for her mom?" Her eyes widened in astonishment.

"Yeah. She's our sister. I'll do whatever I can to help her and take care of her...just like I would have with the baby."

Jess nodded at me, and I knew she believed me, thank God.

"The baby would have been part of *you*. He or she would have had your sweet soul. And there is no way that I couldn't have loved him or her. Because I love every bit of you, including any child you may ever have."

I couldn't believe I had made her feel like I didn't want her to have the baby.

"Christ, I'm sorry, Jess. I've messed up everything big time." My voice was quiet. "I was angry before," I admitted, guilt churning up inside me. "My father and the baby were a constant reminder of how I didn't protect you and how I'd let you down."

"But what's happened didn't change upon your father's death. It's still part of me and will always be a part of me." She was the most serious I had ever seen her. "I'm not the girl you hoped to marry. I'm not the girl who was promised to you. I can't ever be her. I'm broken." A silent tear slipped down her cheek.

"I don't care about that," I said heatedly. "And you're not broken. *You* are the woman I fell in love with—a woman who is not only beautiful, but is also strong, kind, and capable of coping with anything."

She shook her head. "I don't feel like I'm coping. Everything is a mess, including us."

I moved closer to her. "I can help you cope. And you'll help me cope. Together we can support each other through this—it's just going to take time." I took her hand, feeling a desperate need to reassure her and to keep her here with me.

"But it's not working." She wiped away another tear. "We've tried and it's not working. Once the marriage is annulled, we can both move on," she said softly.

"I don't want to move on." My voice was firm.

"What?" Jess's brow furrowed in confusion. She didn't understand—and that was my fault. I had stopped communicating with her and stopped supporting her, and I felt remorse wash over me that I hadn't been there for her.

"I want to stay here. I want to stay in this marriage with you, Jess. This was an arranged marriage. In our world, we don't get to date our perspectives spouses. We don't get to know each other before the wedding, and we don't get to become friends first. Instead, we're expected to wed a stranger and have sex with that stranger on our first night together to fulfil the virgin confirmation tradition. Hell, most Mafia couples have sex before they've even had a real conversation with each other."

"I don't understand..." Jess murmured.

I slowly stroked her palm with the pad of my thumb. "With us, because of what happened, we did get to become friends first before anything else happened between us. Once I got to know you, I fell in love with you. And if you let me, I want us to move onto the marriage and family part when you're ready."

"You want a real marriage with me? And a family with me?"

"Yes. I'll wait as long as you need me to. You don't have to worry or be scared about that side of things." I wouldn't rush her into having sex or even another baby until she was fully okay. "I won't touch you until you're ready for that."

I needed her to know how serious I was about all of this. "I know you can never forget what my family has done to you, but I want to try and make new, happy memories together."

"But...you've been angry at me, after I couldn't decide on the termination and tried to go see Juliana."

"I was angry because it was too dangerous for you to meet with her when we're at war with rival organizations. I was angry because I love you. I was angry because you were hurting and I couldn't give you the support you needed."

"But you've supported me all through this."

I shook my head fiercely. "No, I didn't—because I didn't know how to support you."

"I guess all I needed was for you to be there with me, to make the decision together with me, to be on the same team as me." Her face was so open and honest.

"I've screwed this up so badly. I was so busy being angry at what my father did to you, at the pregnancy he had forced upon you, at the way that he was still hurting you even though he's dead. I was so angry about those things that I couldn't see that I was hurting you too, by not being there for you when you needed me."

She bit her lip as she thought about what I'd just said. "That's all I wanted—for you to be there for me."

"I'm sorry, Jess, for everything my family has done to you, but more for everything I have put you through. When we married, I was serious when I vowed to be there for you through good times and bad, and I know I've failed you in not living up to that promise. I wasn't there for you when things got bad, and I am so sorry for that."

"I need a marriage where we can talk about everything together, like we are right now. I can't do this with you if you shut me out." Her eyes were soft as she spoke.

"I'll never do that again—I swear on my honor. I mean it, Jess, because I love you." And I knew that I really did mean it. "I haven't done enough and I'm sorry for that and I will never stop trying to make that up to you. You mean too much to me. What do you say—how about we try this marriage again?"

"I want to try as well. Because I love you too Rafael."

I pulled out a box. "I got this for you a couple of days before you lost the baby, but didn't know how to give it to you." I handed her the rectangular ivory box tied with a lilac ribbon.

She slowly opened the box, and I saw her first real smile for a long time. "They're so pretty," she said, lifting out a pair of shoes. "They remind me of the very first lilac shoes you got me." They were ballet flats made from lilac suede, each with a small velvet bow on the front. "I've never really got the hang of walking in heels. I think these will suit me much better," she grinned, "although I know I'll look much less sophisticated in them than if I wear skyscraper heels."

"I got them because I wanted to show you that I love you exactly the way you are: your lilac obsession, your inability to wear heels without wobbling, your strength, and your being pregnant—irrespective of who the biological father was. I wanted to show you that we would bring up the baby together and that we'd be parents to him or her. It's too late for the baby, and I'll never stop regretting that, but I don't want it to be too late for us. Nothing else matters except loving you and having a happy family together." I took her into my arms and pulled her into my body, enjoying the feel of her body curling into mine.

"I love you too," she sighed into me. "I've missed this."

"Me too." I kissed the top of her head. "I'm looking forward to starting again with you, but we'll ease into it slowly this time around, okay?"

"Okay," she said in her gentle voice.

"There's no rush," I murmured. "We've got all the time in the world, Jess, and I'm willing to wait for however long it takes."

As she laid her head against my chest, I knew that this was going to work, and we were going to work.

And, at that thought, my heart soared.

EPILOGUE

ONE YEAR LATER

RAFAEL

Looking back at the last twelve months, I thought about how the miscarriage had hit Jess hard and how things had taken a long time to get better for both of us.

For the first couple of months, it had been difficult seeing Jess suffering each day. This was not an emotion I was used to dealing with. Normally, I caused pain and suffering to others, but I didn't stick around to see the consequences.

This was different, though. She was different. She was my life now.

After a long while, we were able to talk about things and started to process everything that had happened. The baby just wasn't meant to be, and slowly we had come to terms with that.

After the miscarriage, Jess decided to go for therapy—to talk about the attack and the loss of the baby. And it helped not only her, but me as well, since some sessions we went to as a couple.

I had never imagined that I, a Made Man, would be sitting in a therapist's office talking about my feelings, but I would do anything for this woman and anything for our marriage.

People always said emotions were a weakness in our line of work and that it was better not to feel; however, therapy taught me that it was more of a weakness to keep your feelings suppressed. Seeing how much talking through things helped Jess made me want to talk about my own feelings too so that I could come to terms with everything as well.

I had felt so much anger after what my father had done. And I, too, felt an immense loss after the miscarriage. The baby had been part of Jess. And, before the miscarriage, I had started to think of it as *my* baby—as *our* baby.

Through the therapy and by talking to each other and processing our thoughts, we began to see that perhaps the miscarriage was fate's way of telling us that the baby hadn't been meant to be. That was the only way we could make sense of what had happened.

I told Jess that she could have all the time she needed before we started trying for a baby again. She really wanted a baby, though, and I wanted to be able to give that to her.

***

Around a year after the miscarriage, we were out one morning for our run. Jess had been more relaxed lately and had also gone back to doing yoga again.

I hadn't been able to resist taking Jess up against the side of the stables. She was just as willing whether it was her ovulating window or not. I could never get enough of her—of the taste of her mouth or the touch of the skin.

Afterward, just as she finished pulling her clothes back into place, she clutched one hand to her stomach and the other to her mouth before dashing a few feet away and violently throwing up onto the ground.

I held her hair back as she emptied her stomach before helping her up.

"I'm sorry," she gasped. "I don't know what happened there. I just suddenly felt really unwell."

"I hope that's not an indication of how bad my lovemaking skills are."

She didn't say anything for a moment. "Well, it wasn't last time..."

"Huh?"

"The last time I was sick during a run, it wasn't because of having bad sex."

It took a few seconds for the meaning of her words to sink in. "No, it wasn't, was it?" I grinned, catching on to her meaning. The last time she had thrown up during our jog, she had found out she was pregnant.

She smiled hesitantly at me. "Come on," I said, putting my hand against the small of her back. "Let's get you home and put that stash of pregnancy tests in our bathroom to good use."

Back at the house, while we waited for the test to do its thing, I thought about how we were in a much better place now than before—how much stronger we were as a couple and how ready we were to be parents. I prayed fate would be kind to Jess this time around. She was desperate to be a mom, and I knew she would make a great one.

I heard a sniff, distracting me from my thoughts, and I looked across to Jess to see a tear rolling down her cheek before she smiled. I looked down at the test in her hand and saw that it was positive.

"You're going to be a mom," I said to her as she broke down in tears and I hugged her to me. I smiled in relief as I rested my hand on her belly, thinking of the new life that was inside her.

This was going to be a new start for us both. We had come full circle and we were ready to have this baby together. "Things will work out this time, Jess—I have a good feeling about it."

"Me too," she smiled.

If positive thinking counted for anything, I knew that this pregnancy was going to be surrounded by it. "I can't wait to start this new chapter of our lives together, Jess. You're the love of my life and I can't wait for us to have a family together."

"I can't wait either," she said, reaching up with her arms and kissing me.

***

After an appointment with Dr. Chiara to confirm the pregnancy, the next appointment was at the twelve-week mark for the initial scan.

"How's the morning sickness this time around, Jessica?"

"It wasn't so good during the first month, but it seems to have settled down since then."

"I'm glad to hear that. Does it mean that you have more energy?"

"Yes, I definitely have more energy. This is what I hoped being pregnant would be like. I've been able to keep up with my running and yoga, and both help to keep me in a positive frame of mind."

Jessica was certainly glowing, and that glow intensified even more when we saw the scan of our baby for the first time. Dr. Chiara printed out photos and I couldn't stop looking at them even after we had left the appointment.

After the scan, Jessica convinced me to go shopping with her. "Any excuse to shop," I said, rolling my eyes.

"We'll be doing a lot of shopping now for the baby, so you better get used to it," she said firmly. "And the lilac flat pumps you got me are a godsend now that I'm pregnant." She looked down at her shoes and smiled. "I can't see myself ever going back to heels, even once this pregnancy is over."

I allowed myself to be dragged into a baby boutique. Whereas normally I would head for the couches designated for the bored husbands to sit upon, today I wanted to go around the store with Jessica in her joy—because it was our joy. It was our child.

And all I wanted was for her to be happy.

She picked up a pair of white booties with a little bear's face and ears on each foot. "These are adorable," she declared.

"But completely useless. They'll stay on the baby's feet for no more than two minutes before they come off with all the wriggling and kicking babies do. They'll be no use in keeping the baby's toes warm."

"They're not to keep the baby's toes warm." Jess looked me in the eye. "They're to make the baby look cute."

I knew I wasn't going to win this argument. "Let's add them to the pile of purchases," I conceded. "What about this?" I asked, pulling a stuffed fluffy lion down from the shelf.

"I think a lion isn't really what you get for a newborn baby. Normally they like animals like a stuffed rabbit or a teddy bear."

"Maybe we could have jungle themed nursery?" I suggested.

"I was planning on something more relaxing, with soft, neutral tones, if you like that idea too?"

"We've got plenty of time to figure it all out—nurseries, toys and everything else. And it's all things I want to do with you. We'll do it all together," I grinned at her.

JESSICA

A couple of weeks later, I thought to myself that I could get used to all the spoiling I was getting now that I was pregnant.

I was sitting on the chair in front of the vanity in the bathroom, watching Rafael run a bath for me in the soaker tub. As I sat back in my robe, I watched the steam billow as the water rushed into the tub, mixing with the scented bath oils he had added, leading to lovely clouds of scent rising into the air.

I inhaled the smell of orange blossom and could already feel the tension easing from my muscles. Not that I had much to feel tense about these days.

It was as if Rafael and I were having our honeymoon. He was ecstatic about the coming baby, as was I, and he wanted to pamper me as much as possible. He was determined this pregnancy would turn out alright and that there would be no hiccups along the way.

Thinking back over the last year, I knew how lucky I was to have a man like Rafael as my husband. It had floored me when he'd suggested that he come to some of the therapy sessions with me. But he insisted that he wanted to do it for me, for us, and for our future together.

Once the tub was full, he took my hand and gently pulled me up to my feet. "Let's get this off you," he said, his hands slipping the robe from my shoulders.

His eyes traveled over my body as his fingertips skimmed my arms.

"Christ, Jess, I love your body when you're pregnant—all the soft curves and dips." His hands ran over my full breasts before reaching my belly and lingering over the small bump of our baby.

He led me to the tub and helped me in, only letting go of my hand once I had safely sat down in the water. He was probably being over-cautious, though I couldn't blame him given what had happened last time. I was being as careful as possible as well, although some sort of inner peace within me told me that everything was going to be alright this time around.

I felt so much calmer this time and there was no stress hanging over my head. I wanted to completely enjoy this pregnancy and for it to be an entirely different experience. Although nothing would make me ever forget the other baby and I prayed for it every day, this time giving me an opportunity to reflect on my emotions.

As I sank back into the water, I watched Rafael walk toward the door. "Aren't you going to join me in the tub?" The bath was definitely big enough for us both and we had come to enjoy soaking in it together. It was a time when he would lie back and relax, and we could enjoy each other's company and make small talk about our day and the baby. We talked about all sorts of baby things, from names to my birthing plan and even our wishes for our child when he or she grew up.

Perhaps it was obsessive talking so much about the baby, but it made me happy and helped me relax.

"I'll be back in a minute," replied Rafael. "I'm just going to get something." I rested my head on the edge of the tub, reveling in the soothing water, which was blissfully hot, just as I liked.

A couple of minutes later, Rafael returned with two glasses of iced water and a bowl of strawberries. "Just in case you get hungry or thirsty." He grinned and I laughed.

"You know me too well. I'm always hungry at the moment." As the heat of the water seeped into my body, I sipped at the coolness of the cold water. Rafael held a succulent red strawberry to my lips, and I took a bite while looking into his eyes.

"This is my idea of heaven," I sighed, as I let the juicy flavor of the fruit explode over my tongue. "Now all I need is for you to get those clothes off and get in the tub with me," I said while raising an eyebrow.

I watched while he undressed in front of me. He had worked from home today and was wearing slim jeans and a fitted shirt. He peeled them from his body and as he pulled down his boxer briefs, I saw his cock spring free and felt my insides stir.

He stepped into the tub and sat down behind me, pulling me back between his thighs and letting my head relax against his chest. "That's better," he murmured. "There's nowhere I'd rather be than with you," he said as he kissed the top of my head.

***

Tonight, Bella was coming over to dinner. I understood now why Rafael didn't want her coming to the Monday Post-Mortem—because that was when the boys talked business—but she normally came over another night of the week. To be honest, it was probably for the best that she wasn't there for the post-mortem, since that might put her off the family even more.

As it was, relations between her and the family were getting a little less strained. We hoped that, in time, she would accept us as her family. The Santinos were happy to accept her; the guys, in particular, wanted to keep her safe. I sensed that she still wasn't entirely comfortable with the criminal element of our world, but that was part and parcel of who we were and wasn't ever going to change.

Nate and Nancia would be at the dinner tonight as well. The war between the Società and the Venetis had escalated after Gabriel told them that we wouldn't honor Nancia's engagement contract. The brothers were determined to keep Nancia safe, and Nate had become much more focused on his training lately.

An unusual turn of events had been the disappearance of Leoluca Veneti approximately six months after the broken engagement. If the Venetis knew where he was, they were keeping that information very close to their chests. It unnerved Rafael and his brothers that they did not know the exact location of Leoluca, nor his intentions toward their sister.

Over the last year, Nancia had become quieter. The knowledge that her father had raped both Bella's mom and me was a shock to her, as was the situation with the engagement contract. We were all keeping an eye on her, especially Nate. She was safe for now, and we would never allow the Venetis to have her.

***

A few days later, Rafael and I were out on our morning run. I could feel his gaze on me.

I looked over my shoulder to see his eyes traveling up my legs. "Are you checking out my ass again?" I giggled.

"Why else would I be behind you on a run?" he quipped, raising a sandy-blond eyebrow at me.

I tried to swat him, but he caught my arm and spun me around, pushing me back against a tree. "Hey, I thought we're supposed to be working out?" I protested.

"You're too hard to resist." He took my mouth with his, kissing me passionately and running his hand up my thigh.

I thought the lovemaking while we were trying to conceive was amazing, but it just kept on getting better throughout the pregnancy. I didn't know if it had to do with all the pregnancy hormones, but Rafael made me feel so desired and wanted.

"You're distracting me," I murmured breathlessly.

"That's the idea." I felt his hands move to my sports bra and he lifted up my top, exposing my breasts, before dipping his head to capture my nipple in his mouth.

"Someone might see," I said as I felt flutters through my belly.

"There's no one around."

I watched the beads of sweat dripping down his muscular neck, disappearing into the neck of his white t-shirt, which clung tightly to his torso. I rested my hands against his strong arms, letting my fingers feel his muscles flex as he moved. His body screamed perfection in every way.

He lifted me up, wrapping my legs around his waist and making me breathless with his kisses. "I want you, Jessica," he groaned as he carried me to the nearby stables.

"What are you doing?" I gasped.

He put me down and catching my breath, I watched while he unfolded a clean blanket and threw it over the hay. He grabbed me and sank down to the ground, pulling me onto him.

"In the stables?" I laughed incredulously.

"I can't wait to get back to the house," he grinned. "I have to have you now." He flipped me over onto my back and pulled his t-shirt over his head in one swift movement before kicking off his shorts and moving on to undressing me.

"Gabriel will kill us if he finds out," I laughed. "He'll say we traumatized his horses."

"Gabriel can go to hell. Now stop talking and kiss me." His whole body glistened with sweat, and I could smell his scent mingled with that of raw, clean sweat. I could never get enough of his smell or enough of him.

"Roll onto your back," I whispered. And as he did, I straddled his bare chest, enjoying the feel of him under my body and grinding my pussy against his rock-hard cock.

He reached for my hips, trying to lift me onto his shaft to get what he wanted.

"Not yet," I said, wriggling free of his hands. I reached for his shaft, running my hands firmly up and down it before taking him in my mouth.

"Christ, that feels so good. Don't stop."

Rafael had pleasured me with his mouth a few times and I wanted to do the same for him. At first, I hadn't known exactly what I should do, and he had to show me. Now when I submitted like this to him, he always said it was so hot and he loved it.

I moved my lips up and down his length before swirling my tongue around the tip and sucking hard on it while I stroked his balls with my free hand.

I positioned myself over him and let him finally guide my hips as I lowered myself onto him, steadying myself by leaning my hands on his ripped abdomen.

"Fuck, Jess, you're going to make me come," he growled as I ground my hips against him, taking him as deeply as I could.

When he could no longer hold back, he bucked his hips and lifted me off him, flipping me onto the blanket on my stomach. I was underneath him now and he moved one of my legs to give him better access before penetrating me from behind, pushing me into the ground with his fierce thrusts.

I cried out with each thrust while at the same time he ran his fingers up and down my spine, kissing the back of my neck and sending shivers throughout my whole body.

"Oh God, I love taking you from behind, Jess. Your ass is perfect." His voice was labored. "I love watching my cock disappear into your pussy, and each time I withdraw, there is even more of your juices coating my dick."

I found the thought of someone walking in on us equally put me on edge and turned me on. Sex with him was never boring and I had never imagined I would enjoy it this much, not after everything that had happened.

Soon his thrusts were coming even harder and bringing me closer to orgasm. And when I couldn't hold out any longer against his harsh thrusts, I cried out and tumbled over the edge. And he finally gave himself over to his climax, continuing to thrust into me as my muscles contracted around him, wringing every last drop of cum out of his cock.

Afterward, he draped his chest over my back, his sweat mingling with mine, kissing my neck and cheek. "Christ, Jess, you're amazing...You never cease to amaze me."

After a quick snuggle as we regained our breath, we got dressed and finished our run and once back at home, he took me again against the shower wall.

SEVEN MONTHS LATER

RAFAEL

"One more push, Jessica! The baby's nearly here," urged Dr. Chiara.

Jessica was exhausted and overwhelmed. She'd been in labor for hours and hours now. My crushed hand could attest to that, but it was the least I could do for her while she went through this to give us a baby.

"I don't know if I can. I'm so tired..."

"I've got you," I said to Jess. "Just squeeze my hand however hard you want, and we'll do it together."

"On three, Jessica," said the doctor.

And then she counted, and Jess pushed with all her might.

And we were rewarded by the sound of a loud cry, making my heart leap with joy. "You've got a beautiful baby boy, Mr. and Mrs. Santino," announced the doctor.

Jessica collapsed back against her pillows. "You did it, Jess, you did it!" I exclaimed, kissing her on her mouth.

"No, we did it," she whispered with a tired smile of relief on her face. "I couldn't have done it without you."

The doctor settled the baby in Jess's arms, and I held them both against me. I was so used to seeing the end of life. This was the first time I was seeing the beginning of life—and the feeling was indescribable.

***

Later, once Jess was showered and rested, I brought out a gift for the baby. For a few moments, I just let my gaze rest on my beautiful wife, who was tucked up in bed, cradling our baby son in her arms.

"I've got a present for Nicholas," I said, holding out the toy I had bought.

"It's the stuffed lion," giggled Jess, recognizing the fluffy lion toy we had seen the first time we went shopping for baby things.

"Yes. I hope you don't mind. I went back to the baby boutique and bought it."

"He is really cute," admitted Jess.

"Yes, it suits our son because he's going to be as brave as a lion."

"Of course he will be with you as his dad," replied Jess.

"No," I disagreed. "He'll be brave because he's got you as his mommy."

Thanks so much for reading. See here for a free **BONUS EPILOGUE** if you are already missing Rafael and Jessica: https://BookHip.com/BZTRWTQ

Continue reading for a sneak peek of the next book in the Marchiano Mafia Series: **MAFIA AND TAKEN (Alessio Marchiano's story)...**

SNEAKPEEK

MAFIA AND TAKEN
A DARK ROMANCE
(MARCHIANO MAFIA SERIES)

BLURB

His obsession. Her ruin...

Cate: When a beautiful stranger rescues me from the Bratva, I think he's my savior.
Little do I know that he will turn out to be the devil in disguise.
My enigmatic rescuer is cruel yet tender.
Demanding yet gentle.

And this ruthless man wants my secrets…
But then I find out the terrifying truth…that he also wants me.

Alessio: As a Mafia Underboss, my first loyalty is to my family.
So, why do I find myself so conflicted by this daughter of a traitor?
Punishing her for her father's sins, our lives become intertwined.
And I place her in a gilded cage where she'll be mine forever.
In a different life, we could have been happy together.
But this is the Mafia life….and here dreams don't come true…

CHAPTER 1

Santa Adelina, Madre di Dio, prega per noi peccatori, adesso e nell'ora della nostra morte.
Holy Mary, Mother of God, pray for us sinners now and at the hour of our death.
— the words every Made Man recites upon a death.

CATE

2.00 a.m.

I woke abruptly to loud voices coming from downstairs.

Squinting into the darkness, I checked the clock and saw that it was the early hours of the morning.

My father was a Captain in the Fratellanza Mafia. He must be talking to some of his men. For some reason, the voices made a shudder run through me. They sounded angry with him.

I reached for my robe. It was thin, but it would cover up my nightgown.

This house always made me feel uneasy now. But the loud voices were making me even more tense.

I silently tiptoed down the stairs.

Creeping to the drawing room, I caught sight of my father surrounded by several men dressed all in black with their weapons drawn.

My heart started to race.

They weren't our men—they weren't Fratellanza.

They were the enemy.

How had they gotten past the soldiers at the gate?

If these men were in our home, that must mean that our soldiers were dead.

My father was pleading with the intruders. "Please, Dmitri, it wasn't anything to do with me, I swear!"

The man he was talking to raised his gun.

I cried out as panic overwhelmed me.

The man spun around and saw me.

And seeing the look on his face, I didn't think—I just ran.

I had a petite frame and ran to keep fit, so I was quick on my feet. I raced toward the front door.

But another man dressed in black was positioned there.

I spun on my heel and made for the opposite direction.

There was a bathroom near the top of the stairs. It had a lock on it. I only had to get that far…

I grabbed the wooden handrail and leaped onto the first step.

The man with the gun was chasing me.

I stumbled on the stairs. My hands propelled my body back up.

I could hear the man's heavy breaths right behind me.

I had gone up and down these stairs so many times during my childhood but my ascent up them had never felt so difficult.

I was panting hard as the top step came into my line of sight.

Only three more steps to go...two more steps...

Then my foot touched the top step.

Reaching the landing I spun back on myself and bolted for the bathroom, whirling around and slamming the door shut.

The door bounced off a hard body...

And in slow motion I saw his face as he came toward me.

With each stride he took, I scrambled a step backward.

Until my back thumped into the bathroom wall and there was nowhere left for me to go.

"Cate Russo..." he said in a deep, foreboding voice. "You're even more beautiful than I imagined..."

The slight trace of an accent in his voice made a shudder run through my body. He was Russian—which must mean that he was Bratva. My father had called him Dmitri. This could only be Dmitri Petrov, head of the Chicago Bratva.

My breaths were coming in heavy gulps as needles of terror pierced my skin.

I tried to bolt past him.

But his arm caught my body and his other hand yanked my head back with a violent tug at my hair.

I cried out as pain ripped through my scalp and neck.

He held my head back at an awkward angle and forced me to look at him—into eyes which were dark and menacing.

I saw his hand moving toward me from the corner of my eye.

"Oh Cate, how I've been looking forward to meeting you," he smirked.

I opened my mouth to scream.

But he forced a damp cloth against my mouth.

I struggled against his hand smothering me, fighting the sickly chemical smell that was threatening to overwhelm me.

But it was no good.

The chemical was taking over the air I was inhaling, slowly stealing me away from my body, and making me fall into a deep black hole of unconsciousness...

***

6 Hours Earlier

"Caterina, it's time you were married," my father said, in his usual commanding tone. "You're twenty-one years old now, and people are starting to talk."

I clenched my fingers tightly around my cutlery. "Father, I don't want to marry anyone yet, especially not a Made Man."

He was the only person who called me 'Caterina'. Everyone else in my life called me 'Cate'.

We were eating dinner at my father's house.

How I hated these weekly dinners. They were nothing like the family dinners we had when I'd been younger—when my mom and brother had still been alive...

My father, Ovidio Russo, carried on speaking, his forehead creased in annoyance. "It's not a matter of what you want, Caterina. You know that in our world you're expected to marry to further the strategic bonds of your family—and just as importantly, to provide heirs for the Fratellanza."

So, there we had it. I was expected to spread my legs to carry on the distinguished line of killers in the Fratellanza.

"Father, you know how I feel about our world and what goes on in it—"

"You've made your feelings quite clear." He interrupted me in a harsh tone. "Which is why I've allowed you to have a job and live in your own apartment since you turned eighteen. Most men in our organization wouldn't permit those freedoms to their daughter."

Although it was unusual that my father permitted me to live in my own apartment, his soldiers still kept watch over me. They guarded me closely every day, even when I went to work as a teacher's assistant in kindergarten.

My father pierced me with his gaze. "Now it's time for you to do your duty."

Duty—it was used as an excuse for everything in our world. For business, for crimes, for murders. Anything could be justified in the Mafia by declaring it to be a duty.

"I've been approached by another Captain. He needs a bride. You would make an excellent match. I've told him that you are obedient and will do whatever he needs."

I felt like shouting that I wouldn't do it, but my mom had brought me up to be polite at all times. Even though she was gone now, I didn't want to let her down, so I answered as calmly as I could. "Father, I'm not ready to marry anyone just yet."

And when I did marry, I definitely wouldn't be marrying someone from the Mafia world—I'd seen firsthand how it could only lead to tragedy and heartbreak.

"Caterina, you should be married by now—or at the very least, engaged. You know that people will be talking."

"They are just a bunch of gossips," I blurted out. "All they do is talk about the nearly-weds and the newly-deads. The women in the Fratellanza like nothing more than to speculate and spread rumors." I couldn't help bitterness seeping into my words. "They haven't got anything better to do."

"Your mom was married long before your age. She was married to me by the time she was seventeen."

That sounded scarily young to me. "Father, I want to choose my own husband when the time comes, not be told who I'm to marry."

I tried to shut out my father's ongoing lecture as my mind wandered.

Every Saturday, I was required to attend dinner with my father. My grandmother, Nonna, was normally here, but this week she was visiting her sister.

I was missing not having Nonna here tonight to fill in the awkward silences and to act as a buffer between my father and me. Without her presence, he was hounding me even more than usual.

But coming here meant that my father left me alone for the remainder of the week. I just had to get through this meal without having an argument with him.

I looked down at my outfit. I was wearing a shift dress and heels. I wore my auburn hair loose over my shoulders and had applied some light makeup—just some eyeshadow, mascara around my hazel green eyes and some pale lip gloss.

"As Nonna isn't here," I said carefully, "I was thinking I wouldn't stay the night like I normally do and skip church in the morning."

"Nonsense! You will stay the night, and I will go to church with you tomorrow."

I suppressed my sigh. What was the point of my father going to church? It would take him at least a decade to confess all his sins.

After we finished our meal, I excused myself, saying that I was tired and wanted to go to bed.

My father went into the drawing room, but I always avoided that room as much as possible—because on the mantelpiece were my mom's and brother's ashes.

Their ashes had been there since I'd been fourteen years old.

As my gaze caught the urn, the all-too-familiar lump wedged in my throat as memories of my mom and brother came flooding back to me.

My mother had always wanted to be cremated so that her ashes could be scattered back in her homeland. My father wouldn't allow me to do this by myself, and he'd never gotten around to scheduling time for us to make the trip to Italy together—as always, work was his sole priority and came before everything else for him.

I slowly climbed the stairs to my childhood bedroom.

It was still exactly the same. Father hadn't changed it after I moved out three years ago.

I took a long, hot shower and pulled on a strappy satin nightgown that fell just above my knees.

Then I climbed into my childhood bed and pulled the covers up to my chin, but as always, it took ages to fall asleep...

This house no longer felt like my home.

It hadn't felt like my home since I'd been fourteen years old.

But I blocked all those memories from my mind. I couldn't go there tonight...

Instead, I watched the stars outside my bedroom window, seeking comfort from their light in the darkness, and eventually I fell asleep...

CHAPTER 2

CATE

4.00 a.m.

I tried to open my eyes.

But my eyelids were so heavy. My head was pounding, and my mouth felt dry.

I could feel movement around me, as if we were in a moving car, perhaps. I didn't know what was going on, but my head was hammering so much that it hurt to even think.

I must be dreaming, I thought, giving in and letting the drowsiness take over.

But then I heard that voice again.

It was the voice with the accent—the man my father had called Dmitri. Dmitri Petrov—the most feared Russian in Chicago.

I forced my eyes open.

Panic engulfed me as I remembered what happened—the angry men who broke into our home, chased me, and drugged me.

I tried to say something, but only a low moan would come out.

The car stopped, and a blast of cold night air rushed in as the doors were ripped open.

Dmitri hauled me out of the car and dragged me towards a warehouse on a derelict industrial estate. Another man accompanied my struggling father. I saw that his mouth was gagged and his hands were zip-tied behind his back.

Entering the warehouse, Dmitri tugged me along as he crossed the building.

But I stumbled as I struggled to keep up with him.

He reached down, grabbed my arm, and hauled me to my feet before continuing toward his destination.

He opened another door and led me down a set of stone steps into a basement. The smell of damp stung my nostrils and the iciness in the air made a shiver skate down my spine.

"W-where are you taking me?"

"You'll see…"

"What do you want with me?" I pleaded.

He pushed me up against a wall, the harsh chill of the brick seeping through my thin nightclothes.

"What do I want from you?" He gave a cruel laugh. "Oh, the things I want to do to you… What do you think you could do to please me, to make me go easy on you?"

I shuddered.

He ran the back of his fingers across my cheek. "I could torture you… But what I really want is to see you on your knees in front of me with my cock stuffed in your mouth, begging me to spare you…"

Panic penetrated my entire body as I felt the blood drain from my face.

"Have you ever sucked cock?" he smirked. "Oh, angelic Cate, I know you haven't—which will make it all the sweeter when you suck mine. After all, the Fratellanza keep all their daughters as pure virgins until their wedding day, to make it all the more satisfying to finally break them in, don't they?"

Terror balled in my throat and I felt a tear betray me and slide down my face.

"Will your pussy get wet when your tongue wraps around my cock?" His harsh laugh echoed in the emptiness of the building. "I can't wait to find out when I test out just how tight your virgin cunt is."

He seized my arm and I couldn't stop the scream from leaving my mouth.

He shoved me onto a hard chair. I struggled but I was no match for his strength as he bound me to the chair with my arms tied behind me and my feet tied to the front chair legs.

"I like seeing you all tied up and with your thighs spread. No need to gag you though—there's no one to hear you. And I want to be able to hear all your screams when I fuck you hard…"

I looked up and saw my father being dragged down the same steps and taken off into a different room further along. He was still fighting, trying to get out of his restraints.

I could see the fear in his eyes. Not much frightened him—he was a Made Man and was used to violence and death. But this was different. I didn't know what the Bratva wanted with us, but I knew they wanted to hurt us.

Dmitri walked away to the room my father was taken into.

The coarse rope was cutting into my wrists and ankles. My head was pounding, probably due to the drug they'd used on me. And I was so tired, but I forced my eyelids to stay open—I needed to work out a way to escape.

My thoughts raced. How could I get away from these men?

Whatever way my mind turned, I could see no way out. I was powerless in this situation but I couldn't just give in.

I had to think of a way to get out of here…

But as these thoughts churned through my mind again and again, a combination of my utter exhaustion and the after effects of the harsh sedative meant that I couldn't prevent my eyelids from falling closed…

CHAPTER 3

ALESSIO

I faced my brother, Marco Marchiano, in the kitchen of our shared mansion.

"Ovidio Russo's men have alerted me that he didn't show up for a meeting this morning and the soldiers at his home weren't answering their cellphones. They checked his house. The two guards there were shot dead."

"What happened?" Marco growled.

Marco was twenty-seven years old and Capo of the Fratellanza. I was a year younger than him, and I was his Consigliere.

"They checked the security footage from the house and grounds," I replied. "It was the Russians. Dmitri Petrov was there."

"Why the hell would they want Ovidio?"

"Well, I'm thinking that both us and the Russians have been having problems with bad drugs over the last few months. It's strange for us both to have the same problem, at the same time, given that we have completely different drug suppliers."

Someone had mixed some shit into our drugs, and the resulting impure product had caused numerous deaths, meaning that we now had the FBI sniffing around us.

"Go on," said Marco.

"Ovidio oversees our drug shipments when they arrive, so he has access to all our drugs. Now it appears that he is also involved with the Russians in some way, otherwise why would they take him? So, it seems that Ovidio is the common denominator in this whole story. The Russians have recently started having the same problem of bad drugs in their supply chain, causing lots of deaths too among the drugs they sell."

Marco understood now and summed up my theory. "Goddamnit, if he's been diluting our drugs with some other shit, that would increase the overall weight of the drugs. Then he could sell the extra weight to the Russians, making himself a tidy profit on the side."

I nodded. "He might have gotten away with it if the drugs hadn't started causing so many deaths, alerting the Russians and us to the fact that there is a problem with the chemical makeup of the drugs."

Marco grimaced. "It seems like he got greedy." He shook his head. "Traitors always eventually get tripped up by their fucking greed."

"What are bad drugs?" asked our younger sister, Debi, who had come into the kitchen.

"Nothing for you to worry about, shortcake," I said gently.

We always shielded our fourteen-year-old sister from the details of our business. Of course, she knew what we did, but I would protect her from the more sordid aspects for as long as I could. "Why don't you take the dog out for his walk?"

"Okay, Alessio. Come on, Mr. Fluffy, do you want to go for walkies?"

The dog didn't need to be asked twice, and he started barking excitedly, bounding toward the door to the garden.

I waited for Debi to go outside before carrying on. "We need to get Ovidio back, find out exactly what he's been up to, who else is involved, and then deal with him ourselves. Plus, the security footage also shows that his daughter was taken too. Ovidio's men told me that she's called Caterina."

"Why on earth did they take the daughter? The Bratva don't usually target the families."

"The house CCTV shows Dmitri Petrov asking Ovidio where the money is. Then Dmitri says something about the daughter's bank account."

"Looks like we need to talk to the girl as well," Marco gritted out. "The whole family might be involved in this fucking shitshow."

"I'll get on it right away."

I went to the office to start work on tracking down Ovidio and his daughter.

My blood was boiling like a blazing inferno—we expected absolute loyalty from our men, and nothing else was acceptable. The whole Fratellanza was built on this.

For a Captain to betray us was shocking. But even worse, it made me wonder how many other traitors were lurking among my men.

The adrenaline started to course through my veins as I thought about the punishments we would dish out and about the violent ends they would meet.

For her sake, I hoped the daughter wasn't involved in any betrayal.

Because even if she was a girl, the Fratellanza treated all traitors the same...

CATE

The next time I woke, it was to the sound of a deep scream in the distance.

I opened my eyes and tried to detect where the sound had come from.

Then I heard it again. It was my father.

Terror crawled over every inch of me–they were torturing him.

But why? I tried to move, but I was firmly bound to the chair. I wasn't sure how long I'd been here, but my arms were aching from being tied behind me.

Then I saw Dmitri prowl toward me.

I tried to shrink back against my chair.

Perhaps I should try to distract him from whatever he had in mind for me. "May I use the bathroom, please?" I wasn't sure why I was being so polite to him, but it was my usual manner and I didn't want him to refuse.

He took out his knife and came nearer, his hooded gaze fixed on me.

The look in his eyes made a violent tremor run through my body.

Slowly cutting the ropes open, I gasped as his hand roughly gripped my arm and he dragged me forward and up the stairs.

But I suddenly jerked to a stop as I heard loud bangs.

Gunshots.

Dmitri ran up the remaining steps to the ground floor, shouting over his shoulder, "Stay here!"

The screaming in the next room had stopped.

The Russians were distracted by the gunshots. This might be my only chance to escape.

I ran up the stairs and got to the top. The door burst open and one of the Russians appeared.

But this was my chance now. I dodged past him.

He grabbed me but I pushed his arm away.

Losing my footing, I felt myself falling back. I tried to grab the handrail. It was just out of my reach. There was nothing for me to hold on to.

And I felt myself falling down the hard concrete stairs.

Tumbling down the steps, each was another harsh blow to my body, sending sharp pains searing through me.

But I didn't care about the pain. All I could think was that my chance to escape was slipping through my fingers.

And that was my last thought before my head hit the hard ground. There was a moment of intense pain, and then everything went black...

ALESSIO

We had tracked down the Russians to this warehouse through a combination of hacking into the Russians' cellphones and gaining illegal access to street camera footage. My youngest brother, Danio, was a computer genius and could get us access to all sorts of things.

Marco and I had come to the warehouse with our soldiers.

The Bratva were a fierce opponent, but we had the element of surprise...

After shooting past the Russian soldiers on the ground floor, we could find no sign of Ovidio or his daughter.

I turned to our men. "Split into two. Half search the top floor. The rest of you search the basement level."

Marco went with the soldiers to the top floor while I headed to the basement level.

I held my weapon close to my body as I made my way down the steps, checking my surroundings for any more of the enemy.

My gaze immediately caught sight of a still figure lying at the foot of the stairs.

It was Ovidio's daughter—the girl that was likely involved with him in his betrayal.

I heard noises coming from elsewhere in the basement. I signaled to my soldiers to carry on toward the sound while I stayed to check the girl.

She was lying on her back with her head turned to one side, her hair covering her face.

I knelt down beside her and slowly smoothed her auburn hair back from her forehead.

I could see the rise and fall of her chest—she was still alive.

The thin nightgown and robe on her body were torn, and her skin was icy to my touch. I checked her over for broken bones. There were no obvious breaks as I ran my hands over the soft contours of her body.

I heard a low moan. And as her body stirred, her torn nightgown fell open—exposing her full breasts and her nipples that had hardened in the cold, dank atmosphere of the basement.

Her eyes fluttered open, revealing exquisite hazel eyes that were an alluring combination of green and amber.

When she saw me, her eyes widened with panic. "D-don't touch me," she cried, trying to push my hands away. She forced the words out, even in her weak state.

"It's okay, we've got you now," I said in a low voice.

And I watched as the frown on her forehead smoothed out in relief.

She thought I was her savior.

I saw one of our soldiers heading back toward me. I didn't want anyone looking at her in her semi-naked state, so I took off my leather jacket and quickly laid it over the girl.

The soldier gave me an update. "Boss, Dmitri Petrov and a couple of his men have gotten away, but we have the remaining Russians rounded up. Ovidio is still alive. He's been tortured and is in bad shape. Two of our men have also been injured and need immediate medical attention."

I nodded at him, and then looked down at the girl, but she had drifted back into unconsciousness.

Marco came down the steps into the basement, and I updated him. "Ovidio been tortured, and the girl needs to see a doctor too."

"Okay, take them back to the garage block on our estate, and we'll question them there."

The garage block was where we took people to torture information out of them. From the front, it looked like a normal garage. But behind the cars parked in it, there was another door leading to our interrogation rooms.

"I'll take the girl with me," I said, scooping her up into my arms.

She felt so fragile.

I couldn't forget, however, that she was a likely traitor. In fact, she had the perfect guise—no one would suspect a young Mafia daughter of being involved in this sort of treachery.

As I wrapped my arms around her petite frame, I heard a whimper escape her lips. She was obviously hurt and in pain.

But I knew that would make no difference to my treatment of her.

I carried her up the stairs and out of the warehouse to my SUV. Then I laid her on the back seat before getting in beside her, while a soldier got into the driver's seat.

Marco would take Ovidio in his vehicle. Ovidio had been beaten badly, but I felt no pity for him. It was unlikely he was innocent in this whole charade. Once we had gotten what we needed from him and his daughter, they would both pay for their deception and betrayal.

As the SUV moved off, I decided to give the girl a more thorough check.

I pulled out the medical kit that we kept in every vehicle, and as I felt her head for any cuts or bumps, I enjoyed the softness of her silky strands slipping through my fingers.

She kept drifting in and out of consciousness, indicating a possible concussion. I also noticed the bruises and cuts on her arms, and more worryingly, around her throat. Her translucent skin had been marred at the hands of the Russians, and that thought stirred up more anger in me.

She belonged to the Fratellanza, and the Russians had no right to touch her...

CHAPTER 4

CATE

I squinted as I felt a bright light being shone into my eyes.

I tried to shut my eyes, but someone was holding them open. The blackness was lightening to a fuzzy gray, finally revealing a man who was checking my injuries.

I'd recognized him inside the warehouse. He was Alessio Marchiano—the second-in-command of the Fratellanza.

I'd never spoken to him, but I'd seen my father speaking to him on a few occasions.

"You've got a bump on your head. I'll get the doctor to look at it." His voice was like a velvet caress.

The relaxing rhythm of his fingers against my scalp made me want to fall into the oblivion of sleep, but I fought to stay awake and focused on the man in front of me.

Even though we were sitting, I could immediately sense that he was tall and strongly built. I looked up at his hands checking me over, noticing his strong wrists, olive skin, and the dark hair that trailed up his muscular arms.

Thank God he'd saved me from the Russians. I shuddered at the thought of what would have happened to me at their brutal hands.

When he looked down at me, my eyes flitted over his almost-black hair and rich brown eyes. "Where are you taking me?" I croaked.

"I'm taking you home."

I breathed a sigh of relief. All I wanted was to be back in my own apartment—back in the safe life I'd built for myself away from this violent Mafia world.

I looked down at myself. A leather jacket was covering my torn clothes.

It hurt when I breathed. It hurt all over. My eyes ached, and my ears were ringing. Just being conscious hurt. "My father?" I murmured.

"We've got him as well."

But he didn't say anything else. His jaw was set in a hard line, and I felt his dark eyes searing into me.

Unease prickled through my body. I had a feeling that my father had done something very wrong...

My father seemed to know our kidnappers. They certainly knew him and were determined to get answers out of him—by torturing either him or me.

As the SUV turned a sharp corner at speed, I winced and inhaled deeply as my sore body was thrown against the car door.

"Take it easy with the goddamn driving," I heard Alessio bark at the driver.

But all too soon, he drove around another bend, and I let out a small cry as my badly bruised arm hit the passenger door.

"For God's sake," Alessio growled.

Before I knew what was happening, he'd undone my seatbelt and tugged me into his arms, settling me in his lap and grasping my body against his chest.

My pulse started beating too fast.

I could feel most of my body in contact with his—and I was acutely aware of how little I was wearing under his jacket.

Sometime later, we pulled up outside a modern estate and I realized that he wasn't taking me back to my own home—this was the Marchiano estate. "I want to go back to my own apartment."

"Not yet."

"Why have you brought me here?"

"We need the doctor to check you." He didn't look at me as he spoke.

I wanted to argue, but I didn't have the energy to. Everything either hurt with pain or ached with exhaustion. I didn't even want to have to think anymore.

As we reached the perimeter gate of the estate, Alessio rolled down his window and spoke to one of the soldiers on guard. "When Dr. Cotrone gets here and is done with Ovidio, tell him that I need him to take a look at the girl as well."

"Got it, boss."

The SUV pulled up in front of the mansion and I gazed at the modern white house surrounded by extensive grounds. But what caught my attention was the enormous stone statue of the Virgin Mary.

It was positioned on their front lawn, the traditional statue clashing blatantly with the modernity of the house. Italian-Americans had a custom of displaying a saint statue in their front yard. I wouldn't have taken the Marchianos, however, as being the godly sort who would follow this tradition. After all, they spent their lives killing people—and enjoying every minute of it.

Alessio got out of the car. I opened my car door and attempted to stand, but as my legs gave out under me, he caught me and scooped me up into his arms.

I felt too dazed to voice anything except for a small gasp. Instead, I let my body sink into his comforting hold, and I relished the warmth of his body against mine.

He was tall, easily over six feet in height, and his whole body was a machine of finely honed muscle, from his broad shoulders down to his powerful thighs and calves. He was wearing dark combat pants, a black fitted top and boots. His clothing, almost-black hair, dark eyes, and very precise movements, gave off the aura of a highly-trained assassin.

He carried me into the garage and headed past all the vehicles and through a door leading to more rooms.

Was this a back way to enter the house? After walking past the luxury exterior of the main house, these rooms were a harsh contrast with their emptiness and desolate air. "What is this place?" I asked, looking around in confusion.

He didn't answer me.

He went into the first room we came to, put me down, and closed the door behind him, the sound echoing with a sinister finality.

I felt unsteady on my feet, but that was the least of my worries right now.

The room felt a few degrees colder than the temperature outside. The room only contained the bare essentials of a table, two chairs, and a storage closet. My breath caught as the realization hit me of what this place was: the closet would be full of torture equipment.

"Why have you brought me here? What are you...you going to do with me?"

"That depends on you—on whether you cooperate." His words were casual but hinted at something much darker beneath his careful veneer.

"I don't know anything," I said quickly.

He prowled toward me, his proximity unnerving me. "Didn't your parents ever teach you not to lie?" His voice was menacing now, in complete contrast to the man who had soothed me earlier, and I realized just how dangerous this man truly was.

My eyes swiftly swept around the room trying to figure a way out. My breaths were coming in shallow rasps. "I thought you came to save me from the Bratva..."

"So, you do know something—you know who your captors were."

I desperately tried to understand what was going on. "I know that my captor is now you," I said harshly. "And anyone would know that those other men were Russians with the accent they had."

"What did they want with you?" As he fired questions at me, he was rolling up the sleeves of his dark top, revealing his strong forearms dusted with dark hair.

A bead of cold sweat trickled between my breasts, making me shudder. He was a Made Man: a man who had been brought up to torture and kill, a man who had no conscience, and a man who thrived on cruelty. I should have known that he wasn't my savior. I should have known that he was just like every other Made Man. He was a person who lived and breathed violence, and a person who could only bring pain and suffering into my life.

"I d-don't know. I was staying the night at my father's house and woke up to find them in the house. I don't know what they wanted with us."

He pierced me with his eyes, and I could sense his mind trying to figure out what I knew. "Tell me, what did they say to you?"

"Nothing, I swear. They barely said a thing to me."

He sighed. He knew I was lying...

ALESSIO

She was lying.

I had dealt with enough deceit in my life to know when someone wasn't telling the truth.

Upon the death of our father, Marco had taken over as Capo at the age of eighteen. And I had been seventeen when I became his Consigliere.

We had taken over an organization that was fraught with infighting and corruption, and it had taken many years of us working our asses off to turn it around into the success it was today.

Betrayals and treachery could easily bring the whole organization down, and I would do whatever was required to prevent that—dishing out whatever retribution was required to set an example to the rest of the Fratellanza.

My brothers and I were known as the Kings of Chicago. Our family hadn't gotten to its position today by being careful and respectful of others—we had gotten here through brutality and being merciless.

The girl's body was shaking, and her eyes were wide. Her father was in a bad way, and we probably wouldn't be able to question him for a while, meaning that it was imperative that the girl talked and that she talked now. And a traitor was a traitor, irrespective of their sex.

I stalked toward her and watched her pretty face pale. She knew how this was going to go.

As I neared, she tried to back away, but after a few steps she came up against the concrete wall. She swiftly looked around herself and realized that there was nowhere left to go.

I slammed my palms on the wall either side of her petite body, caging her in.

I knew what had to be done next.

But first I relished her being trapped by my body...

I slowly raised my arm and ran the back of my rough, calloused hand against her face.

As my skin made contact with hers, she violently flinched.

I cocked my head to one side, regarding her for a few moments. "Do I scare you?"

She didn't reply, however I knew the answer. She was trembling and I could almost smell the fear rolling off her.

The knowledge that she was afraid of me called to my primal senses and to the darkness within me. That side of me thrived on her terror, causing desire to flair through my loins...

She was my captive now—mine to do with whatever I wished.

"What did Dmitri Petrov say when he took you?" My hand continued to stroke her cheek. "I want to know exactly what was said." My voice was low, caressing the air between us.

Her answer was barely audible. "Nothing...he said nothing."

My hand suddenly leaped from her cheek to her throat, pinning her against the wall...

To add **MAFIA AND TAKEN** to your Amazon TBR:

https://www.amazon.com/Mafia-Taken-Dark-Romance-Marchiano-ebook/dp/B0C5B7G4RM

https://www.amazon.co.uk/Mafia-Taken-Dark-Romance-Marchiano-ebook/dp/B0C5B7G4RM

Hi Lovely. If there's enough interest, I would love to write more books about the Marchiano universe. If you enjoyed this book, please could you consider leaving a rating on Amazon? Ratings help new authors like me SO MUCH, and I really, truly appreciate your support. Love Isa xxx Link to leave a rating on your local Amazon store:

https://www.amazon.com/Mafia-Protector-Arranged-Marriage-Romance/dp/B0BW358W7L

https://www.amazon.co.uk/Mafia-Protector-Arranged-Marriage-Romance/dp/B0BW358W7L